AXEMAN: CYCLE OF DEATH

AXEMAN: CYCLE OF DEATH

REVENANT FILES™ BOOK TWO

D'ARTAGNAN REY

MICHAEL ANDERLE

DISRUPTIVE IMAGINATION

THE AXEMAN: CYCLE OF DEATH TEAM

Thanks to our Beta Team:
Kelly O'Donnell, Larry Omans, John Ashmore

Thanks to our JIT Team:

Jackey Hankard-Brodie
Zacc Pelter
Dorothy Lloyd
Angel LaVey

If we've missed anyone, please let us know!

Editor
SkyHunter Editing Team

LMBPN Publishing
PMB 196, 2540 South Maryland Pkwy
Las Vegas, NV 89109

Version 1.00, October 2021
eBook ISBN: 978-1-68500-500-9
Print ISBN: 978-1-68500-501-6

CHAPTER ONE

An uncommon stillness claimed the early morning hours of New Orleans. It was The Big Easy rather than The City That Never Sleeps but there was always a bustle in the streets while music issued from the many clubs, parks, or busking corners. For the last three days or so, it had become eerily quiet after sundown.

Some of it had to do with the murder spree that had raged through the city over the last few months, which made people more cautious. In addition, the rampage on Royal Street that resulted in over thirty deaths in less than an hour must be a record. The monster was vanquished, however, a beast of an individual who called himself the Axman. Until now, the name was only known maybe to some of the older residents of the city and anyone with a curiosity for the morbid history of the crescent city, but it had certainly found a place on everyone's lips since the massacre.

Of course, there was a more obvious answer if anyone cared to look around them. People in white jumpsuits and coats now patrolled the city. On this particular morning, they disrupted the silence of the very early morning when several aircraft suddenly raced toward the city, all carrying more personnel and equipment.

Valerie Simone looked out one of the windows of the police department for District Eight and sighed in annoyance as she finished pouring her coffee and the whir of a hovercraft grew louder when it flew overhead. She replaced the pot and returned quickly to the meeting room, where several high-ranking members of the police and most of the supernatural department awaited.

"And what the hell was that noise?" Police Chief Shemar asked. "Was that another squad of your goons?"

An older woman in a white suit adjusted her glasses. Valerie had learned only the evening before that her name was Sarah Lovett. "That sounds like one of our hovercraft," she replied, her voice monotone. "It's more than likely filled with several members of our recon and lab divisions, along with some important equipment, not goons as you call them."

She was accompanied by three other members of the Supernatural Exorcism Agency, often referred to as SEA or simply the Agency in places with a high ghost residence, which meant anywhere that would be concerned if they knocked on their door.

The young officer sipped her caffeine and remained silent. She was more surprised that it had taken this long for the Agency to arrive in New Orleans. The last time they had been there was reportedly in 2003. This fact wasn't known to her or most of the police department until the day before when Lovett arrived and began to speak to them while her minions hurried to investigate the anomalies left in the Axman's wake.

The department should probably have been more thankful than they were. The Agency had helped to clear up the mess the monster had left. While their presence did alarm some New Orleans citizens, others seemed to be more at ease given that if any supernatural problems remained, the Agency would no doubt deal with them.

Valerie looked at the three agents seated next to Lovett. She didn't know two of them but had met Agent Donovan. Now and then, they would trade looks during the conversation, unlike most of the other officers who didn't want the Agency there simply because they felt they were in the way. From what she'd heard, they didn't want some other force looking over their shoulder or felt insulted that the supposed "calvary" had appeared too late once the problem was already resolved. She had another reason to be suspicious, as according to her new "friend," the Agency might have a backup plan if they didn't like what their investigation uncovered.

One that could lead to serious problems for her beloved city.

"Can you at least tell me when you will be finished?" Chief Shemar asked and snapped Valerie into the conversation again. "Your men keep running around the city and spooking the residents. I thought the Agency was more subtle than this."

Lovett nodded slowly. "We certainly can be, as we explained yesterday when we told you about our previous investigations and missions in New Orleans over the years."

"Uh-huh," he remarked and looked at his tablet. "Your first investigation in the city was in 1922 shortly after the Agency was founded."

"To be fair," Donovan said with a hand partially raised. "New Orleans was merely one of dozens of cities the Agency looked into after its founding. We had only begun to set the groundwork to understand what kind of supernatural presence was in the US and how large it was."

"Almost forty years after the veil tore open?" another officer remarked with a snicker. "It took you that long to do some basic stat gathering?"

Lovett regarded the officer coolly. "The SEA was established in the early twenties, but other projects and missions were run well before then. That was simply our first mission after we officially began. By that point, all the information we had gathered was years out of date." She looked at the police chief. "We routinely returned and checked on cities to measure the fourth-dimensional population and its growth or shrinkage until the invention of the ectograph, which monitored the population on its own within a seventy-mile radius."

"Seventy?" the officer questioned. "New Orleans proper is more than five times that."

She nodded. "Which is why we set up more than a dozen throughout the metropolitan area and at the edges of the city. We are thorough."

Shemar sighed. "It explains why you haven't been back in force since the early 2000s then. Was that when you set them up?"

The woman nodded again. "In 2000 to be precise. The mission in 2003 was to look into a situation that could have been a level-three fourth-dimensional being that was summoned by an overeager unsub who wanted to meddle in forces they had no business meddling with. But they never completed their summoning as they didn't have the correct tools."

"Why does she keep saying fourth-dimensional?" the officer whispered to Valerie.

She shrugged. "It's an older way of saying ghosts from back when they didn't want to believe that what we were dealing with was ghosts."

He tried to stifle a laugh. "Good Lord. I understand being skeptical but once actual multi-colored skeletons fly around?" He looked at the Agency co-chief. "She looks old enough to have been a rookie back when it was founded."

"So you came running on a false alarm and didn't even advise the acting police chief at the time that you were in town. But when an actual supernatural terror causes havoc for months you simply stand by?" Shemar challenged.

"Like we said," Donovan began and stepped forward. "There was some kind of interference, not only with our tech but with our informants, both living and undead." He folded his arms. "I know that to you, it appears we arrived out of the blue. I'm sorry for not giving you a heads-up but we needed to get here as quickly as we could once these... anomalies were discovered and we learned about what was happening in your city."

"Do you not watch the news?" Valerie asked and received a bemused look from the agent.

"We saw the early reports, of course. But news changes quickly and it wasn't a national story after the first couple of weeks." He looked at Shemar. "From my understanding,

5

that was you and your department trying to downplay the situation, right?"

The police chief stared at him with intense annoyance. "Technically, that was Chief Jackson, and he believed it was best to not cause alarm. The people were scared enough when those early pictures got out of what the victims looked like and we didn't need fear to permeate the city if this turned out to be a wraith or demon that could feed on that fear." He leaned forward. "And while he might not have done this as you would have liked, he died defending this city from that monster while you were troubleshooting your damn systems, so the...uh, constructive criticism isn't appropriate."

Lovett cleared her throat. "It's a little late for that now, wouldn't you say?" She adjusted her glasses and the glare on them from the lights in the room obscured her eyes. "While I do commend the forward-thinking, it also allowed your Axman to have more freedom and to act from the shadows and gather strength in a different way by collecting the very lifeforce of a person or fourth-dimensio—"

"Ghost," Valerie interjected and drew all eyes in the room to her. "You can say ghost, ma'am. Most people will be more familiar with that term." She took another sip of coffee. "We made mistakes. I'll even add that I thought we weren't doing enough and exploring leads that were more off the beaten path, but this wasn't like any case I had seen or heard of before. I'm sure it was hard for Chief Jackson to understand the scope of it all along with being in charge of overseeing ordinary crime in the city."

The woman regarded her for a moment, her lips pursed

as she almost seemed like she tried to probe into the young officer's mind. "Officer Simone, yes?" Valerie nodded. "From my understanding, you were something of the spearhead in this operation correct?"

She shrugged, careful to not spill her coffee. "I'm not sure I would go that far, ma'am. I'm part of the supernatural division of the NOPD. I was simply doing my job."

"Indeed, even if it wasn't necessarily sanctioned by your higher-ups."

Shemar glowered at the Agency co-director. "Officer Simone was well within her rights to investigate the case she had been assigned to—"

"I don't disapprove, Chief Shemar," Lovett interrupted with a brief look at him. "I do believe protocol should be followed, but if it is ever bent, at least produce results." She turned to Valerie. "Did you take care of the Axman in the end?"

The young officer paused and tried hastily to think of a way to not get the man responsible involved in this.

"It was a bounty hunter by the name of Johnny Despereaux, ma'am," Donovan interjected, much to her shock and frustration. That little bastard had complicated things merely to earn points with his boss.

Surprisingly, though, Lovett seemed as frustrated as she was. "I am well aware of that, agent," the agent muttered.

She was? Then why had she asked? It must have been some kind of test to see if she would lie. Valerie looked at Donovan, who nodded, leaned back in his chair, and looked knowingly at her.

"Tell me, Officer," Lovett began and fixed her with an

unwavering stare. "Do you happen to know where this bounty hunter is?"

Fortunately, she did not have to lie about that. "I can't say I do. I haven't been in contact with him since shortly before you arrived," she explained. "The last I heard, he intended to look into some haunts for possible leads."

CHAPTER TWO

Johnny slid one hand into the pocket of his jeans and studied the factory, the supposed lead from the shady mobster in Limbo. It was large—three stories tall—and the roof and funnel stacks above were dilapidated, sure evidence that it had been abandoned for years. Graffiti all but covered the walls. To the left of the entrance was a caricature of a demon with a cartoonish bloody heart in its hand with the phrase, *Hell awaits the good-hearted!* in a stylized font beneath it.

He had to agree, at least as far as any good-hearted idiots who had the unfortunate idea to explore there, which had been the case over the last few weeks. The only reason he had decided to do so was because he was able to find a story of some missing "ghost experts" who were last reported searching around the area, even if the factory itself wasn't mentioned. He sighed with annoyance.

Over a hundred years of knowing ghosts were real and that not all of them were exactly friendly or even simply undead humans, and people still ran around acting like they had to hunt these bastards for their big break. Only specters could see ghosts, and anyone else wouldn't see them if the ghost didn't want them to. Unless they were something like a phantom or zombie, of course, and most people didn't want to see those.

The young investigator looked at a nearby tree and realized that the 'ghost experts' might have been right as well. He took a few steps closer, squinted at something carved into the tree, and grunted in annoyance when he recognized the symbol. It was a caller used by witches to summon the dead. While it was too faded to be of much use now, there were always leftovers when someone put one of these up.

Something scraped loudly against metal within. Johnny didn't draw his weapon yet. Although he didn't exactly have to worry about wasting bullets with an ether gun, he also didn't want to give his position away by shooting at a stray cat.

"So what are you thinking?" he asked and returned his focus to the factory. "Is it worth potentially getting tetanus?"

Vic chuckled, appeared next to him, and dug in his coat to produce a loose cigarette and lighter. "That's not a concern for me kid. If that were my only worry, I'd say to go look simply because it's not like we have any other leads at the moment. Or maybe look around the spooky woods some more."

"It's always nice to know you're looking out for my health, partner." He groaned. "See how much longer I purchase your cigs when I have hospital bills to worry about."

"Ha-ha." The ghost fake-laughed before he lit his cigarette. "Speaking of spooky woods…" He nodded at the tree. "That doesn't bode well."

"Does it work, though?" Johnny muttered and looked at the sigil again. "You have to be one of those…uh, spirit callers—that's what Aiyana called them, right?"

"It's more a colloquial term," Vic clarified. "As is the case for most of the more 'mystical' things, to work properly, it has to be done by someone who not only knows what they are doing but can use phantasma. But you don't need an expert to cause problems. You can do that by fucking up right."

He bit his lip as he studied the factory and the rusted doors again. "So you are saying there could be something in there and it has nothing to do with the Axman, merely someone dicking around with occult symbols for kicks?"

"It's possibly like those…what do ya call them? Ouija boards."

Johnny looked incredulously at him. "Wait, do those work?"

"Sometimes, although it's mostly ghosts who are already on this side screwing with some breathers for laughs. But there are types of ghosts like poltergeists that can be invited, and other supernatural beings like the fangs."

"Huh. You can summon a vampire with a Ouija board?"

"You can talk to them. They are a type of ghost in a cursed body."

The young investigator scratched the side of his chin, both bemused and surprised. "I might have to remember that for the future."

Vic made a dismissive clicking sound. "You aren't ready to take one of those on yet, kid."

He rolled his eyes. "It always impresses me that you can do that without a tongue." He drew his gun and looked at the factory. "So we need to reach some kind of agreement here."

His partner craned his neck and shrugged. "Well, I get a bad vibe from this place. And even if we don't find anything on the Axman, I'm sure we could probably get some kind of pay from someone for taking care of whatever spooks may be in there. Then again, we're maybe more likely to run into real rats rather than ghost rats."

With a drawn-out sigh, Johnny reminded himself that it was part of the business to have to creep around old or undesirable places. Still, he would prefer not to if he could find a way out of it, but with no alternatives to focus on, he decided he would at least poke his head around for a few minutes.

Part of him hoped there was nothing inside and if there was, it would be nothing that would want to take his head. He would prefer that too.

The revenant walked through the hall, his third so far. He had heard nothing since entering, but his cautious optimism that there would be nothing too violent to contend with vanished when he saw claw marks etched into doors and along a few of the walls.

These were easily identifiable as the work of ghouls. The dark glow of their corrupted phantasma lined the markings like blood dripping from blades. Dammit, he wished it was zombies instead. Those were easy to deal with, but ghouls were like zombies on a combination of steroids and cocaine—much stronger and a hell of a lot more aggressive.

Considerable dried blood and other fluids were in evidence as well but no bodies thus far. Ghouls weren't exactly the most subtle of creatures so he wasn't sure what they were doing there and how they hadn't been noticed yet.

He stopped in front of the door at the end of the hall. A window in the middle was partially broken but faded lettering on it indicated that this was the main work floor of some kind of assembly plant.

A few dim lights were on, the only sign of activity or that something was there although it wasn't exactly comforting. Why was there power in an abandoned building? Was someone living there? He also saw a couple of small belt lines within, worn and rusted, and noticed something inhuman hanging off one of them.

Vic stopped him as he was about to push the door open. "Hold on a moment, Johnny," he cautioned and looked him in the eye. "I won't be able to help much, at least not with my gun. Spectral bullets don't do jack against ghouls since their ghost form is trapped inside that meat suit. You walk in there and—"

"Yeah, I'm aware," Johnny replied and kept his voice down. "If the ghouls are here, I'm the only one who can deal with them. I always thought we needed to get you real bullets for your gun sometime but we don't use them enough."

The ghost shook his head. "I guess this is why they say better safe than sorry."

"I feel fairly sorry now, honestly," the young investigator said with a dry chuckle. "Don't worry, I got this. I took on that ghoul in Galveston remember?"

"Yeah, but that was only one and we don't know how many—" Something metal landed on the floor inside the room with a loud clang. Johnny adjusted the power level of his gun and nodded to Vic, who returned the gesture. "Be careful, all right, kid?"

He smirked. "If I was careful, we would never have met," he quipped before he pushed the door open and walked in. He looked cautiously around before he approached the conveyor belt. The partially disintegrated arm of a ghoul hung on it and the end appeared to have been torn rather than cut or blasted from the body. A brief inspection suggested that parts of it had been gnawed off. Were the ghouls cannibalizing each other? That would explain why they hadn't made a ruckus in town. Something was keeping them in there and the question was how many were left?

What sounded like a sickly inhale caught his attention and he looked away from the arm. A monster stepped into the dim light of one of the overhead lights, gaunt with long spindly arms and a black-and-gray body. Wispy lines of purple energy wove through its entire being, similar to veins. But the face terrified him as much as it had the first time he'd seen it two years earlier.

It looked like worn, rugged leather stretched over a shattered skull. At the top of its head, it twisted into a crescent-like shape to a long sharp point that was mirrored beneath its chin. Jagged sockets contained no eyes, only holes that emitted a low purple light, and the gaping mouth displayed a long row of spike-like teeth that opened and closed like it was preparing for a feast. This was undoubtedly a ghoul.

Johnny did not back away, however, and simply stood and observed the being as it inched closer. Something tapped against metal and his gaze located another one walking on the railings above while it stared hungrily at him.

Despite the approaching flesh-hungry monsters, another small grin crept onto his face. He recalled the first time he had seen one of these and how he'd been so sure that he would die with it ripping his guts out.

Now, he regarded them much the same as the average person considers a roach—disgusting and a nuisance.

The ghoul in front of him uttered a shriek and lunged viciously. He left his second weapon in his pocket and raised the one already drawn to fire a shot. The power behind it was enough to make him slide back a foot while the ghoul was hurled away. A large hole appeared in its chest and purple phantasma spilled out. It careened into an old machine and writhed frantically, much like a cockroach on its back, as it flailed to grasp at the phantasma as if to try to shove it all back into its body.

Perhaps believing him distracted, the being above took the opportunity to be the first to dine on him. It jumped off its perch but Johnny increased the power on his gun slightly and planted his feet firmly before he fired. He briefly glimpsed the smoky-gray fist-sized projectile that hammered into and then through the ghoul's head, which burst from the impact.

As the body landed with a thump, the other ghoul managed to stand and turned to strike. The young investigator grasped the knife on his belt and unsheathed it quickly to sever its raised arm. He caught the limb in his other hand, turned, and smacked it against the ghoul's face before he threw it on the floor.

The creature recoiled, clutched the area where its arm was severed, and hissed. Johnny lowered the power on his gun before he aimed at the wounded entity and blasted it several times until it no longer moved. He watched it warily until the phantasma dissipated around it.

He snickered as he wiped his nose. "You know, I think all this time shooting something that wouldn't stay dead might have got me a little riled. That wasn't so bad, was—"

"Kid, move!" his partner roared and Johnny spun to fire when something grasped the sides of his head and his vision went black.

CHAPTER THREE

When his vision returned, he was no longer in the factory and Vic was no longer beside him. Instead, he was in a cabin or shotgun house—somewhere rustic. He looked around the darkened walls. The only light was provided by candles in the room.

After a moment, he noticed a window and looked out at what he thought was a night sky, only to realize there were no stars, trees, grass, or other houses—or anything, for that matter, except an unnatural darkness. Crying close by filtered into his awareness and he turned toward a hallway and the sound that came from deeper within.

"Vic?" Johnny called in a muffled tone. "Are you there?" The crying continued and it unnerved him, but not because it was out of place or bizarre. If that were the case, he would probably not be fit for this line of work. The problem was the weeping wasn't from fear or pain but deep, utter despair.

Cautiously, he crept into the hall. Nothing seemed out of the ordinary other than the fact that any picture he saw on the walls was blurry and distorted. Try as he might, he could not make out the faces of the people within. What the hell was going on and where was he?

He found a room at the end of the hall and extended his hand toward the knob, only to pause for a second and look behind him. The hall stretched ridiculously long and he couldn't even see the living room he had first appeared in and that the darkness grew closer. He turned to the door and the sound of sobs and opened it slowly.

The young investigator stood in a room surrounded by the stuffed carcasses of animals, along with jars and boxes of material. The logical deduction seemed to be that he was in the house of a taxidermist, but that wasn't what unsettled him. A young girl knelt in the middle of the room. She was the source of the crying and her shoulders shook with her sobs that showed no sign of abating.

Johnny had no idea what to do. He still didn't know what was happening and adding childcare to the situation didn't help, but he wanted to be gentle.

"Hey," he called, his voice calm as he approached her slowly. "Are you all right? What's wrong?" The obvious answer occurred to him almost immediately. With all the weird things happening, she must have been spooked. Johnny was used to things like this and was still unnerved.

The girl made no reply and continued to weep. "Hey, come with me. I'll get you out of here," he said as he reached for her shoulder. "I promise."

As soon as he placed his hand on her, his vision darkened again but returned immediately. He seemed to be on the floor and wasn't sure if he'd fallen over or knelt when he blacked out.

His vision shifted as he stood but he couldn't be sure that he was standing. He hadn't intended to. A small arm reached to his eyes to wipe them and he made a chilling realization. He was looking through the girl's eyes.

Her tears ceased and there was a loud cry all around her. Boxes, jars, and cases filled with specimens and reagents fell from shelves and rucks and broke. Books of research flew from their positions into the walls of the cabin or were flung onto the floor. She placed her hands over her ears but it didn't seem to stop the noise or even dull it, at least not to him.

The darkness began to seep into the room and nightmarish creatures emerged from within. Their skin resembled bark and spiked vines crossed their chest and draped along their bodies to wind around their appendages. A pair of pure black eyes gazed at her. Although there were no pupils to focus on, she could feel their gaze looking at her and through her.

They were joined by smaller creatures that looked like skinless snakes and crawled along the floor. These appeared to have a set of eight tentacles that followed to leave a black substance behind them. The creatures moved toward her with uncanny smiles of grim delight.

She ran into the darkness. Johnny wanted to scream for her to stop but no sound came out. Frantic, she yanked the door into the hallway open and looked back at what appeared to be two people walking behind her.

"Mommy...Daddy!" she cried, her gaze fixed on her

parents' visages. Their expressions remained neutral as they walked past the other monsters and stopped in front of her. She cried out to them again but no sound left her mouth this time, even though she felt the frantic desire to scream as their features disappeared.

Her parents' skin peeled and flaked as their bodies turned ashen and hair twisted together and dried into cracked horns on their brows. Their eyes turned black but unlike the other beasts, they had white irises. All the creatures advanced on her and with a silent plea, her world turned dark as Johnny yelled for her to run.

When she awoke, sweating and trembling, she bounded from her bed and searched for her parents, desperate for their comfort. She hurried down the stairs of her home, only to be stopped cold by what awaited her.

The monsters from her dream appeared to be very real. The ashen ones hunkered over some object in her living room and the snakes were everywhere. They hung from the ceiling and slithered across the walls and the hallway. She felt the odd sensation of coarse skin rubbing against her and turned to see one of them moving over her hand. It looked at her with its unsettling smile and with a yell, she threw it off and heard a hissing sound from behind her.

One of the monsters with bark skin and thorns was atop the stairs. For a moment, she froze, but as it began to descend on all fours, its limbs twisting over one another as it moved, she panicked and raced down the rest of the steps and out of her home's front door.

The terrified girl plunged deeper into a forest and sprinted along the paths. Johnny could feel her lungs begin to burn as pain flared in her legs. Her fear allowed her to keep moving until she felt a sharp pain in her chest. It was enough to halt her in her tracks and she tumbled into the grass, rolled for a few feet, and finally stopped. The young investigator was desperate for this to end and for whatever bound him to her to let him out so he could help, but nothing changed.

She gasped when she noticed a strange purple mark that trailed up her arm in a long pattern and tailed into eight, starting where that monster had crawled across her. She sat and recoiled with a whimper. The beasts had followed and the two ashen creatures now towered over her with blood dripping from their fangs and claws. A few of the snakes had wound around the thorny ones and uncoiled and glided down their bodies.

Another pulse of pain racked her body and she looked at her arm. The mark had spread and had now reached her shoulder. The creature had done something to her—poison perhaps—and she felt she couldn't hold on for long. One of the two ashen creatures leaned down, positioned its face close to hers, and made a gurgling noise, sickening and deep.

"Go...go away," she muttered, too fatigued to muster anything more than a whisper. The monster seemed to fidget as if it tried to move but was pushed back. The other creatures growled and moved closer and she shut her eyes.

"Stop!" Johnny roared and finally found his voice again. After another blink of darkness, he stood in front of her and faced the beasts as they approached. He drew his gun in one fluid motion, fired relentlessly on the approaching horde, and cursed at them with every shot.

When he looked back to tell the girl to run, she was no

longer there. He blasted the largest targets back and trampled the snake-like creatures, although he still had no idea what they were. These weren't merely ghosts but, thankfully, ether seemed to work all the same.

They seemed endless. He continued to fire but for each one he gunned down, two or three took their place. Finally, he began to fall back and jogged down the hill to get some space between him and them. The darkness mantled the sky again as another howling shriek filled the air.

The young investigator fell to his knees and tried to cover his ears but this time, the pain wasn't only from the loud cry but from an icy chill that began to course through his body—one that was oddly familiar. A hand grasped his shoulder and he spun to fire, only to see a familiar blue-hued skeletal face. "Vic?"

"I found you," the ghost replied, drew his pistol, and pressed it to his partner's head. Before the young man could cry out in shock, he fired.

CHAPTER FOUR

The screech returned and he realized he was on the floor of the factory while shots were fired above him.

"Johnny!" Vic shouted as the young detective winced and rolled onto his back. "Johnny, get up. The phantasm is still here!"

"Phantasm?" He grunted and managed to sit. "Vic, what happened? I was in a cabin with a girl and we were attacked by monsters—you shot me!"

"I had to snap you out of it, kid," the ghost replied and looked around. "Dammit. It's hiding." His gaze returned to his young partner and he extended a hand. "The phantasm got hold of you. What you saw was an illusion. It was trying to warp your mind so it could take over."

"Take over?" he questioned as he grasped the proffered hand and scrambled to his feet. "Some kind of illusion? It felt so real, and it was so…weird. I've never seen monsters like that. What was the point? Shouldn't it frighten me with something I already fear?"

"I can explain more when we're not under attack." Vic handed him his gun. "You dropped this."

Johnny took his weapon and looked around. "Phantasm... I don't think we've come across one before."

The ghost pulled the trigger on his pistol. "Its main intention is to get into breathers' heads and put them into a nightmare like you experienced. Fortunately, I could possess you and get you out by shocking you in the illusion. But it isn't helpless when it's topside and can still manipulate objects, and it has that annoying scream. Do you still have those ectofire rounds?"

He checked his belt and retrieved a diamond-shaped object that burned with a bright green light. "Yeah."

"Phantasms are vulnerable to that. It has something to do with the constant burning that makes it hard for them to keep their form. Change your magazine and use it sparingly. Don't think you have unlimited ammo like you usually do."

Johnny ejected his magazine quickly and replaced the ether with the ectofire. "If it's hiding, do we hunt it?"

"They would normally probably hide in a situation like this, but this one seems...well, hungry."

"Hungry?" he asked and scanned the room. "Well, if it plans to attack us, how long do we have to wait?"

His question was answered by the sounds of concrete floors being torn apart and shattered glass. He turned to where the room was systematically destroyed by something but only caught a glimpse of the culprit. It was so translucent, even to his eyes, that it seemed invisible.

Tricky bastard. The phantasm moved too quickly for

him to get a decisive shot and he decided he would have to wait for a moment when he could trap it.

He fell and pain surged in his left leg. Vic looked at a wound across the young detective's hamstring and a piece of glass embedded in his leg. He fired a few shots quickly as Johnny propped himself up and tried to focus as he yanked the glass out. The phantasm was in a frenzied state, probably pissed that it had lost its potential host.

"We don't have the time to try anything tricky, kid," the ghost told him. "We're gonna have to burn it out."

Killing two ghouls and a phantasm was not exactly what Johnny liked to do in his early mornings, but it certainly got the adrenaline flowing to start the day.

He leaned back and used his good leg to leap out of his position and behind a conveyor belt. The edge of the machine was close enough to use for support as he limped down the room and deeper into the center while Vic continued to keep the quarry distracted. He wished he'd tested the ectofire rounds to see how many shots he had to work with before it ran out of power, but the plan was to need only one so he pushed the power on his gun to maximum and looked for a position to fire from.

The space between the machines was narrow with high ceilings, which gave him some space to work with. Once he found an open location, he signaled Vic to fuse with him so the phantasm would focus on him. When the creature turned its attention to him, he only had to concern himself about striking what was in front of him and didn't have to worry about it flanking him. He turned and positioned himself with his weapon at the ready, and the room fell silent.

Johnny glanced at his original position, which had been torn asunder. Some walls were completely shredded and glass and metal pieces from the lines and machines littered the floor. The phantasm seemed to have vanished, however. He began to second-guess himself and jerked his head in all directions in search of evidence of where it would strike from.

His nervousness made him examine his leg. The wound was bloody but fortunately less deep than he had feared. He still could not put much weight on it at the moment but trying to outrun or outlast this being seemed like a fool's errand.

Reluctant to remain stationary for too long, he moved back with small steps and checked his surroundings constantly. As he passed an old wielding station, he realized his mistake. He saw the swaying chains and it dawned on him that when the creature had begun to attack at random, he'd thought it was enraged. This was a slang term among hunters for any supernatural being that lost its last trace of sanity and simply operated on pure hatred.

But the phantasm wouldn't have sanity to begin with. It was looking for a vessel, which meant it was closer to an apparition—more a ghostly beast that ran on instinct rather than conscious thought.

He took a few steps forward and his foot kicked an unnoticed piece of metal. An idea came to him and he picked it up quickly as he continued deeper into the chamber. He set the power on his weapon to low and squeezed the trigger lightly as he began to trace the metal with the ectofire.

"What are you doing?" Vic asked.

"Making sure I have a backup plan." The metal glowed with the green ethereal fire. "You're a part of it, by the way. This thing is fast but I'll make sure it gets close."

He felt a terrible chill, a tell-tale sign of any ghost that told him the phantasm was close. It uttered another cry, although it didn't help to establish its location and simply echoed throughout the large room. He could not see it but he knew it was there.

A loud crack above his head made him spin to look at the roof where a chunk had been torn off. In the light, he could barely see enough of a shimmer to know that the wraith was bearing down on him from above. He took aim and fired and green fire launched from his pistol. The phantasm dodged it and barreled toward him with a warped piece of metal floating close to it, sharp enough to slice through him.

Johnny had little time to react and had to decide whether to dodge the blow or try to counter. He realized that with his leg still wounded, he would not be able to move quickly enough to avoid the attack. This was probably the best and only time to see if his plan would work.

He glimpsed something aimed at his head and tilted away in an attempt to avoid a direct hit. The phantasm was able to deliver a sharp cut to the side of his eye. Hot blood cascaded down his face but Vic appeared, grasped the jagged piece of heated metal, and thrust it forward to drive it into the angry ghost.

The young detective stumbled as the phantasm uttered a shriek and a blast of phantasma knocked them both back. When he looked up, he smiled. A thin, pale creature with dark-gray skin and large hollow eyes had become visible, and the metal had pierced through what appeared to be its shoulder.

Then, he noticed something peculiar. The being glowed and an ethereal monochrome hue shimmered around it. It seemed to encompass its entire being and swirled like a heavy wind while erratic sparks spewed from its body.

The phantasm whirled, lashed out, and attacked what it must have thought was wounded prey. Johnny held his gun up quickly, set it to maximum again, and unleashed a large blast of flame. He controlled the fire to engulf the being. A thick black liquid gushed down its body and spilled onto the floor as the flames burned its form.

It began to thrash wildly in an attempt to escape the flames that now caged it, and although it was faceless, he could still discern the feelings of confusion, pain, and possible fear that the creature emitted with its gurgled cries. He began to wonder if the controller's feelings were coming through, although he enjoyed the thought that he could make a ghastly being such as this feel fear.

Carefully, he began to compress the flames and force them together to further ensnare the creature before he finally formed them into one large sphere. The wraith was trapped inside it as he raised it high with a clenched fist. He smiled with satisfaction as he opened his hand and mouthed, "Pop," as the orb exploded to obliterate the nuisance.

The fire scattered and small drops of flame rained to set some things ablaze, but they were spectral flames and it took little more than a flick of his wrist to extinguish them. He sighed, walked to a table, and leaned against it as he rubbed his wounded leg.

Vic looked around, careful to avoid the ghostly fire. "Damn good work, Johnny."

"Thanks, partner," he replied and grimaced as he tried to put some weight on his injured leg. "I guess I should feel good about ridding the world of a few supernatural menaces, even if we didn't find anything useful for the case."

"I wouldn't be so sure about that." The ghost detective nodded at something in the distance.

Johnny followed his gaze to another sigil etched into the wall. He wondered if he hadn't seen it before because he was focused on the fight or because the flames now illuminated it. "Another mark, but I'm not familiar with that one."

"It's a prison mark," Vic stated. "Someone was binding these beings here."

He adjusted his jacket and sighed. "Maybe someone simply wanted some exotic pets?"

His partner uttered a low snicker. It suggested that he found the thought ludicrous, even as a joke. "I'll let you keep your hopes up, kid, but we should probably finish our investigation and see if we can find anything else."

The young detective sighed, nodded, and limped toward the door. "Let me go patch this in the car. You get started."

"I'm on it," Vic acknowledged and prepared to start from the other side of the factory. He paused for a moment to turn to Johnny and shout, "Hey, if it helps, drinks are on me after this."

That would raise his spirits. Who didn't like daytime drinking?

CHAPTER FIVE

Romeo placed two glasses and two different bottles on the bar. One of the bottles was filled with a stygia-based whiskey that was one of his top sellers. The other was a new addition to the bar given that it wasn't very popular among his normal clientele. He had decided to get a few bottles for a particularly unique customer because he prided himself on his customer service.

"You look like hell, Rev," the ghost commented as he filled one of the glasses with normal albeit high-grade whiskey and passed it to Johnny.

"It's better to look like hell than be there," he retorted and took a large sip as the proprietor filled the other glass with the stygia whiskey. "There's nothing like starting your morning with taking on a few supernatural terrors to get the blood moving. It's why I never took up jogging."

"I thought it was because you didn't like the outfits," Vic quipped and raised his glass. "I appreciate it, Romeo."

"So what happened?" their host asked as he moved the bottles to the side. "Did you guys find anything?"

"Damn right we did," Johnny muttered and took another swig quickly. "Someone was attempting to open a fucked-up zoo."

Vic chuckled and took only a small sip of his drink. "It's a damn shame. The poor kid got bit trying to hand snacks out."

The bar owner tilted his head. "Is this some kind of code or what?"

"We're trying to use humor to dull the pain." The young detective sighed and raised his glass, only to realize that he had downed it in two swigs. He placed it on the bar for Romeo to refill. "We got a tip from a mobster in Limbo—a runner who works on both sides, living and dead. It led us to a factory in a town a little over half an hour away, where we found both ghouls and a phantasm."

"Seriously?" Romeo asked, filled the glass, and pushed it to him. "And word hadn't gotten out yet? The ghouls alone should have torn the place up."

"No kidding, but whoever was doing it used sigils to keep them in place—the same ones druids and witches use," Vic explained as he fished a cigarette out. "In a weird way, it was a good thing we stumbled across it today. We found evidence of other types of ghosts that used to be there, but whoever had collected these disturbed pets wasn't a very good owner. Most of the residue was left from ghosts who lost their form, were dragged into Limbo after running out of stygia, and in the case of at least one ghoul, were eaten by their starving brothers."

"Damn, man." Romeo gasped and leaned on the bar. "Have you got any clues who did it? Was it the Axman?"

The ghost detective lit his cigarette and took a drag.

"Unfortunately, we couldn't find any of those nifty ax symbols like we did on the letter that led us here. My guess is that he quickly realized it probably wasn't a club he wanted to advertise. We found some messages about shipments and keeping the pets on a leash until 'the day' comes." He bent his fingers in air quotes. "Whatever the hell that is supposed to mean. But given that our letter was similar in tone and that the Axman would probably be the only one with the power to accomplish something like this—"

"Unless one of the mobs is trying a new potential market," Johnny interjected.

"It's probably safe to say he at least has a hand in it. Also, it helps that we found some remnants of the muck that his peons turned into when they were killed. I don't know how he died out there but probably got iced when he drained them for power like he did the poor bastard who died on your floor." Vic turned and looked at the place where the killer had melted. "I got to hand it to your staff, Romeo. I can hardly tell that blood and guts used to be all over the place."

"Eh, to be fair, they had practice," the proprietor responded. "When I first renovated, I had to get all the dried blood out of the floor. Part of the reason why the business went out of business back in the day was how violent this street would get, and a bar was ground zero for the worst of it."

"Speaking of which…" Johnny looked at the eerily silent lounge. "I know it's quite early, Romeo, but your bar seems fairly lifeless—no pun intended."

His partner sipped his drink and nodded. "Yeah, I know

we've only been in town for a little over a week but every time we stopped here, Carnivale lived up to its name day or night."

Romeo sighed as he folded his arms and frowned at his empty establishment. "Yeah, the ghost population has either left for Limbo or stayed inside their makeshift homes. It's becoming more dire every day."

"Even though most people think the Axman is dead?" the young detective asked.

Their host chuckled darkly. "Funnily enough, he's the least of their worries." He reached under the bar and produced a set of photographs. "I got a guy who keeps me informed about things going on in town."

"That is why we came to you in the first place," Vic noted and turned to face him. "In hopes of finding out what was going on in NOLA's dark underbelly."

The proprietor placed the photos on the bar and pushed them forward. "Well, you don't need to look under anything to see these, only to look up." The two partners looked at the pictures and the aircraft darkened by the early morning skies. "Flyers sent in by the Agency."

"Good Lord, how many reinforcements do they need?" Vic muttered as he picked one of the photos up and studied it with a scowl. "It's bad enough that they've arrived by the truckload every day since the fake Axman was eliminated. Now they are bringing air support in?"

Johnny looked at the bar owner with curiosity and concern. "Have they bothered you at all, Romeo?"

He stroked his chin. "Not really, although I kind of wish they had. At least that would be normal. They don't come in here asking questions or trying to run us out or anything like that, but they send patrols through the street and often have groups of guys who simply wander around with these dinky little devices. I've talked to some of the other business owners and none of them have had any of the agents come in. Matty spoke to a couple but that was only because he ran into 'em on the way to his shop."

"Valerie says they've basically tried to take over since one of their co-directors came to town the other day," Johnny told him. "Whoever tried to block them from getting here only pissed them off more. Personally, I hope the Axman shows his face soon, not only for our sake but for the city's. Maybe they will cool off if they can bag a trophy."

Vic finished his drink and handed it to the proprietor for a refill. "I doubt that, kid. When the Agency shows up in force like this, they hang around like... Well, I guess like any American government agency in places where no one wants them."

"And that's what's got most of the ghosts around here so spooked," Romeo explained as he passed Vic his refilled drink. "The Wild Hunt may be scarier since they simply sweep through and reap anything in the way, but the Agency is creepier, even to ghosts. You can never completely be sure what they want, who they are after, or if they simply wanna run tests on ghosts for kicks." He looked toward the bathrooms. "I've had more people using the Ferryman crossing point in the last couple of months than I've had in a year combined—at least heading toward Limbo, that is."

"It's a pity you don't make them pay a cover charge. You could have made bank," Vic quipped and took a drag.

D'ARTAGNAN REY & MICHAEL ANDERLE

The bar owner laughed. "Oh, I've known about the opportunity since day one, buddy. The Ferryman themselves give me a cut to maintain it since stationary crossing points are so rare. And the mob pays me to keep tabs on who is coming and going, so it's a sweet deal." His eyes clouded with worry. "Although I might have to close shop if the agents come looking in here for real. They might do it for me. I've heard they have some type of gadget that can close crossing points."

Johnny rolled his eyes. "I've heard they have a bomb that can nuke Limbo," he muttered. "The Agency plays the ghosts' game against them. At this point, they are probably seen as their bogeymen."

"No kidding." Vic took the last drag of his cigarette. "So, nothing else to report, Romeo?"

He shook his head. "Sorry, guys, but no one's got nothing for me with regard to the Axman. In fact, most people seem to believe he's dead and gone for good. Even that murder that happened the night he supposedly died is being chalked up to a copycat caught in the craze."

Johnny sighed and sipped before he responded. "It's probably for the best. At least we can keep the panic down. If that was the Axman—the real one—he probably did it to keep the fear up for whatever he's planning."

"Or at least keep his name in everyone's minds," Vic agreed, dug some doubloons out, and placed them on the bar. "That leaves us with nothing for now. We should meet Val and Aiyana and see what they've got."

Johnny took his phone from his pocket. "I think Val is still in meetings. She hasn't responded to me about what happened at the factory."

"Then let's hope the spirits were talkative these last couple of days." The ghost detective finished his drink, flipped the glass on the bar, and tilted his cap. "Thanks, Romeo. Stay safe and don't let the Agency bite you on the ass, all right?"

Romeo nodded and took the doubloons off the counter. "I can handle those spooks fine. I ain't the one looking for a demonic serial killer."

Johnny finished his drink and flipped his glass as Vic had. "True enough, but at least it's better that way than the other way around."

CHAPTER SIX

How long had she been awake? Well beyond anything healthy, Valerie decided as she poured herself yet another cup of coffee. Each seemed more ineffective than the last. She placed the pot into the machine and noticed an officer waving to her.

With a sigh, she wandered across the room to her colleague. She had just left the last meeting about the Agency and their plans—which effectively gave them free rein until otherwise indicated—and she had hoped she would finally be able to get out and start patrol. Unfortunately, it seemed that either the homicide team had a new development or they had confirmed something they all suspected.

"What have you found, Jackson?" She sipped her coffee and realized it was only lukewarm. The machine must be having issues or was simply overworked.

"It's what we haven't found that's the problem, Val," he answered and nodded at the tablet in his hands. "It looks like this will be handed to the supernatural department soon enough."

"Is this the elderly couple discovered a few days ago?" she asked, took the tablet, and grimaced at the pictures. "Killed in their bed by an ax?"

He nodded. "Yeah—their ax too."

She pinched the bridge of her nose. "And the hope that it was merely a coincidence that it happened on the same day as the Axman's supposed obliteration is…"

The officer shrugged and took the tablet from her. "It's still possible, I suppose. It could be a copycat but it appears that whoever the killer is, it's very likely that they are a ghost of some kind." He flipped through a few other photos. "We still haven't found any trace of DNA or signs of breaking and entering, but we did find trace signs of phantasma."

"Only trace?" she asked. "I heard police responded to the calls from the neighbors immediately and arrived on the scene only a few minutes after they had heard the last screams. If this was the work of a ghost, the investigative team should have found a heavy presence of phantasma and stygia around the scene of the crime."

Her colleague nodded grimly. "Yeah, that was something I wanted to ask about given that you have gone off the idea that this guy is some kind of spook we haven't run into before. We don't know what his powers are, exactly, and that grimy black-and-white substance you brought in last week didn't have a trace of stygia in it either so…"

"So there is a chance this could be the actual guy?" It was a logical guess and it wasn't hard since rumor strongly suggested that SEA was working on the possibility that the Axman was still active in some form.

She pressed her lips together and leaned toward him to whisper, "I'm sure we'll have it soon. Until then, do you mind keeping this within your department? We already have the Agency scaring the civilians and I don't want them to bring more of their people in until we find out what the hell their plan is should they also decide the Axman is still kicking."

He nodded and held the device closer to his chest as if to hide it. "Sure thing, but I have to tell you that the Agency has kept a watch on all our current cases. Since they are here on their own mission, we don't have to share anything with them, but my guess is that holding back too much will only make them more suspicious."

"Okay, yeah. That's a fair point," she admitted and ran a hand through her disheveled hair. "For now, don't voice your suspicions until we can confirm it. If they draw their own conclusion, I guess it will be Shemar's job to placate them. I don't like passing the buck to him but we can't do much of anything until we have definitive proof." She downed the rest of her coffee and threw the styrofoam cup into a nearby trashcan. "I'll head out. I need to check on some things but thanks for the heads-up, Jackson."

Jackson nodded and they left in separate directions. She took a moment to glance at the officer. Only a couple of years older than she was, he had been diligent even before the attack but in the aftermath, he and the others in the precinct had shouldered many more responsibilities than they had before.

Valerie retrieved her phone and frowned when she

realized she had a few messages, but the one that stood out was from Johnny. She was about to listen to it when someone called her name.

"Officer Simone?" The voice was rapidly becoming familiar.

"Agent Donovan?" she asked and turned as he hurried toward her. "Please don't tell me there's another meeting with your department."

He chuckled, easy-going if a little dry, and shook his head. "No, fortunately. Many of us don't enjoy them any more than you do. We're merely more accustomed to them."

"Mm-hmm." She scrutinized him, curious as always about the almost all-white Agency outfit—a long-sleeved shirt, trousers, boots, and a jacket, which she found odd. It was supposedly optional so who would wear one in the summer? Well, besides Johnny, but he said he wore it because he was chillier than normal as a revenant. What was this guy's excuse? "Is there something I can help you with, Agent?" she asked, her voice somewhat hoarse after being awake for so long.

He looked around for a moment and checked the office before he leaned closer. "I just wanted to again offer my services—"

"The offer has been noted, Agent," she stated flatly and turned away. "But I'm not interested in a shadow."

"It's only a temporary partnership," he replied as he walked briskly behind her. "Look, I understand that no one likes the big bad government agencies to swoop into their town and deal with things their way. Trust me, I would hate to be in your position and I have to admit I'm not big on how the SEA handles things. They don't treat ghosts like they were once humans, more like they are simply a nuisance to be rid of."

"I can certainly agree with you on that," she replied and ducked under the warning tape at the still partially destroyed entrance. "Not that I don't have problems with ghosts from time to time. But for all your offers of help, you've never told me one thing."

The Agent raised an eyebrow as they walked over to the parking lot. "And that is?"

She turned to face him. "What's in it for you?"

His curiosity turned into a grimace. "What? Do you think I'm trying to find a way to make a quick buck?"

"I don't think it is that simple, but you could be jockeying for a raise or promotion, or both," she pointed out. "Besides Johnny and the Maggios, I'm the closest one to the case with the most knowledge. I'm sure the Agency would love to get all the little facts they can out of me. Although that does make me wonder why they haven't pulled me in for a debriefing or interrogation."

"Well, they don't have the power to do that quite yet," he admitted with a sly chuckle. "But I'm sure it will come eventually. You might want to prepare yourself for that because they can be long and quite boring, more so than the meetings." He shrugged and regarded her speculatively. "But if you did want to tell me anything interesting you heard or saw during your investigation…"

Valerie stared at him, dumbfounded at first with a slight flare of anger before she laughed it off and headed into the parking lot toward her car. "Good Lord, you have a terrible poker face."

"I never said that was the reason for my offer," he added quickly. "But you know, cards on the table and all that. Besides, shouldn't you be used to a partner? You're in the police and yet you seem to do everything yourself."

"Specters are hard to come by," she said as she finally reached her car and leaned against it. "Specters who want to work in the police are even more difficult to find so some exceptions are made depending on what we're doing. Going to face a dangerous ghost? Of course we have backup. Hell, the unit is small enough that any real threat is usually all hands on deck, but if we're merely observing or investigating, we go on our own unless it is an active crime scene." She studied him for a moment before she sighed and gestured toward the car. "Look, you get one thing and then you leave me alone, got it?"

His eyes gleamed. "You seemed to have changed your mind quite suddenly."

"I didn't. I'm taking you to the Maggios so you can talk to them about the Axman. We still have no damn idea why he was after Annie specifically and if you have something to offer with your much vaster knowledge of ghosts and their more terrible mutations, I can get something out of you."

Donovan smirked. "That's quite mercenary of you, I have to say."

"Do you want in or not?" He shrugged and nodded and she pressed the button to unlock her car. "Personally, it's been a very long week and I need a shower and nap. Let's get this done quickly."

"Sure thing." He opened the passenger door. "By the way, perhaps you can fill me in on what exactly—"

"I'm running on fumes and I'm very sure I've replaced much of my blood with coffee," she interrupted and looked at him with tired, annoyed eyes. "Let's keep the chit-chat to a minimum, all right?"

The agent nodded politely, leaned back in his seat, and sighed contentedly, which earned a little more of her ire. She was tempted to say something but simply started the car and pulled out of the parking lot. There were currently enough ghost-related issues to deal with and she didn't need to add the ghost of an agent to the mix.

CHAPTER SEVEN

He placed his fingers just inside the confines of the circle and drew the symbol slowly. Once he was finished, he rose and looked at it, noted the curve at the top, then checked the other two symbols he had drawn earlier. He detested making these marks.

They were well outside his forte and with how specific they were, they did not leave much space for error. Should they be off by even a touch, it would render the entire sigil useless at best. At worst, it could tear another hole in the veil or force him back into Hell. He did not mind the former all that much but the latter would be incredibly problematic for him.

Suddenly, the theater auditorium began to shake. The candles on the shrine at the center of the stage, decorated in cigars, wines, and the remains of black chickens, lighted of their own accord. He swiftly closed the jars containing the inky black substance he had used to make the sigil and stood as a cloud of dark essence began to swirl above the shrine.

"Axman!" the voice shouted. Even after all this time, he had not grown accustomed to it. This was possibly because it didn't sound so much like it came from around him but within, a demonic sound that reverberated through his already unholy body.

"What can I do for you today, Baron?" the Axman asked as the figure took shape over the shrine. It settled into the silhouette of a man in a suit and top hat and blood-red eyes glared at him.

"It's not what I need you to do now," his visitor snapped and pointed what appeared to be a cane toward him. "It's what you needed to do before now!"

He tilted his head and the lights of his eyes glimmered against the dark phantasma of his face. "We've had some complications. I believe you were there when they were discussed." He straightened. "Jack sacrificed himself so I could right the course of things. You seemed to agree that it was for the best at the time. What has changed?"

The figure swung the cane wildly. "It's my brother!" he shouted in rage. "He knows about our deal. He was the one who moved against us."

"Your brother?" The Axman considered this as he thought back to that day. "The last thing I remember Jack seeing before our bond was severed was that purple essence covered his body. He had the same form I did and I expended much of my soul to make that happen, yet it was felled with one shot." He probably should have been more concerned but he felt somewhat satisfied that a curious piece had fallen into place. "Well, a keeper certainly would have something to take care of an abomination like me, wouldn't they?"

The Baron looked at his minion with both curiosity and annoyance. "Why do you seem so pleased?" He leaned forward and his large frame obscured almost all the Axman's view. "If my brother is meddling in our business, we will have to close shop soon. An agreement of the likes you and I have is not traditional—"

The Axman chuckled and raised a skeletal hand as the black phantasma oozed off it. "I am well aware of that. The body I have is proof, as is your end of the bargain." He took a moment to stare into the disembodied eyes of his patron. "So your sibling finds out about our little arrangement and the fact that I'm not a panicked mess like you seems to confuse you. And here I thought you preferred a little theatricality."

The figure leaned back and lay in the air as if he'd spread himself on a couch. "I do normally find it most enjoyable, so the fact that I am no more at ease than I was when I came in should let you know how serious this situation is." He swatted at the Axman with his cane again and made contact, but the shadowy object might as well have been nothing more than a shadow as it simply glided through him. "Without real evidence as our agreement is only amongst ourselves, he will find it difficult to convince another keeper to turn their attention to him or us. But as you've seen, he is a big enough issue himself!"

"What was that bullet that obliterated Jack?" the Axman questioned. "Can he make another? Can you make one?"

The darkness seemed to stiffen and the baron's gaze shifted. "I do not have my brother's command over the dead," he stated, his voice low and betraying frustration and perhaps jealousy. "I cannot create the kind of knickknack he did. My abilities and domain are not linked to—never you mind about that!" His focus returned to the Axman and his large form loomed over him. "What is your plan now? Along with this fool's interference, I felt us lose the terrors we had stowed outside the city."

"Ah, so you did notice that," he responded thoughtfully and opened the jar again to place it carefully at the edge of the circle. "It is an annoyance, certainly, but I had mostly given up on that plan once we had to dismiss all the other lackeys. In fact, I think the factory's discovery and destruction could work to our advantage."

"Humph." The baron swung his cane over his head and let it settle across his shoulders. "What makes you think that?"

"It's simple enough. It will act as a red herring," he explained and began to work on the last symbol. "I'm sure they now believe we were stowing them for something, particularly with the ghouls present. I had no plans for them any longer beyond potential phantasma stores but at this point, they would have been almost stripped bare." He sketched one small ring carefully before he connected it to another. "Let them concern themselves investigating a useless plan."

"I'm beginning to see many of those," the being growled, knelt, and tilted his head. "You like to think you are smart, Axman, or perhaps prepared? But given how many plans you've made and how little has come of them, you look to me like you are nothing more than paranoid and incompetent."

The Axman stopped his work and looked up for a moment

but his face betrayed no emotion, anger or otherwise. "I was thought to be the same in life, Baron, and they called me worse as well." He shifted his focus and continued to paint. "But whatever you or they may think, there is one fact I can always retort with." He completed the third connected ring and rolled his hand slowly toward the ceiling to make sure no ink spilled onto the sigil. "I was never caught."

The baron snorted as he folded his arms. "There is still time for that now, isn't there?" He looked at the sigil with mild interest and pointed a pinky at it. "What is this—your fourteenth plan in motion?"

"It's a beacon," he replied, closed the jar, and put it on the desk before he took a bag off the table and opened it to reveal dark dust. "One I came across a week ago amongst the fine collection of literature you provided." He withdrew a handful of the dust and sprinkled it around the sigil. "I still need helping hands to complete the plan. All the souls we have collected—that power—is only an advantage as long as we don't overuse the amount we have." He traced a circle of dust meticulously around the ring of the sigil. "Our previous friends cost too much to maintain. I think you'd agree with that."

The baron nodded and a dry chuckle escaped his throat. "They weren't worth the souls spent on them and needed to find...hmm, alternate employment."

The Axman looked up at the not quite formed image of his benefactor. Flares of white light coursed through him like blood through veins and if he focused on them, he could briefly see faces crying out from it. "I'm sure you are putting them to good use," he remarked, closed the bag, and tossed it onto the table. "I could use your help with this."

"And what would you need?" the baron asked and his eyes narrowed as he growled. "You don't need more souls, do you?"

He finally showed a trace of emotion and grinned as he stretched his arms. "No. Fear is mounting all across the city." That fear felt like lightning in his body and he let it simmer. It was incredible what a couple of dead bodies could accomplish and he realized that he had played perhaps a little too subtle until now. The unusual deaths in the city had people on edge but that had only brought him so far without a name to attach to it. Now that they had his name and there were rumors that he was still around despite the fact that the police believed him defeated had given him the reputation of an immortal killer.

Ironically, his aim was the opposite, but that was a thought for later. "I have sufficient power to keep myself going, but I need more if we want to accomplish ending the madness of your brethren." He snatched one of the candles from the altar. "With two deaths, I have thrown much of this city into doubt. The Agency keeps that fear flowing by their mere presence, but it is all speculation right now, isn't it? They want confirmation. We should give it to them."

"So what now? Will you simply summon more cronies or terrors?" the baron asked with a disapproving click of his teeth. "Maybe I gave you too much credit there, Axman. No, you are merely rehashing your failed projects. What will make this different now?"

"This will be far more straightforward, Baron," he

responded and looked at him as he held the candle aloft. "I need chaos, and that doesn't require ghosts themselves. Their emotions, however, would do nicely."

His patron tilted his head and a small grin formed as he rubbed his hands together. "Ah, you want some shades, then?"

"That is within your domain, correct?" the Axman asked as he held the candle over the sigil.

"Oh yes." The baron's form began to fade as he returned to Limbo. "Start the fire and prepare their cage. You will have an army of rage soon, Axman." He waved his hand as he laughed while his body disappeared. "And make sure to have a little fun. I insist."

CHAPTER EIGHT

"Any word from Val?" Vic asked as he and Johnny continued to drive out into a far more rural part of Louisiana.

"It says she's seen the message but I've had no response. I have no idea what she's been doing. Maybe she crashed—she's been up for at least twenty-four hours," he replied and flipped the screen to the map again. "We're almost at Aiyana's but there's been no response from her either. I wish we didn't have to meet out here. I'm very sure the only living things here are starved and foaming at the mouth."

"What did you expect?" The ghost laughed as he tossed his cigarette out the window. "She communes with nature spirits. Did you think she was gonna do her thing in the middle of a modern city?"

He shrugged as he pulled off onto a dirt road. "Why can't she have the power to commune with the spirits of Google and Alexa? That would be much more convenient."

"True, but also not as special." Vic slid his hand into his

jacket and frowned when he found nothing. "I can technically do that, even if it records my voice as nothing other than screeches and wind."

Johnny smirked as he cut the engine and stepped out of the car while his partner floated out. In front of them stood a forest with a mixture of trees in full bloom and others long dead. He sighed and checked his phone again. "It looks like we'll have to walk through there to find her." He pressed call, hoping she would pick up, but only got her voice message. "Well, there shouldn't be anything to worry about in there, right?"

"You mean supernaturally?" Vic asked, checked his other pockets, and sighed. "No, probably not. Aiyana would have let us know if anything like that was running around. However, those aforementioned starving crocodiles—"

"I didn't mention anything specific," Johnny muttered as he began to stride toward the tree line. "Besides, Louisiana has alligators, not crocs. I'm very sure I mentioned that already."

"Either way, we're talking a pissed-off temperament and way too many teeth." The ghost detective finally realized he was out of cigarettes and his shoulders sagged as he drifted to Johnny. "And look at you, kid. You work out and walk a lot so have nice lean muscle that would make a good meal for anything that—"

His partner held a hand up. "Hey, shut up a sec." They both heard an eerie drone that came from deep in the forest. "Why does that sound familiar?" he asked as he took his phone out.

Vic unholstered his gun. "Try to get Aiyana on the phone again."

"I'm already on it." He held the phone to his ear but was only greeted by the message again. "Dammit." He flipped his eyepatch up. "There are phantasma trails running through here."

"Then we have something waiting for us."

"Maybe Aiyana already took care of it?"

"She can take care of herself but I don't like the fact that she hasn't answered us."

"Agreed," he said with a nod. "Be on the lookout. I'll take point."

They proceeded through the forest. While they probably should have been even more careful, Johnny barreled through the leaves and branches as quickly as he could. He only occasionally checked the map and compass on his phone while Vic flew overhead to make sure nothing could surprise them. "The good news and bad news is that I can't see nothing," he called to Johnny. "I can't see any dangerous animals or ghosts but I don't see Aiyana either."

"I'm sure she's here," Johnny answered as he ducked under a branch. "What I don't understand is what could have happened. We talked to her—what? Twenty or twenty-five minutes ago? All she said she would do was try to commune with some of the nature spirits or elements or whatever in the area. What happened between then and now?"

"Maybe we are blowing this out of proportion," his

partner suggested. "Maybe she's very focused or doing some ritual that requires all her attention and can't be disturbed. The traces of phantasma don't mean there's something evil in the forest. There could be a crossing point nearby that...Johnny?" He realized he was talking to himself, that he had long passed his partner, and could feel their connection pulling him back. "Johnny? Where did you go?" He received his answer when a shot rang out.

"Gah!" The revenant sounded pissed.

The ghost detective located Johnny who struggled with something. What appeared to be clawed hands dug into his ankles and pulled him down from beneath the forest floor.

He began to fire his pistol straight into the dirt. One of the arms released him and he forced himself back but heard a loud crack in the process. When he glanced down, he confirmed that he was free but the arm still grasped his ankle.

Vic floated in and fired a few shots into the earth. "What is it, Johnny?"

The young man yanked off the hand still attached to his ankle and looked at it before he flung it aside when the flesh began to slide off the bone. "Fortunately, they aren't ghouls but—"

Another loud drone issued from both around and below them. The ghost glanced at Johnny who slid his hand into his jacket and produced a small bag which he tossed to his partner as patches of the earth were thrust outward and figures clawed out.

They looked like people in various states of dress but their arms were skeletal with gray and decayed skin. One tried to grasp Johnny but was forced to let go when he tried to slice into its face with his blade. Another shuffled along the ground, twisted, and reshaped itself before it stopped, facing up. It stretched both hands and curved them at a frightening angle to bend back, place them on the ground, and push to its feet.

The being hobbled forward, its head obscured by the hood of its jacket, and raised its head to look at the rest of the group. The face was dark and the eyes were white with yellow at the edges, and it let its jaw hang to reveal cracked teeth and a lolling tongue.

"Zombies," Johnny stated, his voice low and almost a whisper as he aimed. "What the hell has happened to today?"

From above the trees, two more dropped and landed with loud thuds before they forced themselves to stand. "How did they get up there?" Vic asked as he opened the bag to reveal real bullets that he slotted quickly into the pistol. Johnny felt a rumble underneath him and jumped out of the way as more hands emerged to snatch him. When they missed, the owners of the arms forced themselves from the dirt and fixed their attention on the detectives.

"I'm wondering why they are here at all," the young man muttered and turned the power up on his gun when he realized the ectofire shard was still within. "Is there a cemetery nearby?"

"Check the map but I don't remember passing one," Vic answered as he shut the chamber of his revolver. "Looking at their clothes, most of these guys are from modern times." He pointed at a man in an ensemble similar to his own. "With some exceptions."

"What woke them?" Johnny fired a blast of flames as a couple inched closer. The zombies crept around the group with their claws extended as they stared blankly at them with the hollow lights in their eyes. Some of their garments dragged along the ground and all their clothing was in various states of disrepair that worsened as pieces were torn off or fell away when they shuffled toward them.

"Can they be exorcised?" Johnny asked as they closed in.

"Unfortunately, I don't think we've got the time for that, partner." Vic held his gun up. "Nor do we have the ingredients. And since neither you nor I are trained in exorcism without using the party favors, we're gonna have to do this the classic way."

Johnny steadied himself and nodded at his partner. "Either way, cleanup will be a bitch." He fired quickly at one of the fiends and its body erupted in green flames and turned into a melted paste almost instantly. Another swiped his arm and its claws scratched his jacket but bounced off. He placed his hand against its skull and shoved it down before he pressed his gun against its ear and pulled the trigger. The zombie's eyes and mouth lit up as the flames burned it from within to melt it before it turned into the same slime as the other.

Despite Vic being a ghost, he was not completely immune to the hungry nature of the zombies. Due to movies made back in the day when information on the different types of supernatural creatures was less well known and rumors and fear ran rampant, zombies were thought to consume only flesh and this was untrue.

The zombie body needed flesh to sustain its form but the spirit controlling it also needed stygia and phantasma to maintain its hold on the living world like every other ghost. It could get that from other ghosts and Vic looked quite inviting to a few of them.

One leapt at him but he danced easily around the attack. When another attempted to attack from behind, he turned and fired. The bullet impacted the head and blew clean through it and it tottered for a brief moment before it fell.

"Damn, it has been a while since I've heard that sound from my gun," he commented with a chuckle as he turned and fired two more shots in quick succession. Two more fell to headshots and the ghost detective drew the attention of some of the others with his effort. They turned to target him but their shuffling progress meant he didn't have to move all that much.

"Do we know how many there are?" Johnny called as he held a group at bay by firing a stream of flames in front of him. "I should probably change to normal ether rounds before I set this forest on—" A larger blast of blue flames consumed the group of zombies in front of him. He turned to see where it had come from and grinned when he caught sight of the caster. "Aiyana!"

"Hey! Good to see you," Vic called as he dodged to the side of an attacking zombie before he raised his arm and fired through its head. "A friendly face at the party."

The shaman let the flames in her palms fade as she looked at them. "This is my fault," she confessed and surprised them. "I will explain once we have taken care of the monsters, but you must prepare." She turned as the young detective noticed that the earth had begun to shake. "Something worse is coming."

61

CHAPTER NINE

"Something worse than zombies?" Johnny asked as he changed his magazine quickly to his normal ether rounds. "Well, you can go ahead and bring it on. We started the day dealing with ghouls and phantasms."

"I am not sure what to call it," she admitted and ran to him as she launched a fireball at two shambling zombies. The flames enveloped them and burned them to ash in seconds. "But it is a monster like those Axmen clones you battled last week."

"Do these guys have anything to do with him?" he asked as he loaded his gun. "You said this was your fault somehow."

"I also said I would explain when we are done," she snapped and her eyes widened as she pointed behind him. "Look out!"

He whirled and pounded the barrel of his gun into the chest of an oncoming zombie and fired. Bones and fabric spewed and phantasma began to flow out of the wound. He felt something shift under him and immediately expected more zombies to crawl from under the forest floor.

Not this time, he decided. He shoved his gun into the dirt, increased the power to its maximum, and fired. The ground shuddered and two corpses emerged. Their bones turned brittle as they struggled to stand while their phantasma poured out of multiple wounds in their body. One reached for him and he simply smiled and backhanded its skull with his gun. Its head was ripped off its shoulders and the rest of the body fell apart. The zombie behind it fell into the hole and turned to mush.

Aiyana cried out when she felt a sharp pain in her side and she turned to a half-destroyed zombie that had made a small cut in her ribs. "Someone needs to finish their work!" she yelled, kicked the being, and flung it high before she blasted it with a rather large fireball.

"It might have been my bad. I forgot how tenacious these bastards can be," Vic replied. "I'm gonna pop the heads from now on."

She closed her eyes and began to hum as heavy winds swirled around her. "You should both get down," she warned as she held one hand out. The blue flames launched and were caught in the winds, which she manipulated to snake them through the forest to eliminate many of the remaining zombies.

Johnny stood as he watched most of the beings burn in the flames. He fired at a couple that had somehow avoided them, mostly by being flat on the dirt at the time, he assumed. But Aiyana and Vic cleaned out the stragglers. "Damn. Not bad, Aiyana," he told her and prepared to put his gun away. "Not bad at a—"

"We aren't done," she stated and turned to him. "Remember?"

"Ah, yeah, the monster." He looked around as he checked his weapon and twirled it in his hand. "So where is it? Hiding in a cave or something?"

She paused and frowned as she glanced into the forest. "I'm not sure," she admitted and turned to him as Vic floated toward them. "It was chasing me after I had left my sanctuary but I was able to get away because it was still forming—it is large and uncoordinated. I ran into you while I was running from it."

The young detective peered deeper into the trees. "I get the sense that something is there but that could be left from these guys." He pushed one of the bodies away from his foot. "Do we go hunting for it or should we—"

Another rumble shuddered through the dirt but this time, it was not the zombies. The three focused on a group of trees as a massive, bloated monstrosity approached, knocked the tall trunks over, and uttered disgusting moans. It had two massive arms, with two more on its back that clutched large rocks. The group fell back until they stood together while the monster trudged over the bodies and sludgy remains and seemed to absorb them into its form to make it grow even more.

Johnny did not hesitate. He fired on the creature immediately but it held one of its hands out and absorbed the impact, much to his and Vic's shock. They continued to fire while Aiyana studied the goliath and noticed an etching of some kind in the palm. She tried to call a warning to her companions but they could not hear her and were too busy trying to dodge the large rocks the beast threw at them. Vic was barely able to ghost through it but as he reloaded his pistol, he looked at the abomination's hand and saw more clearly what it was.

A mouth opened in the terror's palm and screamed.

The sound was almost enough to incapacitate him instantly and he felt that only his bond to Johnny kept him from being either sent back to Limbo or obliterated. This was the cry of a banshee, something it wasn't—or perhaps it was along with being so much more. It was certainly an abomination, some kind of composite of several different supernatural beings forged into one. Aiyana would have considerable explaining to do once they killed this damn monster.

He looked at his partner, who struggled to stand while he covered his ears. The young detective shook his head and fought to regain his focus. He aimed his gun down the gullet of the hand-mouth and fired a full blast that hurled him back but also unleashed a blast of ether into the screaming maw.

As the shriek stopped abruptly, the arm began to engorge before it burst, and blood and phantasma poured out of the wound as the abomination lurched to the side. Vic took his chance, checked his gun to see that he had four out of six shots, and hastily retrieved the two bullets he had dropped. He shoved them into the chamber as he elevated toward their foe. With his weapon aimed at its chest, he fired all six rounds into where a heart would normally be before he began to fire his spectral rounds and dotted them all along the grotesque body.

"Burn the bastard, Aiyana!" he shouted. The shaman dropped to her knees as she nodded and pressed her palms together, formed the flames again, and blasted them toward the abomination. He nodded as she scorched its flesh and he smiled when the flames began to pour into the wounds he'd inflicted as well and burned it from the inside out.

The monster snatched him with its other hand. He tried to go intangible but couldn't escape its grasp. It brought him toward its mouth and opened it to reveal rows of rounded, stubby teeth leading into a dark gullet.

"Shit, there are worse ways to go and those might be preferable!" He grunted and tried to wrest himself free before another large blast of ether severed the other arm. As he was released, the abomination toppled from the impact with two of its four arms now severed from its frame.

"Nice shot, kid!" Vic called and winced when he saw that Johnny had been launched into a tree. "Walk it off!" He looked to where Aiyana continued to attack the freakish beast and her efforts finally seemed to be succeeding. Pieces of its flesh turned into the same rotting slime that many of the zombies had become.

She stopped the flames as she lowered her hands to her knees and began to draw deep breaths. Vic took a minute to watch the flames consume the abomination and the ethereal light danced off the trees and cast a blue hue on his jacket. He approached it slowly and slid three bullets into his pistol as it uttered a last low groan. With his gun pressed to the back of its head, he fired the three shots before he stepped back as the flames continued to rise.

"This was my fault." Aiyana muttered as she stood. "I came to commune with the spirits. It is better outside cities and in places of nature but here, something was blocking me—or perhaps them—from reaching out."

Although he was listening to her, a glint from within the flames caught his eye. "Maybe it's simply a bad location? The connection between the living and spirit world could be hazy here."

She chuckled. "It doesn't work that way—not like crossing points work. I attempted to commune with a voice I heard here, one that turned into many. I guess I became a conduit of some kind as I reached many waiting souls who crossed over and took control of the bodies in the forest."

"Here in the forest?" Johnny questioned and glanced at the zombie horde. "So they were buried here? Was this a graveyard at some point?"

"My guess is that it is, but not an official one," Vic murmured and plunged his hand into the dying flames to take something from the corpse of the monster. "Bodies dumped by killers, maybe lost hikers and hunters, all piling up over time." He rubbed whatever he had found on his jacket as if it did any good. "Aiyana, could another one of your kind—you know, those spirit callers—can they stop you from talking with the spirits?"

She frowned, scrabbled in her bag, and withdrew a totem. "I suppose they could, maybe. I haven't heard of anything like that. It would be more likely that our powers crossed and interfered with one another. But that would require another being like that to be near—"

Vic held up what he'd found inside the abomination. A figure made out of straw and painted in different inks was bound to a circular pendant with various carvings on it. "Here?" she asked in confusion. "A witch?"

"Your guess is probably better than mine." He threw it to Johnny, who looked at it and passed it to Aiyana.

"Looks like you don't have to beat yourself up too much," the young detective told her as he put his gun away. "We can save that for the necromantic witch."

CHAPTER TEN

"This was my sanctuary," Aiyana said as she showed her companions a small circle drawn on the forest floor surrounded by three totems, flower petals, and leaves. "It's something all spirit callers share—a kind of personal haven we create when we try to access the spirit realm."

"We simply use a door," Johnny commented as he studied the tiny space. "Or something door-like. Although I do have to ask what the totems and flowers are for."

"The flowers are offerings. I keep some with me in my bag. The totems act as anchors. You might not be able to smell them due to the wind but I coat them in a special perfume that acts as smelling salts to some extent and keeps me grounded," she explained as she picked one up and sniffed it. "Fortunately, I didn't start burning them so I can use them again."

"You should probably wait until we deal with that 'interference' before you make another attempt," Vic suggested and gazed deeper into the forest. "Do you think the witch tried to stop you?"

She shrugged as she gathered her things. "I have no way to know for sure. Spirit callers don't automatically assume another is good or evil. We all have different ways to talk to spirits."

Johnny sighed and looked at her. "While I applaud the open-mindedness of it all, you should also remember that whatever she was doing summoned a horde of malevolent ghosts to make zombies and whatever the hell that big bastard was."

"And possibly to control them," his partner added and held up the trinket he had found. "Although since none of us knows what this could be, we're all simply guessing."

"And I told you that we were both trying to communicate with the other side simultaneously," she countered and pushed to her feet. "For the two of you, it may be a simple matter but for even the greatest of callers, it is a very involved process and attempting any kind of piercing of the veil is complex. Having two callers trying to do so at the same time in different ways so close to one another can be very problematic and lead to any number of problems."

"So…what? You think she was inviting all those spirits for tea?" The young detective raised a brow as he leaned against a tree. "I thought you said all callers respected the divide between spirits and humans more than anyone else. Even if there was no evil intent behind bringing spirits over it can still end poorly."

Aiyana sighed as she packed her totems in her bag. "I'm only saying that we shouldn't jump to conclusions either."

"Perhaps we can ask her." Vic shifted his attention to the trees.

"Do you have some idea where she might be?" Johnny asked and looked up to see both his companions staring at him, although she was much more panicked. "What?" He looked slowly to the side and realized that a figure in a dark dress and hood stood directly beside him. Heterochromatic eyes of silver and amber stared at him and he yelped, jumped back, and drew his weapon. "Who are you?"

The woman studied the three of them with eerie interest. She wore a frown but didn't show any obvious anger and twirled her graying hair with her finger as her head tilted from left to right. No one spoke for some time and they merely stewed in an awkward, heavy silence while the woman's mouth moved but made no noise. She finally straightened and pointed at Vic. "You—you will join me, yes?"

The ghost detective cocked his head and slid his hand into his jacket. "Uh...I don't think so, lady."

"And why not?" She hissed her irritation. "You came when I summoned you, didn't you? You accepted my offer?"

"Offer of what?" he asked and produced the trinket. "Does it have something to do with this?"

The woman's eyes widened as she shuffled forward unnaturally and Johnny moved his hand to his gun. She stopped several yards away and pointed. "You have my charm. Where did you get it?"

"Out of the slimy remains of your damned beast," Vic retorted. "What the hell have you been doing?"

She lowered her head. "So it is silent then? I thought as much. Humph. No matter. It can be made again."

"You made that on purpose?" Aiyana asked but received no reply. "What are you doing out here?"

The witch laughed. "I live out here. What are you doing here, shaman?"

"I was attempting to commune with the spirits," she explained and pointed to her sanctuary. "It seems our rituals disrupted one another."

"Indeed so." The woman shifted her gaze slowly from one to the other. "Why do you seek the spirits? Does something ail you?"

"What's with the Ren fair speak?" Johnny chortled quietly as Vic hovered closer and held the charm up.

"You can have this back. It's not like we have much use for it, but perhaps you can help us." This made all three of them look at the ghost with confusion. "We discovered sigils at a factory near here and it was obvious that it was done by a druid or witch like yourself. We believe they were being used to contain supernatural beings for a later use by a deranged escaped ghost known as the Axman."

The witch perked up at the name and Johnny and Aiyana began to shift uncomfortably as she chuckled. "Ah yes, the one who has been causing such chaos amongst both the living and the dead."

"You know of him?" the shaman asked and received a slight nod.

"Are you working with him?" Johnny asked more pointedly. The woman did not respond to this in any way except for a toothy smile that revealed graying teeth as she faded into the trees. "Shit, after her!"

The group pursued her quickly and headed deeper into the forest. Vic took point since he was able to use his higher elevation to search for her but he found nothing. Irritated, he wondered if she had hidden somehow. Then he noticed a break in the trees a little farther ahead and motioned for Johnny and Aiyana to keep moving.

When they pushed through the forest, they stood outside a large field and the crops waved gently in the breeze. The young detective noticed a few fence posts but beyond that, nothing to indicate that these were still active tilling fields.

Before he could ask where she went, a tapping sound made him freeze. It continued with clicking and shuffling through the crops. Aiyana dug into her bag and produced a totem with a small necklace that began to rattle.

"Something is wrong here," she muttered.

Johnny turned, his gun ready as he raised his eyepatch. He immediately located a pair of faint white eyes through the crops and fired. The eyes darted away and his shots hit nothing as he fired twice more and tried to target whatever was stalking around him.

Unfortunately, it caught him first.

Something leapt out of the crops and swooped from the midafternoon sky to land on thin legs made of some kind of dark wood. Its body was sinewy and haggard and covered by a thin cloth, with what appeared to be bones protruding. On closer inspection, however, he decided it was too thin and looked like…straw?

The creature turned and the dimly lit eyes stared at him through a hood that wrapped around its face. A stitched smile was present on its face and it held its hands up to brandish bladed attachments along its fingers and arms. This was a scarecrow—a moving, seemingly living scarecrow. While his mind almost instantly reached the conclusion that it was simply a ghost wearing the form of a scarecrow, that did not make it any less disconcerting.

"Well…you're new," he stated, raised his gun, and aimed it at the being as he adjusted the power and considered switching to the ectofire.

The scarecrow took a few hobbling steps forward and craned its head to the side at an unnatural angle, and the fixed smile seemed to spread across its face.

"You're a damn creepy thing, aren't you?" he asked, slid the scale into place, and pulled the trigger. The scarecrow lowered to the dirt before it lunged at him, its arms wide as the shot sailed overhead. Johnny noticed the darkened spots along the blades. He fired twice and both shots ripped through the scarecrow but didn't slow it. It closed in, reached back with both arms, and cast them forward as he dove away and fired another shot.

This one made the scarecrow spiral out and bought him time to get onto his feet. He opened his gun, removed the ectofire cartridge, and quickly swapped it with the ether magazine as the scarecrow spun its entire body on one leg. "All right, you raggedy bastard, let's see how you handle this." He aimed and the weapon spewed flames to coat the unnatural being. The scarecrow caught fire and he laughed, but that faltered once it turned to him again and extended its now fiery arms as it stalked forward. "Well, shit."

CHAPTER ELEVEN

"What the hell was Johnny chasing?" Aiyana asked as she looked into the sky. "That didn't look like any zombie I've ever seen."

"That's because it's a scarecrow," Vic replied, caught between going to help his partner and the rapid movement among the crops that moved in their direction. "Eyes up, Aiyana. Something is coming."

He unloaded his revolver. If these were merely possessed objects, spectral bullets would work far better than real ones. They stared as figures bounded over the fields directly toward them. His companion pressed her hands together before she thrust them out. The winds picked up quickly and swirled the scarecrows to fling them in several directions.

She then set fire to the fields in an attempt to intercept the other attackers that rushed toward them. Three leapt up, two of them already partially on fire, and she studied them quickly. They appeared to be scarecrows with various sharp weapons along their body. One targeted her and swooped into an airborne attack with sharpened spikes on its legs aimed at her head. She simply jumped back, absorbed her flames into her hands, and cast a large fireball to incinerate it before it had a chance to land.

With a smile of satisfaction, she watched it burn. It opened its maw and something glinted amongst the inferno and several small blades launched out. She ducked hastily to the side but sustained small cuts along her left cheek and arm.

"Ah!" she shouted as the scarecrow finally melted. The other one, still on fire, snapped the arm with the relatively paltry flames and threw it at her. She simply held a hand up and absorbed the incoming fire into her own. A small grin returned as the scarecrow's head tilted, seemingly in confusion, and she sent another fiery blast at it.

Vic fired on the scarecrows with abandon. He was a little cocky at first, as he did not believe these walking garden decorations could hurt him and was sure he would be able to eliminate them with a single shot. However, while his shots did wound them and phantasma bled out of their forms, the scarecrows continued their advance. Even if he believed he could not be hurt, for whatever reason, they certainly believed he could. One of them lunged and caught him in the shoulder. He backed away as he felt a familiar cold hollowness and looked down at a mark through his clavicle. "What the hell?"

"They are guardians for a witch," Aiyana called to him once she noticed his shock. "Is it so surprising that they might have some way to harm a ghost?"

Vic placed his gun to the head of the scarecrow and fired. "And here I was worried about having too much fun."

The creature swiped at him again and he jumped back as the phantasma poured out of its head. "Resilient bags of dried grass, aren't they?"

"The witch is controlling them. We can send them back to the afterlife by destroying their vessels but as long as she's in control, she can keep them tethered longer and potentially summon more."

"Then it looks like we'll have to pay her a visit." The ghost detective fired another couple of shots into the scarecrow's legs and hobbled it as he floated up and looked over the field. He noticed a lone shack deeper within. "I'll bet good coins that's where she's hiding!" he shouted to her, pointed toward it, and took a moment to look around. "Now, where's Johnny?"

As if hearing his name called, his partner barreled through the field and dropped a flaming pile of cloth as he rolled across the dirt. He scrambled to his feet, looked at the pile of scraps that remained of the scarecrow, and spat on it as he heard sounds of battle and saw flames and flashes of phantasma at the front of the field. He raced out, his gun at the ready, only to see Aiyana eliminate the last wounded scarecrows Vic had left. She walked up to him and he sighed with relief.

"I'm glad to see you could manage without me." He chuckled.

The shaman pulled a cloth from her bag, handed it to him, and gestured to his forehead. "And I'm glad to see you in one piece."

"Of course!" he replied and used the cloth to bind the wound on his forehead. "Did you honestly think a bag of sticks and hay could stop me?"

"Normally, no," she replied and glanced at the remains of the golems around them. "But scarecrows don't usually attack on their own and we don't exactly get 'normal' in our line of work."

"Heh, no kidding." He chuckled, ejected his ectofire cartridge, and replaced it with the ether one. "All right. If that's taken care of, we should look for the witch, right?"

Before Aiyana could respond, both were startled when the remains moved and began to twitch and slid along the ground.

"Follow me!" Vic ordered from above and pointed at the shack again. His companions nodded and raced toward the crops. They made sure to glance behind them occasionally in case the killer scarecrows were able to stitch themselves together, but from what remained of them after Aiyana's attacks, they would be lucky to make even one.

When Johnny heard a ravenous shriek, however, he realized that might be exactly what was happening. "Shit. Keep moving!" he ordered when they finally cleared the field and approached the shack.

As they reached it, he prepared to kick the door before Aiyana stopped him and pointed out a small sigil above the door frame. She burned it with her flames, nodded, and stepped aside so he could kick the door in and enter with Vic, who hastily began to block the doors and windows with whatever spare furniture and items he could find.

"Hey, kid, did Val give you a blockade by chance?"

He nodded, retrieved it from his jacket, and backtracked to place it on the door. "This will probably hold off anything out there better than an old sofa."

"Can you see her?" the ghost asked and both his

companions shook their heads. "This place isn't exactly big. Is there a cellar or…"

"Are we sure she's here?" Johnny looked at some charms hanging from the ceiling. "We saw her head to the field and this is probably where she lives unless the occult has become chic recently. But maybe she's hiding somewhere else."

"That is certainly possible, but spirit callers of every kind require sanctuaries for our strongest connection to the other side. If she's controlling or at least summoning this many spirits to work for her, she would need to be in her primary sanctuary, which would most likely be her abode."

Something thudded against the side of the house and Johnny and Aiyana turned to where what appeared to be a scythe attempted to cut through the walls. He chuckled. "Honestly, I'm merely glad it isn't an ax."

"Hey kids, look here." They turned to look at Vic, who stood in front of a grandfather clock. "There's a passage behind this."

"How can you tell?" the shaman asked as she walked closer to study the antique.

"Because I flew through it," he replied casually and moved to the side. "It's some kind of secret passage. I can simply ghost through it but you two will probably have to find out how to open it. I suggest starting with the clock-face and—"

He didn't finish as his partner interrupted him when he stepped to the side of the clock and drove his boot into it. His first kick dislodged it slightly, his second cracked it, and it toppled with his third to reveal a narrow passage behind it.

"I can see both phantasma and ether on the walls. Someone or something is definitely down there." He glanced at his companions while whatever was outside continued to pound into the barrier. "Let's try to finish this quickly before we're the ones strung up in the fields, yeah? I have a feeling this witch is more wicked than nice."

CHAPTER TWELVE

Although they attempted stealth as they descended, it was a pointless endeavor given how old and rickety the steps were.

"If she is down there, she's probably heard us by now." Johnny winced when one of the boards broke beneath his boot.

"Which makes me wonder what the hell she is doing down there," Vic muttered as he inserted a couple of bullets into the chamber of his revolver. "It must be important if she is simply going to ignore us."

"She could be doing exactly that," Aiyana told him and produced a small flame to light their way. "We spirit callers are trained to tap in and defend against the supernatural. Our powers do little against the living."

Johnny regarded the small flame a little dubiously. "So you're saying that would not burn me?"

"Well, I'm not exactly sure, given your existence as a revenant." She looked thoughtfully at him as she moved the flame closer. "I could check if you would like me—"

He stopped in his tracks. "No thanks. I guess I'll have to stay curious." He pointed farther down the steps. "Look ahead. It seems we found her."

A shadow on the wall was created by flames in the room ahead. The witch's silhouette was motionless, her palms together and her head down, deep in a trance. An enraged shriek from above made Vic look back and mutter, "How long do you think the ether barrier will hold?"

"It should hold for up to half an hour," Johnny replied as he focused on the area ahead. "But we've seen one breached before."

"Do you want me to keep watch while you deal with her?" his partner asked and surprised the young detective, who looked questioningly at him. "It's only a precaution in case whatever is out there gets into the house. Plus, this witch controls spirits. I don't think she has any control over me right now but I don't wanna take the chance and get too close. You got this, right?"

Johnny held his gun up and glanced at Aiyana, who shrugged at him. He looked at the ghost detective and nodded before the two of them descended while Vic stood guard on the stairs. They reached the bottom, stepped into a small room, and held their hands over their mouths as smoke began to fill the space.

The witch now stood in front of a small firepit. Although a hatch had been constructed above it, this appeared to have not been cleaned in quite some time. Other charms and decorations hung around her. The young detective noticed bones among them and for once, had the macabre hope that they were merely animal bones.

They both stared at the witch for a moment, unsure if disturbing her would make the situation worse. He was the first push past their hesitation and held his pistol up as he said, "Do you mind calling off your pack of mutant killer scarecrows?"

The witch was unmoved, however. He prepared to fire, if for no other reason than to get her attention, when Aiyana stepped forward and approached her.

"Fellow caller, we are sorry...I am sorry for disrupting your previous ritual. If you are simply defending yourself, let us know and call your summons off." The words hung in the air for a moment.

A quiet snicker preceded the response and the woman tilted her head as if in thought. "Defending myself? I suppose so, in a manner of speaking. But more importantly, I am defending him." She turned in almost an instant and her pure white eyes focused—or, at least, he assumed they did—on Johnny. "The Axman."

"Oh, come on!" He aimed his weapon at her again. "He even has witches on his payroll."

"I don't work for him." The flames in the pit began to grow. "Not yet, but I believe in what he is trying to do. No separation should exist between us and our lost loved ones. There is no point in a divide between the planes."

"What the hell is she rambling about?" Johnny asked loudly as the fire behind her began to crackle loudly. He waited to see if Aiyana had any tricks up her sleeve, but that appeared unlikely and it also seemed like this would get out of hand far too quickly.

"Separation from our loved ones?" the shaman

muttered and took a totem from her bag. "Is she talking about the veil?"

"That is why I will contact him now and offer my aid again!" She cackled with glee and pointed to the two of them. "You are marked by his essence. Surely he will want to know where his strays have gone."

"Marked by his essence?" Aiyana repeated and looked from the witch to Johnny. "The Axman's essence?"

"Strays? She thinks we're strays? From what? She thinks we're his flunkies?" he muttered in annoyance.

His companion ignored him. "What do you mean we are marked by his essence?"

"Do not try to lie to me!" the witch roared as the flames began to contort into a circular shape behind her. "I see it on your bodies. You have seen the Axman with your own eyes."

"She must be talking about the one who attacked the police precinct," Aiyana suggested and held the totem up as it began to glow.

"The fake? I guess it could have had some of the Axman's actual phantasma. It looked exactly like the photos." He reached behind his belt. "Look, she's losing it and I don't think we have much time left to—"

"Kid, I heard something break up there!" Vic yelled, and loud thuds moved rapidly toward them. "Wrap it up!"

The witch beamed a grin and revealed her gray teeth. "I'll let my pet deal with your flesh." She turned toward the flames and purple phantasma poured from her hands as the blaze formed what appeared to be a portal or window for her to look through. "I will deal with your souls and prepare them as an offering."

"Aiyana, do you still wanna try reaching out to her?" Johnny asked and she looked at him with real concern as gunshots were fired behind her.

"End it."

The young detective nodded curtly and fired at the witch, and the ectofire streaked toward her. She turned and held a hand out, and the supernatural flames divided and warped around her as she laughed mockingly.

"Ha! Was that supposed to kill me? I have control over all supernatural forms of pow—hurk!" A knife was embedded into her head and her body slumped as Vic swooped down the stairs. Behind him, a large, misshapen scarecrow creature began to spasm and fall apart as phantasma burst from its body and flowed into the floor.

"The fire was only a distraction," Johnny stated as he walked to the witch's corpse, knelt, and removed the blade. "This is what was supposed to kill you—why am I talking to a dead body? I'm not a caller."

He sighed and flicked the blade a few times in an attempt to get the blood off. As he looked around for something to wipe it off with, both Vic and Aiyana stared at the firepit with shining and wide eyes respectively. He turned and realized that something was in the portal the witch had created that was fast unraveling. The figure was skeletal like Vic but black-and-white lines shimmered around his body. He looked exactly like the decoy that had attacked them only days earlier.

"The Axman," Aiyana whispered as the trio stared at him. He appeared to stand in the middle of a sigil of some kind, his eyes dark and boney hands pressed together. Behind him, Johnny registered rows of seats, battered and damaged, and off to the side what appeared to be a large burgundy curtain. This strongly suggested that he was in a theater of some kind.

"She found him?" Vic muttered and watched the image cautiously with the others.

"I think she already did before," Aiyana replied and rubbed her arms as she took a step back. "She said she was offering her services again." She looked at the totem. "I guess he didn't want to work with her for some reason."

"That is because," a hissing, irate voice began, "a witch can often be more trouble than they are worth." Suddenly, the eyes of the Axman shined like stars in the void of his face as he studied them. "And it seems I shouldn't have spared her the first time." He stood and raised an arm toward them. Johnny and Vic snapped out of their stupor and readied their guns. "I should learn from my mistakes—starting with you."

"No!" Aiyana cried and flung the totem at the blaze. It touched the fire in a blaze of light and the flames turned white momentarily before they were absorbed into it. She fell to her knees as the two partners looked at one another in shock.

The young detective wanted to ask what she had done but she trembled violently and he pushed the question to one side. He put his gun away and knelt beside her as he reminded himself that she was a shaman and able to not only see ghosts but feel them in a way that he couldn't understand. As he placed a hand on her shoulder to comfort her, he looked at the firepit.

He wondered what she'd felt coming from that demon that scared her so.

CHAPTER THIRTEEN

"They still aren't answering." Val sighed in frustration as she turned her phone off and placed it in one of the cup holders.

"The Maggios or your other friends?" Donovan asked as she slowed the car when they approached a crosswalk.

"Johnny. I tried to call Aiyana as well but she barely uses her phone for anything." She looked both ways and noticed two ghosts staring at her. "Tell me something, Agent—what do you see over there?"

Donovan raised an eyebrow. "Two ghosts." He folded his arms. "Probably travelers or looking for a way out of the city."

"Do you see them as former humans?" she asked as she continued down the street again. "That they were alive once?"

He closed his eyes and nodded, her insinuation not lost on him. "If you have questions you can simply ask them outright. I know you take issue with the way the SEA handles the supernatural, but I'm telling you we aren't all like that."

"So you are making a change within the organization?" she asked, genuinely curious. "What would cause something like that? Especially with old souls like Lovett in the higher ranks."

The man smirked and gestured vaguely with his hand. "It's true that the Agency has a fair number of the old guard still in the ranks, but that's how almost all government agencies are, right? What's changing is how much new blood is coming in, both by traditional means like training or being scouted in other organizations or the military. Or scouted at a young age like me." A small white orb formed in his hand and surprised her, and her gaze darted constantly between it and the road to make sure to not hit anything. "Neat right? It's my empath—a ball of ether that can trap phantasma and track it. As you can imagine, it is quite useful in both recon and hunting missions."

Valerie felt a pang of jealousy. "How did you manifest it?"

Donovan closed his hand around the orb and it disappeared. "It simply happened like it does with most specters who get an empath. I don't know what made it take the form it did. Maybe it's simply because I liked hide and seek as a kid? But I was scouted when I was a kid and was made an offer once I turned eighteen to train with the Agency."

"What? Did they see you messing around with it one day in an ice cream shop or something?"

He frowned a little and tapped his thigh in thought. "You know, I never got the complete story about that. I guess between all the flurry of those early days at the facility the question kind of got lost in the shuffle. I am registered as a specter and my empath too. That was the most likely story I came up with."

She chuckled as she shook her head. "You are a far more trusting person than I am. I'm not entirely sure what I would do if some person dressed in all-white tried to tell me to join their special organization. Well, I guess I would be confused that they were talking to me rather than about me, but after I realized it was a government agency and not a militia, I would probably go about my bus—"

Her phone rang and she snatched it up as Aiyana's name flashed across the screen. She pressed the button to answer. "Aiyana? Where have you been? Did you...a witch?" Donovan straightened in his seat. "She's dead? Summoned ghosts to do what? You saw the Axman? Aiya— Aiya! Calm down, please. You are speaking too fast...

"You're with Johnny and Vic, right? Look, I'm on my way to see Annie and Marco. Can you meet me there? All right, cool. Also, I'm bringing someone new in. You'll meet him when you arrive." She bit the inside of her cheek. "The body? I should arrange for someone to collect it. Send me the coordinates. All right. Thank you, Aiyana. See you soon."

She hung up and her phone chimed as the shaman sent her a text with pictures and the coordinates for the location of the dead witch. For a brief moment, she considered sending it to Shemar, but with how hectic everything was at the station, they could all use a break and the Agency did seem eager to do...well, anything.

"There's a dead witch at that location." She handed her companion the phone. "she sent some photos."

He took the device and looked at the message. "Should I apologize for overhearing?"

Valerie shrugged. "I guess it's preferable to you trying to block your ears as you sing 'la la la' while I'm talking." She drew a deep breath and asked, "Can you send it to some of your Agency friends? Ones who won't ask a ton of questions? Maybe that will distract them enough to give my people some breathing space."

Donovan nodded, retrieved his phone, and sent a message. "Sure. He'll probably be thankful for the diversion. Besides, he's a spirit caller so he'll be able to take care of anything your friends missed."

"I doubt they did but I guess it doesn't hurt to make sure." As she slowed for a traffic light, she noticed an Agency truck pass them in the other direction. "I've seen them taking tech and parts all over the city. What are they doing?"

"It depends where they are going," he answered without looking away from his phone. "Probably updating the ectographs if they are in the city. If they are part of the teams heading to the outskirts of the city, they are probably preparing the dome."

"The dome?" she asked and didn't like the sound of that. "What is that?"

"Think of it as a big-ass ether barrier," he responded casually as he placed her phone into the cupholder. "It's used to contain any supernatural presence in a large area like a city. Any ghost are trapped within and they can't even use crossing points."

"And you guys can simply do that?" she demanded and almost side-swiped another car when she tried to move to the next lane. "We have to prepare the civilians for that. They will freak!"

"They won't even notice." He sounded indifferent, almost to the point that it annoyed her. "Even specters have a hard time noticing anything other than a slight glimmer on occasion. It's high-grade, fancy tech. The generators are a tad loud but the devices themselves are out of the city so it will probably not bother anyone."

He folded his arms again. "I wouldn't worry about it too much. We can't simply do it like you suggest without either permission from the governor of the state or mayor of the city, or we have confirmed the existence of a level-five or six 'fourth-dimensional'"—he used air quotes and a thin, reedy voice for the last words—"threat in the area. Under those conditions, we can activate the barrier but they set it up just in case."

Valerie rolled her eyes as she looked reflexively into the sky in an attempt to see the glimmer he'd mentioned. "The Agency is a fan of the idea that asking forgiveness is better than permission, huh?"

Donovan laughed with genuine amusement. "I wish they could be that considerate. Most of the higher-ups would merely say that getting permission slows things and forgiveness is unnecessary in all but the most extreme cases." For a moment, he had a deeply troubled frown on his face. "I don't think the people of Savannah got an apology, for whatever good it would do."

They maintained a tight-lipped silence for the remainder of the journey to the Maggios. She looked at the sky again as they pulled up. While she didn't see a glimmer, she did see rain clouds approaching in the distance.

CHAPTER FOURTEEN

Johnny pressed the doorbell as Vic continued to admire the house. "Man, it's a damn shame what happened to their old home, but Marco and Annie certainly got an upgrade."

"It's not their place, technically," he muttered and stepped off the porch to look at the windows of the second floor. "It's their parents' vacation house—or second house? Whichever. They ain't here so let them use it while their place is being repaired."

"Well here's to hoping they don't need to get this fixed too." The ghost detective scowled at the dark clouds rolling in. "It's starting the sprinkle."

"Are you still worried that he has minions at his side?" Aiyana asked and joined Johnny on the porch as the rain picked up.

"Not from what we know. Hell, he vacuumed the souls out of his last batch," the young detective recalled with a queasy look in his eye. "But anything could have changed since then. And we saw him in that portal or fire window, whatever the hell it was. He stood over some sigil."

"You don't happen to know what that was, do you?" Vic asked Aiyana. She shook her head and looked like she was about to speak but they stopped when the doorknob jiggled.

"Hey, guys!" Marco greeted them warmly as he opened the door. "It looks like it's starting to rain. Come on in."

"I appreciate ya," Johnny responded as he and Aiyana stepped inside onto the white tiled floors.

"You seem chipper to see us, Marco," Vic noted as he tipped his hat. "The last time we visited you, we were attacked by one of the Axman's flunkies."

The slick-haired young man grinned. "Yeah, but we took care of it and if it happens again, we'll take care of it too." He clapped him on the shoulder but his hand met no resistance. "Besides, it's not like he has more guys to throw at us, right?"

The ghost shrugged, walked inside, and left Marco hanging, which confused him slightly. He looked beyond the door as if something might be waiting for him out there before he closed it slowly and headed to the living room.

"Hello, Annie." Aiyana greeted the young woman with a hug. "I'm sorry I haven't returned your messages over these last few days."

Annie Maggio smiled and waved her off. "It's all right, Aiya. Valerie told me you are often busy in your line of work. I only wanted to make sure you were all right." She looked at Johnny. "Same with you, Rev."

"Hmm?" he muttered, waved at Valerie, and noticed the stereo system around the TV. "I've responded to your messages."

"Only in the vaguest ways, man," Marco retorted and fell onto a loveseat. "I like to think surviving an assault by a supernatural terror from the depths of hell would bond us a little more."

The young detective tucked his hands into his jacket and nodded. "And it did, Marco, truly—so much so that I've schlepped all around the city and Limbo to make sure we can finish this bastard off."

"Yeah, I've wondered about that," the other man mused. "Are we sure he isn't dead? The only guy who says he isn't was a freak from Limbo who wouldn't give you his name, right?"

Johnny and Aiyana shared a despondent look. "I had hoped for that myself. But we saw something today that snuffed that completely."

"What did you find?" This voice was new to the revenant and he turned to a man several years older than him in an all-white outfit with the Agency emblem on the right breast.

"Uh...howdy." He gave the newcomer a half-hearted wave. "And who are you?"

The stranger extended a hand to him. "Agent Donovan. It's nice to finally meet you, Detective Desperaux."

He responded with an equally half-hearted handshake. "You can call me Johnny, buddy."

"What's the spook doing here?" Vic asked and tilted his head to regard the Agent with disapproval.

Valerie shrugged. "I didn't think we would all get together like this. I brought him here on a... let's say a trial. I was only gonna have him interview Marco and Annie and report to his superiors to hopefully get them off our backs, but then everything else happened." She looked at Johnny. "I still don't have a good grasp of what, exactly, so do you wanna fill the class in?"

The young detective studied Donovan with a mixture of curiosity and bafflement. "Are you cool to discuss this with him around?" he asked as he folded his arms. "Look, nothing against you buddy. I'm sure you are perfectly nice. But the Agency isn't known for handling situations with much tact."

"Subtle at times, certainly, and professional—almost infuriatingly so," Vic added. "But this situation is very sensitive and we would like a guarantee you won't run off to your superiors so you can handle this the Agency way. Speaking as a ghost, I know that many of us tend to be caught in the crossfire or go missing after the Agency has been to town."

The agent chuckled as he leaned casually against the wall with his hands in his pockets. "I guess I should get out in the field more and talk to the locals. I knew the Agency had a mixed reputation but I didn't expect that so many were suspicious of our motives."

"That's mostly because the mixed reaction comes from people who fear ghosts and those who know that not all ghosts are out to possess you or haunt the attic you haven't cleaned in months," Johnny pointed out. His gaze flicked to the window and he noticed that the rain fell heavier. "The Agency simply barrels through every ghost like they are dealing with a feral animal."

"I agree with you." Donovan sighed with a trace of dejection. "That's what we've become known for. It's a reputation that's unfortunately well earned but many are trying to change it—mostly people on my level but it is gaining traction amongst the old guard as well."

He looked at Valerie. "The situation has changed but I don't plan to do anything different here. I merely want to hear you guys out and learn what you know. I'm not in the highest of positions but I am in charge of important tasks and run with a good group of other agents. If we can find this Axman—should he still be around—and eliminate him with no harm done to the greater city for both the living and ghosts, that's good enough for me."

"Heh," Vic muttered, took his hat off, and scratched his skull. "He's an earnest one, isn't he?"

Johnny shrugged. "Well, it's not like they won't find out on their own anyway. The SEA is also known to dredge up even the coldest cases and find something." He looked at the young officer. "We—and by we I mean myself, Vic, and Aiyana—can confirm that the Axman is indeed still alive."

"And how's that?" she questioned.

"We saw him," Aiyana replied and Marco and Annie straightened. "The witch summoned some type of connection to him. We caught a glimpse of him after she was vanquished. He appeared to be standing on a stage of some kind and performing a ritual."

"A stage?" Donovan repeated, retrieved his phone, and opened a notepad app. "Is there anything else you can describe?"

"Rows of seats, but broken and dirty," the young detective added. "I saw a thick reddish curtain at the side. But beyond that, nothing else was clear outside the sigil he stood in."

"A sigil?" The agent looked at Aiyana. "Do either of you happen to know—"

"We have no idea, but he was pissed off to see us." Johnny looked at the stereo equipment again. "I don't know if he recognized us but he certainly didn't fear us at all."

"Hey, Johnny, are you good, man?" Marco asked and nodded at the stereo. "You keep looking over there."

He sighed and ran a hand through his hair. "I guess I've become a little paranoid in the rain," he confessed. "I keep waiting for that creepy jazz music to play."

"Jazz music?" Donovan asked.

Valerie looked at him. "It's kind of a calling card of the Axman and probably has something to do with his attachment to it in life. Jazz music would play in radios or speakers whenever he—or more specifically, one of his flunkies dressed as him—would arrive, along with rain."

"It kind of gives him away, doesn't it?" the agent commented.

"Yeah, but good luck fighting him if he comes after you." Johnny sighed and leaned against the couch.

"I thought you had."

"Oh, yeah. Several times!" He dragged a hand over his face. "It doesn't mean I want to deal with another anytime soon if I can."

As if to punctuate his statement, the power cut out and gloom filled the room as loud bangs issued from the front yard. The revenant groaned as he drew his pistol. "Please let that be a very dedicated mailman."

CHAPTER FIFTEEN

A dark presence stood in front of the door to the Maggios' temporary home. It held an ax in one hand, which it raised to hack through the door. When it swung the weapon, however, the blade did not strike the wood but the tile of the doorway instead. The figure looked up at several guns aimed in its face and an orb of flame.

Before it could yank the ax free, all the guns fired and it seemed to shatter before it lost its form and became a shapeless mass of darkness. Vic pushed to the front of the group and scowled as it began to unravel and fade away. "Well, it's been a while since I've seen one of those."

"Has it come in yet?" Marco demanded, slid down the side of the stairs, and brandished his bat. "Let that bastard get in here. I'll—"

"We took care of it already Marco," Annie told him and held up the pistol Valerie had given her in the aftermath of the fake Axman's attack. "It wasn't him."

Her brother strode to the door and looked around. "Where's the body? Did it get vaporized already?"

"In a manner of speaking." Vic stared at the ax still embedded in the doorway. "It wasn't the Axman or even one of his lookalikes again. It was what we call a shade."

"A shade?" Donovan looked at him over his phone. "I've never heard of something like that and the Agency's database only brings up speculative information."

"That's why you need more friends on the other side, buddy," Johnny commented as he twirled his gun lazily. "Shades are rather unique when it comes to ghosts. As much as we ragged on the Agency for treating all ghosts like rabid animals, if there is one that technically fits that description, it would be the shades."

"And even then, it would be only very technically as they are not a ghost specifically but are made from ghosts," Vic continued but paused when he realized that the group now all stared above him. "Is something the matter? Are there questions from the class?"

"Sure, Vic," Marco began and pointed his bat into the air. "What the hell are those?"

The ghost detective turned and scowled again at shapeless masses of darkness that hovered above the grass outside. They landed quickly and began to take shape to look exactly like the Axman from a few days earlier and even formed the ax.

Marco smiled and rested his bat on his shoulder. "You guys can hang back. I've got these jerks." He strode confidently across the front lawn as the two partners shared a look before they aimed their weapons.

The shades walked forward and held their axes up as the young man hefted his bat and prepared to swing. Two different shots rang out. Johnny hit his target in the chest and gouged a large hole, while a smaller, glowing hole burned into the eye of the other shade from Vic's shot. Both shades began to unravel, but Marco was either too excited or oblivious to notice and swung with all his strength. His bat sailed through them as they fell apart and he spun and landed with a thump. "What the hell?"

"Sorry, man. We were only being cautious," Johnny called as he jogged to help him up.

"These don't seem like much of a threat." Valerie holstered her weapon.

Donovan put his gun away and began to type messages on his phone. "No, but they are probably scaring the New Orlenians. I'm getting reports that dark figures are appearing all over the city, some in the form of the Axman."

Valerie shrugged. "Between the police and the Agency, they'll be wiped out in no time, given how fragile they are."

"That's only because we weren't afraid," Vic stated as he drifted toward them. "And there aren't that many of us."

Donovan, Valerie, Aiyana, and Annie all looked expectantly at him. "What are you implying?"

The ghost detective took a fresh pack of cigarettes out and pounded it in his palm. "Like I was saying, shades are made of ghosts but are not ghosts themselves. Specifically, they are made of negative emotions—like a crude phantasma strung together by sadness, fear, and anger."

"How does that work?" Donovan received a disinterested shrug in response. "You don't know? But aren't you a ghost?"

Vic broke the seal on the box and extracted one of the cigarettes. "Did you know that flamingos can only eat with their heads upside down?" This seemed to catch the agent off-guard as he opened his mouth a couple of times before he shook his head. "No? But aren't you alive?" The ghost fumbled in his coat for a lighter. "I'm a detective, kid, not a scholar. Moving past that, shades aren't normally seen out of Limbo since every ghost needs stygia to keep themselves here. Shades are essentially phantasma blobs so they would simply be obliterated immediately."

"So how did they get here now?" Annie asked.

"Well, I would guess that the Axman has something to do with it," Johnny said as he and Marco joined the group and he passed Vic a lighter before he slid his hands into his pockets. "Given the fact that the shades took his form and all."

"Could it have been that sigil we saw?" Aiyana asked the detectives. "Maybe he found a way to summon them here and control them?"

"Possibly, but even if he isn't controlling them, we have a bigger problem than you probably realize," Vic warned and lit his cigarette. "Shades can also grow stronger by feeding off the strong, negative emotions of others, ghosts or breathers." He took a long drag. "Like fear," He finished as the smoke billowed out of his skull.

Valerie checked her phone. "I'm getting reports from all over the city. There's an alert at a church nearby."

"I'm getting the same," Donovan added and looked at the group. "I need to get out there."

"Agreed. It seems the timeout the Axman had called is over." The ghost detective took another drag. "I'd like to think I was responsible in some way."

"Will you guys help?" the agent asked and looked at

Johnny, Vic, and Aiyana.

Marco answered first. "Of course we will. Point us in a direction and we'll—"

"Nuh-uh, Marky," the ghost said dismissively. "You, Aiyana, and Annie are getting the hell out of Dodge—or New Orleans. Take your pick."

"Huh?" He balked. "And go where? Do you expect us to run every time this guy shows his face?"

"That would be helpful, yeah." Vic nodded to his sister. "Look, Marco, I get it. You are a fighter. But we already had an issue with the fake Axman and we no longer have the special bullet. We still don't know exactly why he wants your sister so badly but it's probably not because he prefers blondes, all right? The fact that he is saturating the city with these means he's trying to either accomplish something through the chaos or send a message. If it's the former, we should probably consider the very real possibility that his intention is to kidnap Annie. Given that, it's best she skedaddles, yeah?"

The fiery man let the thought simmer for a moment before he nodded silently and turned toward his car. "I'll drive."

Vic looked to the shaman. "Sorry. I volunteered you there—are you okay to watch over them?"

Aiyana nodded. "That would be smart if it turns out you were right, but where will you and Johnny go?"

The partners held their guns up. "Doing what we do best," the young detective answered with a grin. "Sending bad ghosts back to where they belong."

"Or merely obliterating them." The ghost chuckled and took another puff. "Whichever is faster is preferred."

CHAPTER SIXTEEN

"We still have a situation at Christ Church Cathedral. An ax-wielding supernatural being has been seen in the building. Are you on it, Simone?" Shemar demanded.

"I'm on my way there now, sir. I'm with an agent who will assist me," Valerie replied as she raced down the street. Donovan frowned out the window at the shades that flew past.

"An agent? You sure you won't need backup?"

"I'll be fine, sir. Besides, if we had the people to spare, you would probably have already sent them." She looked at her companion. "I'm with Agent Donovan and have confirmed he at least knows how to pull a trigger."

"Understood. Report in when you've dealt with the situation." Chief Shemar hung up before she could respond and she put her phone away. "Is there any news on your side of things?"

"Nothing to be concerned about. Even if you and your friends don't have the highest opinion of the Agency, you can all agree on one thing at least—we are good at obliterating ghosts."

"Let's hope no innocent ones get caught in the crossfire," she retorted as she slowed on the approach to the church. "We're here."

Donovan straightened in his seat. "If the shade is still here, it's probably inside." He looked around the street. "It seems clear but we should check to see if anyone is inside. We'll need to get them out of the way."

"For their safety and so they don't power the shade," Valerie agreed and nodded as they unbuckled and slid out of the car. She was the first one up the steps and hissed when she noticed blood on the concrete. "It looks like we have wounded but I'm not sure if they are still here."

"Any dead?" he asked and drew his gun from its holster as he shuffled slowly to the door opposite Valerie.

"I haven't seen any but guess we should take a peek." They both looked into the entrance of the church and scanned the area. "No one in the lobby," she whispered as she crept inside with him directly behind her.

"Why would it come here?" He looked around for signs of life or the shade. "It's not even a Sunday service...or even Sunday."

"It could have been an evensong or maybe a meeting of the church staff," she suggested as she noticed stairs and wondered for a moment if she could go up. "I don't think they necessarily have specific points to head to. They are merely here to cause chaos and spread fear."

"Fear of the Axman," he added darkly and gestured to the stairs. "Should we go up?"

"He might be on the upper floor, but my guess is he's

still down here somewhere. We haven't even checked the main hall." She turned and strode to a large pair of double doors. "Follow me."

Donovan complied slowly and made sure to check above and behind them. "He must have gotten impatient since his plan with the elderly couple didn't pan out."

Valerie almost snorted. "If he expected us to play into his little game and get the people riled up, he needs to catch up with the times. We would never be his hype squad."

"I think he noticed." The agent gestured to a large slash in one of the walls. "Now he's making his own hype squad."

"The doors are ajar." She pointed ahead. They hurried forward and he looked inside, then nodded at her to confirm that the shade—or something, at least—was within. She drew a breath and leaned closer to him. "I don't know how much you were told about our fights with the Axman's goons but listen to me. Even if this isn't as powerful as those were, do not stop until it is down completely. There is nothing we can gain from trying to interrogate it or capture it. We are here to destroy."

"You are starting to sound like a member of a SEA oblivion team," he quipped in a jovial tone as he double-checked his gun. He glanced at her irate face. "Don't worry, I copy. I didn't think we could talk to them anyway. Like the ghost bounty hunter said, they don't have minds of their own."

"He's a detective," she corrected.

"Really?" He considered this. "He seems far more trig-ger-happy than most PIs I know."

"He's from a different era." She smirked. "Let's do some-

D'ARTAGNAN REY & MICHAEL ANDERLE

thing we can boast about later." With that, she turned toward the door and snuck through with him on her heels. She moved to the far wall while he circled the shade Axman, who seemed to patrol up and down the pews.

Valerie soon discovered why as she could see hands and feet under the seats a few rows ahead, and the shade was rapidly closing in. She powered her gun up and stopped to aim and fire a charged shot. The shade looked at her before it was caught by a blast of ether that removed an arm and shoulder. It toppled over the pews and a mother and her son scrambled to their feet and bolted out of the room. The woman had scooped her child into her arms.

Once she made sure they had left safely, she focused her full attention on the shade. It had reshaped its arm and now surged toward her and crushed the pew under its feet as it prepared to bisect her with one strike of its ax. Another blast of ether struck it from behind her and it hurtled overhead. She ducked and crouched close to the floor as it tried to swipe her in passing.

As she fell back, she set her gun's power to maximum and the shade landed and tried to get to its feet, its back caved in from the blast. It attempted to reshape itself but she aimed her gun and held the trigger—one second, then two, and all the way to six—before the shade lunged at her and she fired.

The impact was large enough to completely disintegrate the upper half of its body and the lower half dissolved before the feet met the floor again. She drew a deep breath as its form began to dissipate in front of her.

"Nice gun you got there," Donovan commented and

looked at his similar weapon as he extended a hand to help her up. "Where did you get it?"

Valerie took his hand and pulled herself to her feet before she ejected the ether magazine and replaced it with a spare. "A friend got it for me from the Limbo markets."

"Is that right?" He scrutinized the weapon again before she slid it into her jacket. "Man, Agency tech isn't as classified as they like to believe, huh?"

"I can't say I know what you mean," she responded as she headed to the door. "Come on. I got to call this in and then we should go find another. We don't want Johnny and Vic to have all the fun out there, do we?"

CHAPTER SEVENTEEN

"And pull!" Vic shouted as he leaned out of the window and fired at a shade in the sky while he and Johnny roared down the street. His shot struck it in center mass and it plummeted. He looked back and adjusted his cap "I had hoped that would obliterate it outright."

"We're getting deeper into the city so there's more fear to go around," his partner explained and moved the slider on his gun down a little so it wouldn't jerk too hard when he fired.

He noticed a group of civilians who ran from another shade, aimed his gun at it, and fired a baseball-sized shot. The blast flung it into the wall of a building before it vanished. "Still, they are only shades. As long as we catch them outside areas with a high volume of people in the vicinity, they shouldn't be all that much of a problem, right?"

His phone chimed and the ghost detective picked it up after he fired twice at another shade. "Okay, it's an updated list of locations from the agent. It looks like the closest emergency location is a hotel about ten blocks away."

"A hotel?" Johnny groaned and leaned forward to locate the building. "Well, I guess that's exactly what we wanted—the opposite of what we were hoping for."

"What were you hoping for?" Vic asked with a chuckle and checked his revolver. "I think about it like this—the more of these we take care of at once, the sooner this will all be over."

"Who's to say the Axman doesn't have a limitless supply of them," the young detective countered.

"The fact that he's using shades to begin with," his partner replied. "He's gathering energy for something, right? He has enough to spare or at least found a way to get a boatload of shades cheaply, but he isn't using those mutant mindless clones from last week because he can't cash the check. If he was seriously trying to spread chaos and stoke the city's fears, those would still be more beneficial."

"I doubt the general populace can tell the difference between the fake Axmen and these faker Axmen," he retorted. "Especially since some of them have taken on his last seen form. Hell, that's the one most people are probably familiar with since it rampaged through one of the busiest streets in the city."

"Okay, that's a fair point," Vic conceded as he blasted a shade through the head before it could phase through the wall of a store from an alley. "I'm not saying it isn't effective, but this comes across as a little desperate on his end."

"I'm not sure I'd call the guy we saw in that portal desperate but I'll take a dose of optimism." Johnny sighed and slowed the car as they approached the chain hotel. The traffic was currently backed up due to a group of cars that had collided. "Dammit. Hopefully, there won't be a too-high body count in all this madness."

The ghost detective was silent for a moment and let the cigarette in his mouth burn out. "Let's get in there before we worry about that," he said flatly, tilted his head, and pointed to the sidewalk. "Hey, do you see those guys standing in front of the entrance?"

His partner leaned forward and was barely able to see a few heads over some of the cars. "Yeah, what are they doing? They are simply standing there. Did the cops or Agency already take care of the problem?"

Vic looked around. "I don't see any cop cars or Agency vehicle, so I don't think we're that lucky." He floated out of the car. "Watch yourself, kid. They might be possessed."

"By shades?" he asked as he stepped out of their car. "They can possess people?"

"Not the conventional way," the ghost stated as he moved slowly around the car. "They don't take control of a person, but they are manifestations of negative emotions. It's likely that these guys are either extremely depressed or violent psychos. We're gonna have to make sure that we take care of any possessed individuals along with the shade-man. Treat them like you would any other possessed individual."

"Fill them with ether?"

"You got it!" They jogged immediately to the unmoving group and Johnny hoped they were all simply despairing rather than the angry mob they could be. Unfortunately, it seemed he was doomed to experience a recurring theme.

His hope was dashed as soon as one turned. His eyes rolled back in his head as he pointed and roared before his three buddies turned and did the same.

They should probably have simply attacked. It would have been somewhat effective but instead, each of the four staggered under the impact of a shot of ether or spectral round. The shades erupted from the back of the bodies in clouds of dark mist before they disappeared and their hosts fell.

The men all rolled around and moaned in a daze. Vic continued to the entrance while Johnny checked on them.

One of the victims blinked, shook his head, and looked at him. "What happened? I…I blacked out but I remember feeling so…" He squinted with the effort of trying to recall the events. "I was angry at someone. Was it you?"

"You were possessed by a terror called a shade," he explained and helped him up. "Although since I did shoot you, I could understand you being a bit pissed off at me now."

"You did what?" The man gasped and checked his body for injuries.

He shook his head and clapped him on the shoulder. "It only hurts ghosts. You should be fine besides a headache. Get out of here before any more arrive." He began to run off but paused to look over his shoulder. "And fill them in too, all right?"

"The lobby looks clear," Vic informed him from the doorway as he caught up. "Of bodies, anyway." Most of the furniture had been upended and glass, chipped tile, and paintings littered the floor. "I'm not looking forward to having to comb through this entire building but we should get started as soon as—"

"Vic!" Johnny shouted and pointed toward the elevators. Three people stepped out of one and the first held their arms and shook visibly while the two others screamed at each other. "Stop talking and let's get in there."

The ghost detective's only reply was a swift nod and they strode into the hotel. The revenant fired three shots at the two who were possessed and drove the shades out of them while his partner scanned the opposite hallway. Once the shades had vanished, he joined Vic, who scowled silently down the hall.

A moment later, he saw what had held the ghost's attention. A body was slumped under a table against a wall. "He was probably wounded and tried to hide," Vic suggested and gestured at the pool of blood on the ground. "He bled out."

Their discussion ended abruptly at a crashing sound farther down the hall and neither said anything as they hurried forward to find out what it could be.

When they reached one of the banquet halls, Johnny felt like an idiot for a hopeful thought that it might be something other than one of the Axman's shades.

The terror flipped tables and destroyed chairs without restraint. At least three bodies sprawled on the floor and he was sure the shade-man was looking for more still hiding in the large room. He looked at Vic, who motioned silently for him to increase the power of his weapon.

With a nod, he complied before he held three fingers up and counted down to zero. They thrust through the doors and fired on the shade-man, but this was not one of the weak clones from the house. His shot struck it cleanly in the chest and it merely jumped back like it had been punched in the gut.

The ghost detective landed two shots, one in the ribs and the other in the left temple. They bored holes in the doppelganger but very little phantasma leaked out. The shade-man looked at them with glowing eyes.

"Ah, hell," they muttered together as it raised its ax and hurled it toward them. They both dove out of the way and it broke through the wall into the hallway behind them. Johnny fired another shot but the shade bounded onto a nearby table, snatched one of the chairs up, and flung it at him.

He rolled out of the way and stopped under a table behind a shaking woman. Urgently, he motioned for her to run but she seemed to be too shocked to move. Before he could try to convince her, he heard a pained shout and crawled out. The shade-man loomed over Vic, who fumbled for his gun which had been dislodged from his hand. His attacker held him beneath one of his boots as he raised a hand and his ax returned to him.

"Vic!" the young detective shouted, raised his weapon, and set it on full before he fired. The force catapulted him into the table and it toppled. With impressive agility, the shade leapt off Vic and over the shot and once it landed, it charged at Johnny. His partner called to him as he attempted to retrieve his gun.

He felt a sharp pain in his shoulder and realized it had almost been dislocated, but he still managed to turn and raise his weapon as the Axman clone held his ax over his head. A loud boom rang out and the shade was knocked aside. The sound of a shotgun being racked followed before more shots were fired, not from either of the detectives' weapons but from machineguns and shotguns.

Finally, the shade was felled by a barrage of spectral bullets. Johnny stumbled to his feet and Vic helped him before they turned when members of the ghost mafia ran past them to check the room.

"The mob?" the young detective asked. "The mob is here?"

"My associates thought it would be a good time to give back to the community," a deep, familiar voice said with a drawl. The young detective's eyes widened as he turned to a figure he'd thought he wouldn't see for a long time and certainly not living side.

He was certainly smaller than in Limbo but still towered over the partners. As always, he smoked his signature cigar as he dusted his purple suit off and draped his shotgun across his broad shoulders. "Well now, I wonder who is luckier—you boys or me?"

Vic and Johnny both gaped before they exclaimed in unison, "Big Daddy?"

CHAPTER EIGHTEEN

Marco's driving was impressive. The number of near misses and the speed at which they occurred would make almost anyone think he was either a professional or psychotic.

"Marco, don't you think you are driving too recklessly?" Aiyana asked as she clutched the headrest in front of her in a death grip.

"Hey, the job is we get my sis out of town so we'll do exactly that!" he retorted without easing his foot even slightly off the gas. "And I'm not the kind of guy to do things half-assed. Especially with all these ghosts running around."

They hit a bump and all three passengers almost knocked their heads on the roof of the car. Annie groaned in frustration. "If you aren't careful, we'll be ghosts."

"Is that so bad?" His voice carried an angry edge. "That was your plan a few days ago, wasn't it?"

"What?" She gaped at him in shock. "Are you talking about when we faced the Axman? You're upset about that?"

Marco shifted in his seat but fixed his gaze on the road. "I wasn't exactly happy that you threatened to kill yourself, no. I tried to get over it because I thought we had dealt with the bastard but now that we know he's back, I'm worried it will be your plan again."

"That was a last resort!" she exclaimed and held onto the railing on the side of the door as he made a sharp turn. "I'm as interested in living as anyone else but if it comes down to saving my life or yours—or hell, the entire city—I'll choose that."

"We could have defeated him," he protested feebly. "I don't want you to throw yourself off the ledge at the next available opportunity, okay? We'll protect you this time around—I'll protect you, all right?"

"Marco, are you seriously saying that you wouldn't do the same if you were in my position?" She gritted her teeth. "In fact, you are doing exactly that. He's not even after you and you throw yourself in danger."

He made another sharp turn and almost collided with a parked car that had been abandoned by its owner. "Yeah, and I'll keep doing it to keep you safe. I'm your older brother. I have to look out for you, and like hell will I let this creep come for you again."

Annie huffed in growing fury and held his attention. "That's not an answer. And defend me? I'm nineteen now, Marco. I'm not some little girl you need to look after all the time. It feels like you are deflecting—"

"Guys!" Aiyana shouted. Marco focused on the road and cursed when he realized that two large trucks blocked the road. He braked desperately and turned the car sideways while everyone held on as the car that had moved at eighty mph came to a complete and sudden stop. After a shocked moment, they checked each other and themselves to make sure none of them were injured—or more to the point, that they were all still alive.

"What the hell is going on out there?" He growled as he reached behind his seat to grasp his bat and shoved his door open.

"Marco, I think those are Agency vehicles," Aiyana warned as both women scrambled out of the car to follow the irate driver. Sure enough, after they'd walked only a few yards closer, several agents in their all-white uniforms stepped around the vehicles to check the noise of Marco's car grinding to a halt. They rushed forward to make them stay back.

"You need to leave," one warned and held up some type of rifle with a glowing chamber. "This area is not secure. You need to get away from here."

"Yeah, that was the plan," Marco retorted and pointed behind the vehicles with his bat. "We're trying to get out of the city, so move your big-ass trucks."

One of the agents stepped forward and gestured for the others to leave before he stared at the young man. "It's too dangerous here. We are dealing with the situation and you can proceed out of the city once we have eliminated the current supernatural threat. It would be in your best interest to—"

"Go back the way we came?" he demanded and rested his bat against his shoulder. "Why the hell do you think we came this way? If you want to offer an alternative or a shelter you would think is a better option, I'm all ears, pal."

The agent straightened and looked like he was ready to

unleash his ire, but something behind the three civilians caught his eye. "Shit!" He gasped and primed his rifle.

"Get back. We have possessed!"

They turned to look at more than a dozen people who surged toward them. At first, Aiyana thought they were merely desperate civilians trying to run from the shades, but she felt her warning totem tremble and held her hands out.

"Get behind me!" she ordered as she held one hand out. It lit up with her blue flames and she retrieved another totem with a mark that looked like a falcon. She tossed it toward the crowd and it erupted in a blast of white light. The wave cascaded through the group and shades were torn from their bodies before she raised her hand and her flames spewed to burn through the released shades and leave their hosts unscathed.

"Nice one, Aiyana!" Marco cheered as the agent looked on in surprise. He turned to the man with a cocky grin. "I think you can see that we can take care of ourselves."

This somewhat sarcastic assurance was met with a disinterested expression. "I think I see that she can take care of herself."

The young man sighed dramatically and shrugged. "Yeah, well. She's with us, all right? Can we please go through?"

The agent paid no attention to him and instead, issued instructions about the no longer possessed civilians behind the line. "Look, we didn't set this blockade up to keep anyone in. There are supernaturals behind these vehicles, both loose and possessing people. In addition, a figure that has been identified as the Axman is destroying the store behind us."

"The Axman?" the three asked in unison. Aiyana stepped forward. "No, that is probably not the Axman but a shade that has taken his form."

"A shade?" the man asked as his colleagues who'd come to investigate earlier stepped behind the barrier and hurried past them to tend to the civilians. "I thought those hadn't been confirmed. What makes you so sure?" He regarded her sternly. "You are a shaman, right?"

She nodded. "I am, but more importantly I've seen them copy the Axman's image. You must surely know that multiple Axmen are running around the city, correct?"

"We've received reports but that doesn't mean they are all fakes. We have to assume that at least one could be real. If you were in this city when he attacked before, you know how dangerous he—"

A loud crash behind the vehicles cut him off and he turned and ran past the barricade. The friends looked at each other before they followed him. "What's going on here?" the agent demanded. Two agents lay unmoving on the street and a horde of people ran out of a store toward them and the agents while a dark figure strode behind them.

"The Axman," Aiyana stated and flames encircled her hands. "Or one of his copies."

"There's a fast way to find out which." Marco held his bat in both hands, growled belligerently, and marched forward.

"Marco!" Annie cried as one of the agents shouted at the others to fire. Aiyana ran to the young man's side and he wielded his bat with determined efficiency against the horde. Each swing forced a shade to emerge to either be shot by the volley of ether from the agents or torched quickly by the shaman.

The apparent Axman noticed the two young civilians. A few ether shots struck him but with little effect. He grasped his weapon in both hands and launched himself high, raised it over his head, and swung it as he landed. Marco clashed with him and the impact made him lean back but not falter. This certainly wasn't the Axman, or at least not on the level of his copy from a few days earlier. If it had been, his reckless charge would probably have ended differently.

He was able to push his adversary away thanks to Aiyana blasting the side of the shade's face with her flames. As he readied himself for another swing, two possessed shoppers barreled into him, flung him off his feet, and dislodged the bat from his hand. The shaman tried to help but the shade-man's hand connected with the side of her head and she tumbled.

Her companion shoved his two assailants away but now stood beneath the shade-man's looming frame. It stared at him with eerie, glowing eyes. When he turned to retrieve his bat, he noticed it wasn't where he last saw it. Annie brandished it and prepared to strike the shade. He wanted to call out to her to get away but the bat flared in her hands exactly as it did in his and even looked brighter, and the color was a bright white instead of his icy blue.

She pounded it into the chest of the shade-man and on impact, it launched a wave of phantasma similar to Aiyana's totem but reached far wider. The Axman lookalike began to evaporate and all the still possessed people crumpled as their shades dispersed on contact with the wave.

The agents were stunned by what they had seen. Aiyana looked at her friend in shock and Marco grinned hesitantly. "Damn, Annie. Since when could you do that?" he asked as he got to his feet.

She didn't answer and her body trembled as the bat fell from her hands. "Annie?" he called again as she fell to her knees. "Annie!"

In his den, the Axman felt a great force cascade across the city and a flash of white light struck him and hurled him off his feet. Dazed and his power sapped momentarily, he struggled to his knees as his arms sank into the floor and his body shifted between tangible and intangible. It passed after only a few moments and his strength returned, aided by the fear of the city siphoning into him.

One thing did not return, however. His connection to the shades was severely compromised and he felt less of them as the seconds passed. When he tried to see through one, the white light struck it and the connection was severed. He was perplexed at first but when he looked at his hands, he could see trace amounts of human phantasma.

As he studied it, a smile began to form. It seemed he could no longer simply stalk from the shadows, not when an opportunity such as this presented itself.

CHAPTER NINETEEN

Donovan stepped behind the shade-man and fired a shot into the back of its head. Its skull shattered and the rest of the body followed. He blew the tip of his gun dramatically despite no smoke coming from it as he turned toward Valerie. "That one went down even faster than the last." He looked around the restaurant with a smile. "I wonder what the special is?"

"It's not like anyone is here to make it for you," she replied flatly and checked her phone. "Come on. There's another report from a neighborhood about three miles from here. Plus, we should check the street and see if any of those poss—"

She was interrupted by a ring of light that cascaded through the restaurant. They held their hands up to shield themselves but it simply passed through them and didn't even shake the tables or rattle the walls.

When it passed, they lowered their guard gingerly. "What in the world was that?" Donovan asked in awe. "It felt like...phantasma?"

"It certainly wasn't a ghost's phantasma," she responded and checked her body before she looked at the door. "Come on."

The young officer ran out with him on her heels. They stepped into the parking lot and stared at the remains of shades in the air that shifted their forms erratically before they vanished completely. She turned toward him with a questioning look. "Was that some type of Agency weapon?"

He shrugged. "If it was, I'm certainly not in the know." He looked at his gun. "Besides, it was some form of phantasma. We can contain ether or stygia, which means it had to come from an empath or ghost."

Valerie frowned at her phone and opened her contacts. "It might be a long shot, but she would probably be our best bet." She selected Aiyana's name and rested the phone against her ear.

After a couple of rings, the shaman answered. "Valerie, you need to get here."

"Aiyana? What's wrong?" she demanded and gestured for Donovan to walk to her car. "Get where? Did you see that light?"

"It was Annie. I'm not sure how she did it but it came from her when she attacked one of the shade Axmen." The shaman paused to draw in a rasped breath. "She collapsed afterward. Marco is tending to her but I'm worried the Agency on site will want to take her in."

"Like hell," she declared as she slid into the driver's seat. "Send me your location. I'm on my way—and get Johnny too." She ended the call and buckled up as she started the car. "It was Annie. She made that light."

"She can do that?" the agent asked skeptically as he clipped his seatbelt on.

Valerie looked back as she reversed the car. "It seems so but it's news to me too." Her phone chimed and she checked it for the location. "They are with a group of your people and Aiyana is worried they might try something."

Donovan opened his mouth to speak but considered it for a moment before he shrugged. "Perhaps. That was an unusual event. Given the situation, though, I doubt they will focus on that with all the shades around."

She accelerated sharply enough to push both of them into their seats. "Maybe, but you saw what it did to the shades. If that went through the entire city, the shades are no longer a problem." She held two fingers up. "Which means two things. One, with the shades gone, there will be many questions about what eliminated them, and that looks like Annie right now. And two..." She gritted her teeth as she formulated her next words. "I'm worried that it's not only us who noticed."

"Do you boys need a ride?" Big Daddy asked as they walked out of the hotel and headed toward a fleet of vans and escalades.

Vic looked back at mafia members who continued to run inside. "We've got wheels, BD, but we could use some answers."

"Like are you here to kill us?" Johnny inquired, and both ghosts turned to look at him. He glanced at Vic. "What? Wasn't that the first question on your mind too?"

His partner dug in his jacket pocket and withdrew his pack of cigarettes. "At first, yeah, but if that was his goal, he would probably have simply taken care of us in the banquet room and blamed it on the shade if anyone asked."

The other ghost chortled as he ashed his cigar. "That's why I like you, Vic. You're sharp and reasonable." He looked at Johnny's gun, still grasped in his hand. "I see you're making good use of that money I gave you."

"Gave us?" The young detective questioned as he thought back to the last time they had seen the dealer. "From what I recall, we stole it. That would be the reason I asked my last question."

Vic sighed and rubbed his temple. "Kid, if someone doesn't remember details—whether they are lying or not—you play along. It gets you out of more bad situations than not."

Big Daddy laughed. "It seems you still aren't done mentoring the kid, eh, Vic?" He took a deep drag of his cigar. "I assume the next obvious question is why I'm here," he began, but his two companions were too distracted by what was going on behind him. A wave of white light headed directly toward them.

"Look out!" Johnny shouted and shoved his partner down before he caught hold of Big Daddy and forced him to the ground as the wave washed over them. They remained still for a moment. When the revenant opened his eyes and looked around, both ghosts were still there. He rolled and narrowed his eyes as some of the mafia members who were posted at the doors pushed to their feet and looked around in a daze.

"What was—" Vic was cut off by gurgling from above as

several phantasms emerged from the building and twisted and turned as if they were in pain. Moments later, they shrank into a dark mist and evaporated.

The three stood and allowed themselves a little time to take it all in. Johnny cleared his throat as he dusted his jacket off. "Well, I guess that worked out. Good job, team."

"That felt like phantasma," Big Daddy muttered and checked his suit. "Human phantasma."

"Agreed." Vic scanned the asphalt and sighed in contentment as he picked his cigarette pack up. "But from who?"

"Someone who seems to hate the shades as much as we do," the revenant remarked as his phone rang. He took it from his jacket pocket and checked it. "It's from Aiyana. She's sent her location and wants us to get there as fast as we can." His eyes widened. "She says that white light came from Annie."

Vic was almost slack-jawed "Annie? She's an empath?" He tilted his head. "Okay, I guess that makes sense since Marco is, but to be able to do something like that is crazy."

Johnny flipped through the rest of the message and turned hastily toward his partner. "We need to go, Vic. Aiyana says they are surrounded by agents."

Big Daddy grunted and scowled with displeasure. "So the Agency is here? I thought I saw a couple of their trucks along the way." He looked at the others. "How bad is it?"

"Fortunately, I haven't had to deal with them until now so I can't honestly say." The ghost detective shrugged. "But their numbers have grown more each day as they've brought more tech and people in."

"Hey, Big Daddy!" They turned as a mobster descended

the stairs with others behind him. "The hotel is clear. Whatever that light was, it spooked those spooks."

The dealer nodded and clamped his teeth on his cigar. "Then get in the cars and let's head out. We'll follow the revenant."

"Wait—what?" Johnny looked from Big Daddy to the mobsters who all hurried to the cars. "You lead the mob?"

Big Daddy chuckled and smoke escaped from his skull. "Nah. Technically, I'm here representing parties in Limbo but their don is hosting me." He took a few steps toward one of the vehicles. "We'll need to parlay with the cops and agents anyway so might as well join you in keeping the peace since it seems our work here is done."

One of the mobsters opened a sliding door in one of the vans for him and he turned, pointed ahead, and told them to get moving before he sat and the door was slid shut.

"Did they seriously need to open the door?" Johnny looked nervously at Vic. "Does this seem like a good idea to you?"

The ghost detective took a cigarette out and lit it. "Honestly, what we think is irrelevant right now." He turned and drifted toward their car. "Besides, he didn't kill you and obliterate me so maybe we should play along."

His partner agreed silently and hurried to their car, sat behind the wheel, and maneuvered carefully around the other vehicles. The fleet of mafia vehicles followed him when he headed out. Whatever was waiting for them, they had backup, at least.

CHAPTER TWENTY

"Annie!" Marco cradled his sister and looked at Aiyana. "What's wrong with her?"

The shaman dropped to her knees and pressed a palm to her forehead. "It's only shock, I believe. She released a large amount of phantasma—honestly one of the greatest I have ever seen at one time. Even experienced empaths would be affected by that and I wasn't even aware that she was one."

He seemed to relax slightly but while his trembling subsided, his worry was still evident. "I didn't either. I suppose it makes sense. Our parents are both specters and our pops is an empath. But she hadn't manifested anything and she is way older than I was when I did."

"It takes time for some," she explained as she retrieved one of her totems and some string. She threaded the string through a small hole in the item and eased it over Annie's head. "This should help her recuperate faster." She touched the totem again and a green glow emitted from it. Her eyes narrowed as she looked up and behind him. "It seems we have other concerns for the moment."

Marco looked up, confused at first until he followed her gaze to the agents who talked amongst themselves while some stared at them. He glared as he lowered Annie gently and grasped his bat. Aiyana stayed his hand. "All they have are those ether rifles," he muttered and his hand tightened around the grip of the bat. "I won't let them try anything."

"We don't know that they don't have conventional weapons. It seems foolish for employees of a government agency to not carry at least a handgun." She did her best to stay calm. "I have already made contact with Valerie and Johnny and they are on their way. For now, we should focus on making sure your sister is all right until she wakes."

As much as he seemed to be itching for a fight, he sighed, nodded, and relaxed again, although it was only for a very short moment. Two agents approached, one of which was the man they spoke to at the barrier. Their rifles were slung over their shoulders and they gave no indication that they would attempt to take Annie. Still, both fixed their gazes on her for an extended amount of time.

The two friends rose, an uncomfortable silence in the air as everyone simply stared at one another. Finally, the agent cleared his throat and said, "We need to get you out of here."

"After we helped to take care of the mess?" Marco muttered and folded his arms. "If you had simply let us through, we would probably be out of the city by now."

The other agent tilted her head. "It seems we might have been quite lucky that you had not left."

"Why is that?" Aiyana asked.

The first agent looked behind him into the sky. "After the initial shock of that...explosion, we've had reports that those beings—the shades—were banished on contact with the light. It seems she felled them all in one swoop."

He looked at his sister in shock. "All of them? Through the entire city?"

"Yes. We saw a massive spike in human phantasma energy in our readers, at least until they overloaded," the female agent confirmed. "But we have concerns that it could draw him out. We think it would be best if you accompany us to—"

"Aiyana...Marco!" Valerie shouted. The four in conversation looked at her as she tried to get past the line of agents, who only moved when Donovan arrived and ordered them to. She ran closer. "What's happening?"

"Annie is unconscious but seems well aside from that," Aiyana explained. She nodded at the agents in front of them. "They seem to want to take us somewhere."

"Only into our care," the woman assured them. "We are concerned that the release of such energy will force terrors to come searching for it."

"Terrors?" the young officer asked. "Or the Axman?"

The agents stiffened but the man nodded. "I saw that one of them took his form. If he is controlling them somehow, I'm sure he is aware that his plan was foiled. We don't know how he will react and he could come out here himself."

Marco waved a hand dismissively. "He's nothing but a coward. All he's done is send clones and minions out to do his dirty work. He's probably not even all that powerful and once we find out where he's hiding, he's done for."

"We?" the agent questioned. "You aren't seriously looking for him yourself, are you?"

"Not by choice." The young man rested his bat on the ground like a cane. "He, or his goons I guess, keep showing up and we've had to deal with him."

Valerie folded her arms and closed her eyes. "Marco, I think you should listen to them."

"Do what?" he exclaimed and recoiled. "Go with these weirdos? I thought we all agreed that we didn't like them."

She opened her eyes and stepped forward. "I may disagree with their practices but I can attest that they don't seem all bad—or at least malicious." She looked at Annie's sleeping form. "Sending you home is out of the question and with the police in chaos, I'm not sure how effectively we would be able to protect you like we did last week."

Marco still seemed hesitant, but Aiyana seemed to understand the gravity of the situation, even if she wasn't exactly thrilled about it either. She rubbed her arms and frowned at Valerie. "I suppose my question is, if he does come for her himself, would anywhere be safe?"

"Captain!" an agent called out and everyone turned toward him. "I've got something on the ectograph—a large spike in phantasma, but not any kind that is in the data—" He didn't get to finish. With a loud screech of metal, the tank behind him began to fall apart, cut in two. As the upper half of his body, along with several of his comrades, slid off the bottom half and the vehicle collapsed, a dark figure appeared behind it.

He stood taller than any of his clones. The black phantasma flared off his body like a crackling fire. His eyes shined pure white, almost blinding as he gazed at Valerie, Marco, and the others before it settled on the one who was resting at their feet. He stepped on top of the Agency vehicle and began to march toward her.

The agents, still shaken by the sudden attack, aimed their weapons and fired on the Axman. Although a few shots connected and bursts of the dark phantasma flurried from his body, he swung his ax without seeming to hit anything and continued toward Annie. The other agents were all cut down and their blood flooded the street.

The three friends and the remaining two agents prepared to attack, but the Axman stopped several yards away and studied them for a moment before his shining gaze settled on Annie again. "She will have a hard enough time understanding what is to come," he said and seemed to direct this as much to himself as to them. His next comment, however, was undoubtedly addressed to them. "Do you want to add to that misery when I tell her you died pointlessly?"

"Fuck you, you bastard!" Marco roared and brandished his bat at the killer. "You were a coward who killed people in their sleep. Now you wanna act like big scary dick out of Lord of the Rings?"

The Axman chuckled darkly. "Yes, I suppose you would see it that way today. My little celebration with that elderly couple didn't have quite the effect I wanted it to. I suppose much can change in a century." He grasped his massive ax in both hands and stared at them with eerie delight. "Including me and how I kill."

Before he could strike, a car horn broke the tension.

Everyone, including the Axman, looked at a familiar Camaro that raced toward them, followed by a parade of black vehicles. Windows in the vehicles were rolled down and ghosts in suits hung out of the sides with guns at the ready.

The first shot was fired by the ghost detective in the Camaro.

CHAPTER TWENTY-ONE

The Axman's head jerked back when Vic's spectral bullet burrowed into his skull at least partially. He eased it out and it disappeared between his fingers. "The revenant." He smiled as Johnny's car stopped with tires squealing and the two partners all but threw themselves out. The vehicles following them began to stop and mafia members filed out and ran toward the Axman amidst gunfire and shouts.

"It's the Axman!"

"There he is!"

"Ice that son of a bitch!"

"Obliterate the bastard!"

Though their target seemed to be able to withstand much of the gunfire, he was not prepared for the blast of flames from Aiyana, followed by the impact of Marco's bat. He uttered a low rumble as he slammed his foot into the pavement, turned, and swung his ax. Everyone ducked as it sliced overhead and into several cars to chop their roofs off. A streetlamp began to topple as well.

The Axman turned to the approaching mob and placed

a hand on the ground as his dark phantasma began to snake out of his palm. Soon, a wall of the black substance surged up to block the salvo aimed at him. The shield extended over him and his prey as he turned to deal with Annie's guardians.

Three mobsters tried to bulldoze through the wall of phantasma, only to be hurled back as the color drained from their bodies.

"Whoa, whoa! What's going on here?" one of the mobsters asked as he stopped to tend to his friend. He held him up as he turned from a bright red to a monotone gray "Frank, hey! Keep it together, buddy!" He turned toward the wall. "Ain't that only phantasma?"

"It came from the Axman," Vic explained as Johnny took his eyepatch off. "I doubt that it's only phantasma. Do you see anything, kid?"

The young detective stared at the wall but shook his head after a moment. "It would be easier to try to see through ink. But if it's ghost phantasma, I can probably get through it." He turned and extended his hand. "Are you with me?"

His partner tilted his head. "Are you sure that's safe? I might be able to get through by fusing with you but you are a revenant."

"Sometimes, you have to gamble. Even if I can pass through myself I can only go so far without you. Besides, we don't have the time to experiment and I'd rather take you with me."

Vic looked hesitantly at the wall before he nodded and holstered his pistol. "Ah, well. I'm fairly sure that if one of us dies, the other goes with him."

trees. "We'll need to get him to drop her so we can grab her and get out of here."

Johnny looked at the broken piece of the baseball bat. "Maybe she can do that," he ventured and held it up. "Marco tossed this to me before we entered. I wanted to ask why because it's not like I can use it as he does."

"But maybe Annie can." Vic gestured ahead to where the Axman looked over his shoulder at them. "He's seen us, kid. We may not have much to work with but it's time to make our play." he stopped in his tracks and began to fire at their target. His initial shots were to the head before he focused on the legs in an attempt to cripple and slow the killer while his partner circled.

The revenant was able to move along the rows to where he was on the Axman's left side and about twenty yards away. As he slid the power switch to full, Annie began to kick her captor's chest, evidence that she'd fully regained consciousness. He aimed and was about to fire when the Axman turned toward him. The lights in his eyes appeared almost like flames as he swung the ax.

He flung himself prone and trees all along the path were sliced through. They toppled and he flipped himself and fired a split-second before he touched the dirt. The force of the shot rocketed him toward the killer at an alarming speed and he barely missed the falling trees that threatened to crush him. He flipped the baseball bat handle and held it up.

"Annie!" he shouted and lobbed it to her as he careened past. He landed hard, slid along the soil, and tried to stop himself as she grasped the remains of the bat. It illuminated with the same white phantasma he'd seen before and she drove the pointed end deep into the Axman.

After all the horrors and killings he had been a part of and how many people he had made cry and scream in terror, it was his turn to utter a pained shriek. His hold loosened enough for her to finally break out of his grasp. Johnny bounded forward and whipped his coat off as Vic streaked to him and they fused.

Their adversary yanked the bat out of his chest and turned toward them as the revenant reached Annie and held his jacket up. The Axman roared as he brandished his ax and arced it vertically to bisect the young detective.

When the blade buried itself in the ground, the only thing that remained was two halves of the jacket.

CHAPTER TWENTY-TWO

"Hey, Vic?"

"What's up, kid?"

"Are we alive?"

The ghost chuckled dryly. "Not me, but you should have known that. As for you? Well, you might have taken a hit to the head but you still seem to be breathing."

He groaned as he pushed himself off the floor and checked his chest and head for wounds

"Ah, good. I merely wanted a second opinion." A muffled sigh drew his attention to Annie, who pushed slowly to her knees. He reached over to help her. "Hey, easy now. You've been through a hell of a wringer."

Her eyes fluttered open and she looked briefly at him before she focused on her surroundings. "Johnny? Where are we?"

It was a good question but a cursory look around the place where they ended up after crossing over from Limbo did not give him the answer. It appeared to be an old house with only a couple of dusty chairs and a small desk against the wall. Faded patches on the paintwork indicated that pictures had hung there once but no longer.

"I'm not entirely sure," he admitted as both of them stood carefully. "It looks like a house but no one seems to be home."

"Not now nor in the last couple of decades at least," Vic added and grimaced at one of the dirty chairs. "I guess that means we don't have to bother with awkward explanations, at least. Nothing ruins family dinner like two breathers and a ghost appearing out of thin air, especially if there isn't enough stuffing to go around."

"The real question is whether we are still in New Orleans." Johnny scrutinized the room again and realized there were no windows or doors. He took a couple of steps before he stumbled over a folded ladder attached to the floor. "Oh, we're in an attic." He looked at the wall where the odd blank spaces were. "Did someone used to live up here?" He looked at Annie, who had turned her attention to the top of the desk. "Have you found something, Annie?"

She turned toward him with something in her hand. "Only this picture on the desk." She handed him an old photo of a woman in her thirties holding a baby. Her head was bandaged. "Something about it caught my attention."

"I'll say," He muttered and tilted his head as he studied it. "I wonder what she went through to get those bandages. It looks like she was in a car crash or something."

"That probably would have been preferable." The statement followed by a low snicker made the two partners whirl and draw their guns as Annie gasped. The face was familiar, even if they still didn't know his name.

"You again?" Vic snapped as he aimed his gun into the air. "You show up at the strangest times."

The stranger chuckled and took a drag of his cigar. "Strange is normal for you, though, isn't it?" he remarked, took a few steps forward, and twirled his cane theatrically. "I can tell you this much—you are in New Orleans thanks to my intervention."

"You were able to direct the crossing point?" Johnny relaxed slightly and lowered his weapon. "Why bring us here?"

He blew a plume of smoke out. "I wanted to bring this place to your attention and more specifically, that photo." He tapped his cane on the floor before he pointed it at the photograph in the young man's hand. "This place is quite special. It belonged to a woman named Anna Schneider— the same woman in the photo."

"Anna Schneider?" The revenant looked at his two comrades. "Does it ring any bells?"

Annie shook her head and Vic frowned in thought. "I knew a dame in Chicago with that name. She was a singer in a jazz club—a great pianist too. It didn't look like her, though, and she never came to New Orleans as far as I know."

"She was one of the Axman's victims," the stranger stated and captured all their attention again. "One of the few who lived. On top of that, the baby in that photo? She gave birth to her in the immediate aftermath of the attack. As a result, she was often referred to as the ax baby."

The lights in the ghost detective's eyes brightened and grew. "She gave birth after having her melon battered? Strong woman."

Annie took the photo silently and studied it as Johnny folded his arms and approached the stranger. "Why are you telling us this? Why now? You've crept around this whole situation ever since you showed yourself to us. Now you wanna be an informant?"

"If you hadn't botched the job thus far, I wouldn't have to intervene more than I already have," the stranger said dismissively, ashed his cigar, and frowned. He took another puff and waved his hand. "But that is in the past, and I have realized that there is no way to avoid the consequences of my failure and my brother's plot." He walked past the two partners to one of the chairs and sat, his demeanor rather glum as his top hat was pulled down and cast a shadow over his shining eyes. "I still cannot intervene in a more tangible manner—and before you comment about how I'm a fool or coward, there would be great consequences should I try to deal with the Axman or my brother."

"Worse than the rampant killing and potential destruction of New Orleans?" Vic demanded with thick sarcasm.

The stranger was unmoved. "Yes, indeed. In this situation, should there be something that a keeper has to take care of themselves because the living and dead cannot do so...well, the others will have to make sure it can never happen again." He looked into their eyes. "And they prefer a showy, very permanent method. Although given what those white-coat-wearing idiots have done, maybe it isn't so different, hmm?"

"Are you talking about the Agency?" Johnny asked and sat next to him. "Why? What have they done since we've been gone?"

He shrugged. "Cleaning up, mostly. I wasn't talking about what they've done here in my city but what they've done in the past."

"The desecration of Savannah," Vic interjected. He received confused looks from Johnny and Annie but a knowing nod from the stranger. With a sigh, he removed his hat wearily to scratch his head. "But in all fairness, I must say it wasn't intentional. From my understanding, it was an accident. Some agents played with forces beyond their knowledge. But in the seventies—after I kicked the bucket—they were hunting a coven that was opening a portal to release a demon or something. Although they were able to stop it, some type of explosion was unleashed that not only destroyed the city but obliterated both any living and dead inhabitants in the area. A by-product of the incident is that anyone who was alive during it forgot Savannah even existed."

Annie and Johnny stared at him, aghast, and the revenant raised a hand to his head. "Wait, what? Where did this happen?"

"The state of Georgia," his partner explained, replaced his cap, and took his pack of cigarettes out. "You've heard of the Phantom Crater, right? That tourist attraction everyone thinks was either a meteor strike or some kind of government experiment? I suppose they are partially right on that last one. The Agency might have done it accidentally but rumors abound that they've found a way to recreate it just in case."

"In case of what? Jesus Christ, that's way too much!" the detective protested as he tried to wrap his head around what he had been told. He looked at the stranger with wide, shocked eyes. "Wait—are you saying the Agency is considering doing the same thing in New Orleans?"

The visiting ghost tilted his head speculatively from side to side. "Marsan's informants believe as much. They've been quite accurate in the past, although others claim this is merely one interpretation by those who are virulently anti-Agency."

Vic stopping flicking his lighter and looked quizzically at him. "Marsan? As in Big Daddy? You two are in cahoots?"

"We work together on occasion. A keeper sees and hears much but not everything. It helps to have associates who can help you keep track of the little things in both worlds, and a loa is always happy to help their worshippers."

"Loa?" the ghost detective demanded with grim intensity. "So that's what you are, then?"

"What's a loa?" Johnny asked.

"They are spirits worshipped in Voodoo," Annie informed them and clutched the picture to her chest. "With what we know now, most believe that all loas are keepers serving God like all other deities who were once worshipped throughout history."

The keeper gave her a slow clap. "The girl is familiar with the basics at least. Bravo. Although we weren't deities as such but close enough." He tilted his top hat and grinned broadly, an eerie look when paired with his skull-like face paint. "Since we will be working closely now, I suppose I should provide a proper introduction."

He stood and a purple fog filled the room as he became a dark figure. The lights of his eyes turned purple and as he seemed to grow taller, his form became more skeletal, and his eyes formed deep pits. He removed his top hat and bowed.

"My name is Baron Samedi, head of the Gede family and a loa of death like my other kin and one of many keepers over the living and dead." He spun his top hat in one hand before he flipped it onto his head and chuckled confidently. "Although if I may blow my own trumpet, I am the best there is."

CHAPTER TWENTY-THREE

"The best there is?" Johnny folded his arms defiantly. "If that were the case, how the hell did we get into this situation in the first place?"

"On top of that, you said your brother plays a part in this?" Vic added and finally lit his cigarette. "I've heard that keepers don't bother with one another unless they already have a connection of some kind. But if he's your brother, I would think you would at least keep an eye on him."

Samedi slouched, sighed, and waved a hand to disperse the mist around them. "You try for a little panache and no one appreciates it. I hate working with you specters."

Annie cleared her throat and bowed slightly. "It's an honor to meet a keeper mister...sir—sorry, Baron Samedi," she stated and straightened. "And I liked the atmosphere."

The baron smirked with satisfaction. "She's a warm one, this girl," he remarked cheerfully as he flipped his cane and tapped it on the attic floor. "At least one of you is capable of showing proper friendliness. You better hope you don't get me when your time comes to cross over, Johnny boy."

The young detective rolled his eyes. "Yeah, well, I'm from Texas, not Louisiana or Haiti, so I don't think I have to worry about it."

His partner blew out some smoke. "That's...uh, not how it works, kid."

Johnny raised an eyebrow as he looked at him, gritted his teeth, and muttered, "Shit."

Samedi laughed, walked closer, and placed a large hand on his shoulder that not only covered it but wrapped around his back and down his arm. "I'm not so petty, little detective. Let's clean this mess up and we'll call it square, hmm?"

He looked at him with an amused expression. "Is it that easy to get a ticket to heaven? Do a favor for a keeper?"

The baron laughed again and clapped him on the back a couple of times. "Heaven? No keeper can promise you that. It's up to the big man—well technically, I suppose—but you know what I mean. Still, I can promise you a gentle ride into Limbo and maybe even some perks!" He tapped his cane on the floor a few times before his form shrank. "But that's hopefully far into the future for you, boy. Or it could be soon depending on however this turns out."

"Or never," Johnny replied and drew puzzled looks from both Samedi and Annie. "I'm a revenant, remember? I'm missing a part of my soul." He flicked a thumb at Vic. "Or have you not met my chain-smoking Halloween decoration of a partner?"

"That's me," the ghost detective said with a casual wave.

Samedi frowned and stroked his chin. "Ah, right, it is

funny that I forgot that. It is something that makes you the talk of the town whenever you come by and what got Marsan to nominate you for the gig in the first place."

"We'll talk to him about that when we see him again, by the way," Vic stated.

The revenant bit his lip and nodded. "Agreed."

Once he'd shrunk to his normal—or at least normal to Johnny—height, the other ghost collapsed onto the chair and rapped his fingers on the arm. "It was a strange thing that happened to you, wasn't it? Are you still no closer to finding anything out about it?"

Johnny recalled seeing the...what was it? Remains, apparition, ghost clone?—whatever it was near the Big Dark when they faced the fake Axman. He decided it was best to not bring it up for now. It didn't seem like something that could help but rather confuse. "We've only been making our bones in this business for the last three years or so. I've been too busy to try to look into it further."

Samedi nodded and leaned back in the chair, and his gaze drifted in thought. "I see. Well, maybe old Samedi can help you out with that."

"What? Do you think we haven't resolved this sooner because there isn't enough of a reward?" Vic demanded cynically and flicked his cigarette toward the keeper. "We want to get rid of this guy as much as anyone. It's not like we can pack up and leave at this point. Unless he is destroyed or at least sent back to hell, I doubt he'll simply let bygones be bygones."

Johnny pointed at the other ghost. "By the way, if he does go back into the furnace, make sure to use chains and deadbolts, not merely a pinky promise that they won't escape, all right?"

Samedi looked at Annie but specifically the picture she was grasping. "Speaking of which, do you want to know how I knew about Anna Schneider?"

The ghost detective shrugged indifferently. "I assumed it was merely keeper knowledge or BD's informants like you said."

The baron nodded. "They confirmed my findings. Despite what you may think of me and my kind, we don't sit behind fancy desks and stamp travel papers. We have our jurisdictions and our duties and a century ago, I was the one to take the Axman to the pits."

"Is that right?" Vic muttered and took another drag as he thought about this. "Then how did he escape both the guards of Hell and your supervision?"

"Or is it only a lock the door and throw the key away situation down there?" Johnny asked.

Samedi placed the cigar held between his fingers into his mouth and lit it again with a small pillar of purple fire that erupted from his thumb. "Well, that normally works, yes. Despite the belief that no one escapes Hell, that is not as true as we would like to believe."

"Why am I surprised?" Vic replied gruffly.

"As for how it happened, it was the work of my brother Baron Kriminel."

"Kriminel? Like criminal?" Johnny raised an eyebrow. "It seems a little on the nose."

The ghost waved him off. "We keepers have been around far longer than any of your languages. It happened to work out like that." He raised his head and blew a plume of smoke out. "Kriminel was the one who was going to take the murderer's soul but I took that pleasure for myself. He is usually responsible for the more aggressive souls and either helps them work through their troubles or drags them fighting to the fire. But I intended to be the one to take care of the fool who caused such chaos in a city I hold so dear."

Johnny waved the smoke out of the air. "I imagine that however grateful your worshippers might have been about that, they probably would have appreciated it more if he hadn't killed so many."

The baron looked at him from beneath the rim of his hat, neither sad nor angered and merely contemplative. "He has killed far more than you know but we keepers cannot throw a cloak on, grab a sickle, and play reapers. As I said, we have rules."

"And bad things happen when you don't abide by them," Vic added and tapped his cigarette to ash it. "Which keeper's fault is it for vampires again? I'm very sure I've heard several different names and many people would like to have a word about that."

Samedi stretched his arms and yawned. "We have a sacred duty, certainly, but we get bored as well and there are repercussions for such foolishness. Trust me when I say that keeper will no longer be a problem."

"Eh, it's good to know, I guess."

"Um—excuse me?" Annie interjected and held the picture up. "Could you go back to what you learned about her? I can't shake the feeling that I know who she is."

The baron clicked his tongue in affirmation. "You are

quite right, young lady. By the way, it was impressive what you did back there with the shades."

She gasped and looked at her two companions. "The shades! With everything that happened since I woke up, I completely forgot about—"

"If you're worried about Aiyana and your brother, they're fine," Johnny assured her before he looked away and asked the baron, "They are, right? Did the Axman go back?"

"I cannot sense him. My brother is no doubt protecting him in some manner," Samedi explained. "But he has not returned. Even hidden, he can only do so much. If he were rampaging around the city again, I would know. Your friends are safe for now." He took a drag of his cigar and turned his head lazily toward Annie. "Now as for you, little one, I'll get back to my story. I've seen her picture before because the Axman made one." He slid his hand inside his jacket and produced a scroll that glimmered with the phantasma of Limbo. Carefully, he unrolled it and showed the others a sketch of the same woman but with long, dark hair.

"The Axman made this?" Vic asked and ran a hand over it.

"I have to say, it is impressive work," Samedi conceded as he studied it. "I don't think he was much of an artist in life, although it seems some of them do take a dark turn. I've sent many a starving artist to either Hell or Purgatory. It's a shame they don't use them to liven the place up— make some murals and the like." He handed the picture to Annie, who took it gingerly in her other hand. "That was in a hovel the Axman was living in."

"A hovel? Like a shack or something?" Johnny asked, bewildered. "I thought Hell was eternal damnation. Lakes of fire, monsters gnawing at your body, and torture with innumerable pointy things."

"Oh, there certainly is all that and more," the baron told him with a firm nod. "Hell is rather like Limbo. It's an ever-stretching land that is decayed, blighted, and burning, at least in some places. In others, it is frozen to a degree that is not possible in the world of the living, where outcasts exist in a state where they are iced to their core. They are only able to will themselves to move now and then until they can leave those lands, and they are conscious all the while.

"There are forests filled with creatures that can harm a soul in various devious ways. Some swallow them into their stomach where they will be stuck eternally, burned by their acids. Others will capture you and take you to their lair to feast on your damned soul until they are sated, then give your body time to rejuvenate so they can do it repeatedly."

"It sounds like the best tourist attractions," Vic snarked.

"You will find many more such areas, always changing and always horrid. There are torturers and the like. Some escape and are rarely pursued. Even the calmest areas of Hell are worse than anything you can run into in the world of the living or Limbo. Some even return to those prisons after escaping. I suppose the horrors you know are better than the ones you don't." Samedi considered this for a moment and his cigar hung limply. "But the Axman decided that living in the wilds was what he preferred. I'm surprised he lasted so long. I didn't see him as a huntsman or survivalist."

Johnny sighed and collapsed in the chair next to the ghost. "Can I ask you something?"

Smoke poured out of the baron's nose. "It would be a nice change from all the lip you are giving me."

"Why do you keep calling him the Axman? You must know his real name."

"Does it matter?" he asked seriously. "When you die, even if destined for Hell, your ghost form takes on elements that you were strongly attached to—hairstyles, beards, clothes, and the like. Your name is among those things. You may have been born Jonathan, but you prefer Johnny so that will most likely be your name when you die."

Vic seemed to understand where this was leading. "So you're saying he was so attached to the Axman moniker that it is now his 'real' name?"

"Indeed so."

The young detective sighed. "Still, we could look into his past and see—"

"He was a former hitman and used other people's weapons—a trick he picked up in his profession to allay suspicion. He had a hatred for immigrants, particularly Italians, and he was no stranger to murder and eventually got involved in a cult that no longer exists," Samedi explained. "Beyond that, there is nothing of interest. He was killed by a rival hitman when his employer thought he was becoming a liability, a fate many hitmen fall to. My hope is that by the end of this, no one will care about the

Axman more than any number of psychotics who have existed in the past."

Vic leaned against a wall and stubbed his cigarette out on the ceiling. "It was technically too late for that even before all this happened. Although that does make me concerned."

"About what?" Annie asked.

"I don't think sending those shades was an elaborate plan to kidnap you. No offense, but if that was the point, why not send them all toward you? And he didn't have a problem coming to get you himself."

"I see your mind has finally started to work again, Detective." The baron smiled. "You are right. It was to sow fear."

"Fear? I assume for power?" Johnny replied.

"That would be my guess too," his partner added. "Going for souls didn't work out like he wanted it to. But having an entire city in a panic...if he can siphon that like wraiths and shades can, it means he'll have enough juice for...whatever the hell he is doing."

"He wouldn't need such power for himself," Samedi stated. "It's for my brother."

"What could he want with it?" the ghost detective asked. "He's a keeper. Doesn't he have enough power?"

Samedi stood from the chair and walked a few paces away from the group. "Power is nothing more than a tool. Only a fool gathers power merely for the sake of it. What you build with it is the frightening thing." He turned to face them and the revenant was shocked by the grim expression, almost of fear, on the loa's face. "My brother is using that power to become a god."

CHAPTER TWENTY-FOUR

"A god?" Vic was incredulous, as were the other members of their little party. "What kind of god are we talking?"

Samedi regarded him with a look that was both intrigued and made it clear that at least part of him thought he was being an idiot. "Maybe I have not been keeping up with modern English vernacular, but does 'god' have multiple meanings now?"

"Well, it means all-powerful being, sure, but are we talking a Cthulhu type of deal—tentacles and madness and all that—or more like the all-knowing, loving God the Christians are into nowadays? The one you'd invite to the cookout to share stories and a cuddle?"

"Does anyone hear thunder and lightning?" Johnny asked and Annie listened intently before she caught his joke and she frowned.

Samedi mimicked her expression and narrowed his eyes at him. "Is this attempt at humor your way of dealing with the severity of the situation, Detective?"

He shrugged. "Hey, in this gig, you gotta be able to look death in the face and laugh."

"Especially if you've already dealt with it once," his partner quipped.

The baron sighed but gave what looked like an appreciative or at least understanding nod. "I suppose so. Perhaps that is necessary to carry you through to the end of this." He looked around the room. "I suppose if you won't take my warnings seriously with only words to convince you, I should show you what awaits if we do not stop Kriminel and his partner."

Before they could ask what he intended, he appeared in front of Johnny and Annie, raised his hands, and clamped them on their heads, and the world quite literally went gray. The room seemed to disappear and they stood in a purely monochrome space.

Johnny knocked the loa's hand off of him. "What the hell did you do?" he demanded.

"I brought you to the path." He looked at Vic. "Ah. good. It seems your connection allowed me to bring him along as well, which saves me a trip."

"The path?" Annie looked around. "What is the path? I've never heard of it."

"That's not surprising. It is mostly the domain of myself and my fellow keepers." He gestured around the blank domain. "Although every ghost travels through here on their death, they do not remember it. This is where their soul awaits their judgment. It does not have a fancy name and is simply the path that leads from life to death—or vice versa in special circumstances but there hasn't been one of those in over a couple of millennia."

The young detective looked down and froze for a moment as all he saw was a seemingly infinite void of nothing. "All ghosts forget they've been here? That seems convenient." He craned his neck casually. "I guess that means you can't vouch for what he's saying, eh, Vic?" No response came from the often surly ghost. "Vic?" He looked at his partner, who stared above them, seemingly mesmerized by something. "Samedi, what's wrong with him? Does this place affect ghosts differently?"

"That ain't it, kid," Vic croaked and continued to stare into the space above. "I'm a little distracted, is all."

"Distracted? By wha—" Johnny's words died in his throat as he and Annie looked up. The skeleton of a massive creature seemed to hover above them. It was molded from a dark force of some kind, but what appeared to be a maelstrom of white light surrounded it and poured into it.

"What is that?" Annie whispered, her eyes wider than seemed possible. "It looks like...him."

"The Axman?" Johnny studied it with a scowl. "It looks like him if he were the size of a skyscraper."

Samedi rested his cane along his shoulders and looped his arms over it. "My thought is that the Axman's form was something of a progenitor to this. Creating an army of shades is nothing for my brother, but creating an entirely new being from scratch is not something any keeper is familiar with."

"Your brother made that?" Vic demanded and finally snapped out of his stupor. "Is it some kind of monster he intends to unleash?"

The baron uttered a dark, dry snicker. "A monster?

Perhaps not in the traditional meaning. It is certainly an abomination, however." He gestured around them. "Think of the path as a reality sectioned into hallways or domains. Where we are is Kriminel's domain and where he brought souls over. He's been hiding this body in here where no others can see."

"Then how are we here?" the ghost detective asked.

The baron placed one hand on his chest. "You remember when I said that most keepers don't bother with one another unless connected? Well, those connections work similarly to the bonds between ghosts. I can travel into his domain due to our connection, something he either did not consider since I do so no more than I have to, or perhaps he simply had no alternative."

"What is he doing with it?" Johnny asked, his gaze fixed on the morbid creation above him.

"As I said, becoming a god," the loa answered. "We keepers might have more power and presence than a ghost, but we are not of the living, not as you consider it." He pointed his cane toward the skeleton. "All that white you see swirling around it? Those are souls—the ones who were supposed to be handled by my brother. He uses them to form the body he will inhabit."

"Those are souls?" Annie gasped, darted closer to him, and grasped his arm. "Mister Samedi, you have to free them! You are a keeper so you can do that, can't you?"

He did not jerk away from her or admonish her in any way. Instead, he looked remorsefully at her and placed a hand on her head. "If I could do that, my dear, I would have done so already. I might be able to travel into my brother's domain, but those souls are in his care."

Johnny finally looked away from the unfinished body. "So what? Is that it for them? They get a bad dice roll and they are destined to be turned into blood cells for your brother's pet project?"

Samedi shook his head. "That does not have to be their fate. Assuming we succeed." He sighed and adjusted his hat. "If we can defeat the Axman and sever his connection to Kriminel—which is the only thing that allows Kriminel to inhabit the world of the living in a permanent way—I can deal with him, destroy that abomination up there, and release the souls to move on to where they deserve to go."

"Why does he need it?" Vic asked and pointed upward. "From what you're telling us, it's merely a fancy body. I might not know much about resurrection but I'm fairly familiar with possession. I would imagine a keeper could possess a body if necessary."

The baron nodded, released Annie, and floated to the side, where his form changed to that of a young African American man in a well-tailored suit. "Indeed we can, as well as take many different forms. His body changed once into a purple-scaled snake but continued to speak even in that form.

"But Kriminel does not want to merely possess a body —not that a mortal body could contain a keeper for longer than a couple of days, at best. As I said, this body is so he can achieve godhood. Souls are different than ghosts. They still hold a vestige of life, which is what makes them so powerful and prized among the supernatural terrors."

He returned to his normal form, spun quickly, and pointed at the big skeleton. "He is using phantasma and stygia to make the body, but the souls are like concrete to seal it together. It won't stay in that skeletal form. He is making it in his image and once he inhabits it, he will have a form that can interact with the living world, Limbo, and the path. No realm will be beyond his reach and I doubt he will keep them separated. Why divide your kingdoms like that?"

Johnny recalled the words of the witch. "The Axman is breaking down the barrier between life and death," he muttered as his eyes widened in realization. He looked at the baron. "But you're saying this is Kriminel's plan, right? What does the Axman get out of this?"

Samedi landed in front of him. "That is why he is your focus, while my brother is mine. I am still not aware of what the Axman gets out of all this and how it would be of any benefit to him if what I believe Kriminel is up to is true." He placed his hands on Annie and Johnny's heads again.

"But my hope is that what he is planning is of little consequence. We must stop them both and put an end to this nightmare before they can bring it to life." His eyes lit up and when the gray world disappeared, they had returned to the attic. "Find out how Anna Schneider fits into all this. That might give you some clue as to what he is after and his next steps. Keep the girl safe. We know he is after her at least."

He tipped his hat as his body began to fade. "I will be in touch, my friends. I leave this up to you as I prepare for what I must do." A sad expression crossed his features just before he vanished entirely. "And the consequences that may ensue when it is done."

CHAPTER TWENTY-FIVE

Johnny lowered the attic door, extended the ladder, and climbed down. He paused and looked around the empty house. "It's clear, Annie," he called as he continued to explore the hall.

She descended, still clutching the picture. "This kind of feels like breaking and entering."

He laughed. "After what we saw, that's what concerns you?"

Vic floated past her as she blushed and looked away. "Don't let him knock ya. He doesn't have a problem because he's a degenerate."

"Pardon?" he responded with an irate look. "Do you wanna remind me who taught me how to pick locks and do all those degenerate things in the first place?"

The ghost shrugged. "Hey, you were all for it."

Annie walked forward to look through half-open curtains at the streets. "If there is nothing else here, we should probably go and find Marco and the others."

"Oh, right!" Johnny fished his cell phone out of his

pocket. "I guess I'm forgetting things too. Huh? I have no bars in here. What is this? Communist Russia?"

Annie checked her pockets. "Sorry, I must have forgotten my phone when we left."

"Don't worry. I'm sure I can get a signal somewhere out there." He walked to her and peered through the windows. "We should probably get out of here, though. I can't think of a good excuse for why we would be in here if someone does catch us walking around."

"We could always tell the truth," she suggested.

He looked at her and tried to stop himself from rolling his eyes. "Do you prefer an asylum over a brief stint in jail?" He dropped the curtain into place and walked out of the hall to find the living room and front door.

She frowned. "We'll have to tell the others about what we saw. Do you think they won't believe us?"

"Valerie, your brother, and Aiyana? Sure, but the others? Even the Agency members might have a hard time believing everything we saw. It certainly doesn't help that our inside source is a keeper. We might live in a time where the crazy people are those who don't believe in ghosts, but that's where they tend to stop. Most people don't like to think about the keepers and that all religions are technically right." He jiggled the door but the deadbolt was locked and the lock itself had a double keyhole. "Speaking of lockpicking," he muttered as he retrieved a lock pick from his inside shirt pocket. Quickly, he manipulated the mechanism and opened the door. They had stepped onto the front lawn and headed to the sidewalk when they heard a police siren.

"Oh, that is terrible luck there, kid," Vic commented with a wry grin.

He gritted his teeth and scowled at his partner. "What? You don't think the NOPD has prisons for ghosts?"

The ghost detective considered this as two officers stepped out of their car. "Hmm, good point. How fast can you run?"

"Annie Maggio and Jonathan Despereaux?" one of the officers called and drew surprised looks before Annie nodded slowly. "How did you end up here? Whatever. Officer Simone asked a few of us to look for you after you disappeared. Your brother's worried sick, Ms. Maggio."

She sighed, both relieved that he was still alive and seemingly flustered by his protectiveness. "Thank you. I need to call him."

"Reception is a little spotty around here," Johnny told them and held his phone up.

"Officer Simone and your brother are both at the station. She arranged to get your car towed there as well. Do you need a ride?" the cop asked.

Johnny put his phone away and nodded. "This isn't the way I thought this would go but it's certainly not unwelcome." He and Annie walked to the car.

Vic fused with him and muttered, "Whoever tows it had better not scuff the paint."

───────────

"Understood, thanks," Valerie said, ended the call, and turned to Marco, Aiyana, and Donovan. "Johnny and Annie were found. Two patrol officers are bringing them here."

"Oh, thank God!" Marco sighed with relief. "I thought that bastard finally had her."

"After seeing what she did to those shades, I don't think I would be surprised if she could take him on herself at this point," Aiyana commented.

Donovan looked to where several agents and cops headed into a meeting room. "It looks like it's about to start. Do you wanna get in there?"

Valerie and the others noticed a few members of the ghost mafia enter the room as well, including Big Daddy. "We probably should," the officer replied and stood from her chair. "To see the spectacle of the Agency, NOPD, and ghost underworld trying to work together if nothing else." She glanced at Marco. "Do you happen to know the leader?"

He looked at a green skeleton with sculpted silver hair and a neat pinstriped suit. "Sergio? Fairly well, but I didn't think he was the head of the mob. I remember he used to work with my uncle. My uncle didn't work for him." He considered this for a moment before he shook his head. "Still, with what happened to uncle Gabe and the mafia trying to take care of it themselves for a while, I guess it isn't hard to think that many mafiosos were killed, which probably left a power vacuum."

"My question is whether he's trustworthy or not," Donovan stated as he watched Sergio and his bodyguards head into the room.

The young man shrugged "I don't remember anything that would make me think he's gone power-hungry. Besides, the ghost mob doesn't operate like living mobs— not like they are peddling drugs or anything. They focus on the ghost population, which means they have as much of a stake in this as any of us." His gaze shifted to Big Daddy. "I want to know who the jolly purple giant is. He seems to be the one calling the shots. He and his boys rode in with Johnny and Vic so I guess they know each other?"

Marco, Aiyana, and Valerie looked at each other to see if anyone had anything to say about it but they were all clueless. "I guess we'll have to wait until he arrives," Aiyana declared.

This got a nod from Valerie as she began to walk toward the room. "I guess so. For now, let's get in there."

———

"Thanks for the lift," Johnny said as he, Annie, and the cops who had chauffeured them walked into the precinct. "Do you have any idea where Valerie and her brother are? We have information we need to share with them."

"Well, the last I heard before Officer Simone came back was that they were going to have a meeting with the Agency," one of the cops replied.

"And the mafia," another added. "Er...the ghosts, not the living one."

Johnny smirked. "I don't think there's been a real mob in New Orleans in decades."

Vic drifted out of him and startled some of the specters in the station. "Or in much of America since the eighties. I have to admit I kind of miss them. They made for easy cases as so many thefts and murders in Chicago turned out to be mob-related."

His partner ignored him for now. "Which way to the meeting?"

The cops looked at one another. "I know—or at least I assume—you are an informant or consultant working with Officer Simone, but I'm not sure they will allow you into a meeting."

He pointed to himself and then to Annie. "Maybe, maybe not. But since she was taken by the Axman and I pursued them and we both escaped, don't you think they will want to know what happened? Personally, I think our chances are good to receive an invitation."

One of the cops snickered as the other nodded and pointed them deeper into the station. He thanked them and he, Vic, and Annie strode to the meeting room. When he saw Big Daddy, he stopped her. "Hey, Ann, would you mind doing me a favor?"

The door to the meeting room opened and everyone present looked at it as Annie walked in clutching a picture.

"Annie!" Marco shouted as he ran closer and hugged her. "I'm so glad nothing happened to you. Are you okay?"

"I'm fine, Marco," she replied, and despite her previous pushback against her brother's fretful behavior, she hugged him and tears stung her eyes. "Johnny got me out but I have so much to fill you in on—all of you." She looked at the giant purple skeleton among the mob delegates. "Mister...uh, Big Daddy?"

The dealer chuckled, removed his hat, and bowed

slightly. "It's a pleasure to meet you, darling. How can I be of service?"

She pointed outside the room. "Johnny and Vic want to see you." Everyone looked outside at the revenant who stood with his arms folded while his partner waved sarcastically.

"Ah, right." Big Daddy replaced his hat and looked at Captain Shemar and Director Lovett. "Excuse me for a moment. Sergio will take over from here." He cracked his knuckles and floated toward the wall. "It seems I have to take a moment to square things with two of my best bounty hunters."

CHAPTER TWENTY-SIX

When Big Daddy exited the meeting room, he gestured to an empty office and the two partners followed him there. Johnny walked in and sat on one of the chairs while Vic closed the blinds.

"Are there problems, gentleman?" the dealer asked as he leaned against the desk. "You seem somewhat perturbed. Although since you pursued the Axman into God knows where in Limbo, I suppose there are worse things you could be right now."

"Perturbed?" The revenant folded his arms. "That's one way to put it, I guess."

The ghost raised an eyebrow and the lights in his eyes shined. "Why are you all fussy? You seemed fine enough at the hotel."

"That was before we know what we do now," Johnny answered. "Besides, we were shocked to see you at the hotel."

The dealer reached into his pants pocket and produced a cigar. "That I wasn't there to smoke your ass? Heh, heh, we've been over that already." He used a fancy golden lighter to light his cigar. "So what's got you so morose there, fellas?"

"We met the baron, BD," Vic responded flatly. "He told us you set us up for this gig."

He nodded as he shut the top of the lighter and put it away. "You met the baron, eh? Old Samedi is something, ain't he? I'm surprised he let you know who he is already. He usually holds that close to his chest." He took a drag of his cigar and let the smoke trail slowly from his skull. "That's right, I told him to look at you. But you should remember that you investigated it yourselves. I merely gave you the gig that pointed you in that direction. I didn't even have an official listing. You have to remember that I tried to keep it all on the down-low."

"And we're starting to wonder why." Vic walked up to the giant ghost. "I thought it had something to do with the mob not wanting what was going on to get back to Limbo. It ruins the tourism and the flow of ghosts who come back and try to find a place in their old hometown, which means less business for them. But Samedi told us about his brother's involvement and the body he's trying to make."

This seemed to catch his attention. "You saw it? Samedi took you to the path and you saw the body his brother is making?"

Johnny tilted his head. "Have you?"

Big Daddy shook his head. "Nah, but the loa told me about it. He said it was only half a skeleton. What does it look like now?"

Vic relaxed slightly and slid his hands into his pockets as he wandered to the window. "Mostly complete, I guess.

There were pieces missing. Samedi said he's trying to make it in his image so he's gonna need more than a skeleton for that."

"Shit, that'll come easy for him," the dealer said with a grimace. He took a longer drag on his cigar. "Kriminel still has those souls coming to his domain. This city is in a panic and no amount of cops and agents telling everyone to calm down will help—not that they'd believe them anyway with everything that's happened. The Axman will be juiced up by all that fear."

"It doesn't take a genius to realize that he won't hide for much longer," the ghost detective reasoned. "Samedi said he couldn't detect him normally because his brother is probably hiding him. But if he storms around, he's out in the open. The Axman probably wants to get powerful enough that he won't have to worry about that."

Johnny straightened. "Say what? Can a ghost become more powerful than a keeper?"

"He's not merely a ghost," his partner corrected. "He's some kind of demon or at least a close approximation. And keepers don't have the same type of absolute power they do in Limbo."

"A keeper can only bestow power or gifts on others. They can possess a body, sure, but that only gives them limited strength in the world of the livin'," Big Daddy added and chewed on his cigar. "In a possessed body, especially a willing one, they are far stronger than any breather or ghost. But seeing what the Axman has been able to accomplish…" He whistled. "I'm not too sure who I'd put money on in a fight if he gets enough power."

Johnny sighed in exasperation. "Fuck me. It's not like

we'll find a willing host for a loa here." He rubbed his temple before he noticed that both Vic and Big Daddy stared at him as if he had asked what addition was. "What?"

"You do remember we're in New Orleans, kid?" Vic asked.

He nodded. "Yeah. What? Are you saying he still has worshippers?"

"To make sure, New Orleans, Louisiana, right?" Big Daddy added.

"Yes, dammit! Look I know that Louisiana Voodoo was a thing at one point but in the time since the ghost world was discovered, there can't still be a large population of worshippers left."

"Sure, not large, but they are still there." The ghost detective pointed to Big Daddy. "The baron told us he used to be one."

The dealer chuckled. "Well, when I was a hunter, making deals with a keeper who had domain over death seemed...well, appropriate." His eyes glinted as he seemed to get lost in thought. "I had many a close call but I could never tell if it was my skills, luck, or Samedi deciding it wasn't time to dig my grave yet."

He looked at Johnny, who studied him curiously. "You were a worshipper? I thought you only did that to make deals."

"That was certainly a bonus," he admitted.

"But knowing what we know now about the afterlife, what kept you around?"

Big Daddy shook his head. "Louisiana Voodoo still worships God, kid, but in its own special way. Besides, I'm still in Limbo with a while to go before I got to worry about all that." He dug inside his jacket pocket and produced a card. "There's a priestess you should talk to if you have any questions you need answered about Samedi and his brother and all that. Also, if it comes down to it, she might be willing to help us."

Vic took the card and read the name aloud. "Catherine Leveau." He looked at Big Daddy. "How did you meet her?"

"I knew her mama when I was alive. She's a spirit caller. It runs in the family."

"Spirit caller?" Johnny took the card and glanced at it before he handed back. "We might want to pass this to Aiyana."

"It would probably be nice for her to meet one who isn't trying to kill her this time," the ghost detective noted as he put the card away. He frowned and looked from his partner to Big Daddy. "You know, I'm not as annoyed as I was when we walked in here."

The dealer responded with a satisfied laugh. "That's the charm that has led me to become one of the biggest gig dealers in Limbo." He took another drag. "In both stature and accomplishments, before you make the obvious joke."

"It seemed too easy," Vic replied. "The truth is I have more questions but they are probably best left until we are back in the meeting. We need to decide where to go from here and how you and the mob play into it."

Big Daddy snorted as he ground his cigar out in a nearby coffee cup. "That Agency director was asking similar questions. I'm not a fan of her attitude."

"And I think both Vic and I would prefer to not work with the Agency at all, but they did their part during the shade attack, at least, and they aren't obliterating ghosts on sight, so I guess we can find some kind of compromise," Johnny suggested.

Vic moved to the door and turned the knob before he looked over his shoulder. "We'll have to. If we don't take care of this problem, there's the chance the Agency blows New Orleans up, the Wild Hunt purges New Orleans, or maybe even God himself smites New Orleans."

The dealer pushed off the desk and stretched. "Whew, New Orleans is dealing with some shit now, ain't she?"

The revenant sighed as he stood. "Yeah, well, you know what they say. There's always something going down in New Orleans."

CHAPTER TWENTY-SEVEN

When Johnny, Vic, and Big Daddy returned, no one in the room turned to look at them as they opened the door. Instead, a loud ruckus of many voices shouting over one another exploded inside the room as they walked in.

"Man, it's a good thing this room is soundproof," Johnny muttered as he closed the door behind them.

"Sergio, what the hell is going on?" the dealer demanded as he floated through the group of mafiosos who were busy squabbling with the agents and cops.

Johnny and Vic moved to Valerie, Aiyana, and the Maggios. "Val, what happened?" the ghost detective asked as the rumble of shouting voices continued. "We were gone less than ten minutes."

She looked at him, her fatigue evident in her eyes as was her desire to be done with this bullshit. "The short version is the Agency wants to quarantine New Orleans with an ether dome to trap the Axman. The mob and cops don't. They might agree on that but some loudmouths don't want to work with mobs and some don't want to work with ghosts."

He rolled his eyes. "You might not want to mention that I've helped out."

"It's a little too late for that," Marco interjected.

"I thought it would help but yeah, nothing going for me there. Not all the cops here are specters. They probably haven't seen this many ghosts in corporeal form ever so are already on edge and that doesn't help," Valerie admitted and glanced at Johnny. "Annie filled us in on what happened after you two disappeared."

"How did that go?" The revenant grimaced at what he thought was the crash of a mug hitting the wall. "Did that have anything to do with what is going on now?"

She held her thumb and index finger up close together. "A little. Some believe it, some don't, and some don't want to believe it but do. All in all, a good mix."

Annie sighed and stared at the photo. "It seemed to work out how you expected, Johnny."

He nodded and glanced at the Agency director, who stood silently at the head of the table beside a frustrated captain Shemar. "What was the agents' response?"

"Surprisingly, some seemed to believe it immediately," Aiyana revealed and glanced at Donovan. "Valerie's new friend backed Annie up. He seems more open-minded than the others."

Johnny recalled what Vic had said about the Savannah incident and the Agency's hand in it. "Or they are familiar with how bad things can get when you mess with the after-life." The agent seemed to catch this and looked briefly at him before he returned to avoiding his gaze.

"It's been like this for the last few minutes," Valerie stated and frowned at Shemar. "I hoped they'd burn out quickly or the leaders would step in, but they don't exactly see eye to eye either. They seem to have more sense than to squabble right now but maybe not enough to stop this mess."

Johnny drew his gun and lowered the power. "Allow me to have a shot." He pointed it at the ceiling and fired, and a ball of ether streaked up through the ceiling and out the building. The sound was enough to stop the argument, but the ghosts were on high alert as they were far more familiar and concerned about the sound of an ether weapon. He lowered his weapon and looked around. "Are y'll done barking at one another?"

"Who the hell are you with?" one of the agents asked.

"Us more than you," a mobster retorted.

"That's the revenant, isn't it?" another agent asked. "I'm surprised he hasn't skipped town."

"He's with Valerie, right?" a cop asked another. "Is he a consultant or something?"

Johnny pointed to the officer. "Sure, let's go with that. Anything to get this meeting rolling again and focused on the Axman instead of me."

Lovett turned to him. "And what have you to add about the Axman, revenant?" Johnny had heard himself called by that title many times, mostly in Limbo, but this was the first time that it sounded less like awe or curiosity and more like an insult. "Can you verify the claims this young lady has told us about—"

"Meeting a keeper, visiting the path between life and death, and seeing some kind of body being made there by another keeper. Yeah, those are the basics," he interrupted. This seemed to stir renewed, albeit quieter, discussions in the room. "Look, the long and short of it is that the Axman has a plan. Despite there being three completely different groups here, I don't hear anything from any of them"—he pointed a finger at the director—"that doesn't involve putting New Orleans under supernatural lockdown."

The woman adjusted her glasses. "Do you have one, revenant? Because as I see it, we don't want this Axman to leave the city when we have an—"

"He won't leave the city," Big Daddy stated coolly. "Not when he's set himself up here so nice. Hell, I wouldn't be surprised if doming the city is exactly what he wants."

"What do you mean?" Shemar asked.

Sergio stepped forward and removed his shades to reveal shining green eyes. "Me and my men, we keep an eye on the ghost populace. More and more have disappeared and not only because they have fled to Limbo. Either they are all holing up in a place we don't know about—which I can tell you is very unlikely—or they are being taken. The Axman might play like he's a mastermind hiding in his lair and making grunts do the dirty work. But we know he doesn't have any more flunkies in his employ. He's out there hunting."

Vic stepped forward. "That dome of yours—it stops ghosts from crossing over as well, right?"

Lovett raised an eyebrow. "And how do you know that?"

"Well, I'm familiar with ether blockades and by the sounds of it, this dome is merely a big version of that. Plus, the SEA was working on tech like that even when I was alive over fifty years ago. I'd like to think the tax dollars are getting some use." His gaze shifted to Johnny, who looked down and seemed deep in thought.

"That's a good guess," the woman replied.

"It's simple deduction," he retorted. "I agree with Big... Marsan on this one. The Axman ain't going to leave New Orleans, not when he has everything he needs and wants right here. And to add to what Annie and Johnny said, I saw the body too and it's close to finished. We need to get to work to deal with him now because with the city in fear, he will have far more power soon and we don't have anything to take care of him when he decides to stop skulking about."

"You think so?" Sergio asked. "We've got spectral weapons, explosives, and even a few ether cannons and some mystical crap we had spirit callers make for us."

"Ether cannons?" Shemar narrowed his eyes at him. "How did you get your hands on those?"

Sergio grinned wryly. "Perfectly legally, I assure you, Officer."

"And I assume you have permits for all of them?" Lovett demanded.

The mob boss shrugged. "Sure. I'll show them to you when you and your agents get this cleaned up and are on the way out. If you had gotten here sooner, maybe we wouldn't be in this mess in the first place."

Her lips tightened. "We were briefly compromised—almost as if someone didn't want us here to begin with. You seem to have numerous connections."

He snarled. "The ghost mob is bigger than only one city,

sure, but you ain't placing the blame for your incompetence on us, lady."

"Enough!" Shemar thumped his tablet on the table. "We won't start that shit again. For now, we need to do the groundwork before we can build a decent plan." He looked at his officers. "I'll have every available officer, both specter and non, combing the area. Officer Simone's associate shaman told us that the Axman seemed to operate out of a theater or auditorium of some kind so fan out, search all abandoned buildings that could fit that description, and radio in anything you find." The officers looked at one another for a moment before they nodded agreement.

Lovett stared at him, seemingly impressed by the police chief's outburst. "Very well. I will have our technicians look into the unique phantasma readings we got off the Axman and examine the sigils the shaman saw to identify other possible things he could do with them. I will also send some agents to patrol the city and others to assist your hunt."

Sergio adjusted his jacket. "I'll bring those weapons in, just in case the Axman flips the script and sends another batch of spooks out. My guys will keep the ghost population safe—what is left of it—and check the haunts around the city."

Big Daddy folded his arms. "I've got my informants in Limbo keeping me up to date on anything going on that side. I have numerous bounty hunters who owe me favors. If it comes down to it, I can call them in to help with the search or deal with him if we get a bead on him."

Vic nodded, finally happy that they all seemed to be doing something for once. "All right. That wasn't so hard, was it? And while you are doing that we will be—huh?" He felt himself being dragged out of the room as Johnny left. "Getting an early start it seems—best of luck!" He tipped his hat quickly as he was dragged to the door and disappeared from the meeting room.

CHAPTER TWENTY-EIGHT

Johnny was already outside the station by the time Vic caught up with him. "Hey, kid, what's the matter?" he asked and floated in front of the young man as he looked around. "Things were finally coming together in there."

"Yeah, that was good," he answered almost absent-mindedly. "Do you think they dropped the car off in the parking lot?"

His partner scratched his skull. "What? You don't wanna get in on this?"

He pressed his lips together and his expression indicated that he was lost in thought. "Of course I do, but a thought occurred to me that could help us hobble both the Axman and his buddy—but I need a nap first."

The ghost detective folded his arms. "What? Why's that? Spit it out, kid."

Johnny brushed him aside as he headed toward the parking lot and retrieved his keys. "You're going to tell me that I'm too tired and not thinking straight." He pressed the unlock button on his remote and heard a beep at the back.

Vic clicked his tongue. "Seriously? Try me and see."

He stopped, turned, and looked his partner in his lights. "I think we should confront the Wild Hunt and bring them in on this."

The silence between the two stretched for a long moment. Finally, his partner placed a boney hand on his shoulder. "Partner, you are too tired. You need to rest."

"Why did Johnny up and leave?" Marco asked when the parties in the meeting finally began to disperse.

Valerie shrugged and finished typing a message on her phone. "I couldn't hazard a guess right now, but I'm sure he'll get back to us." She closed her messages and put her phone away. "I'm more interested in that photo your sister has."

Annie handed it to her. "This is Anne Schneider. She was one of the Axman's victims who survived."

The officer nodded and passed the picture to Marco so he and Aiyana could take a look. "I know of her. After the attack, she went into labor and gave birth to a baby girl."

"Yes, the baron told us that the Axman seems to have some kind of obsession with her."

"The baron?" the young man asked and handed the photo to Aiyana. "Who's that?"

"Baron Samedi," she replied. "He's a loa of death and a keeper. I guess he's the one who helped Johnny over the last few days."

"You met a keeper?" Aiyana gasped and almost dropped the photo. "When the Axman took you?"

She shook her head. "After Johnny rescued me. The baron was able to direct us to an old home when we crossed back, which is where we found the photo. He was the one who told us all this and showed us the skeleton body."

"Wait—why didn't you tell us that in the meeting?" Valerie asked. "You said you overheard it from the Axman's ranting and when he took you into Limbo."

Annie frowned and shrugged. "Johnny asked me not to mention him. He said everything would probably be hard enough to swallow without revealing that a keeper told us."

"And you are telling us now because?" Her brother raised an eyebrow.

She looked frankly at him. "He believed that all of you would be more willing to believe it given everything we went through."

They exchanged glances and either nodded or shrugged. "He's not wrong," the shaman conceded.

Annie dug in her pockets. "He also wanted me to give this to you, Aiyana." She handed her the card Big Daddy had given him. "He passed it to me before he left."

She took the card and raised her eyebrow. "Catherine Leveau? A Voodoo priestess?"

The other woman nodded. "She's a spirit caller like you. Big Daddy said she might be able to help us in the future. She's one of his worshippers."

"Well, we could certainly use any potential allies we can find," Aiyana responded as she placed the card in her satchel. "Maybe I can meet her later. For now, I wish to talk to the Agency."

"The Agency?" Marco looked at her in bewilderment. "What for?"

"They will look into the Axman's use of sigils," she explained and adjusted the strap of her satchel across her shoulders. "I wish to do so as well, and they probably don't have any spirit callers amongst their ranks. We might all have our differences and we like our personal space for the most part. You don't seem to get much of that in the SEA."

"How long will you be gone?" Valerie asked and glanced at Shemar, who conversed with a small group of police.

"Hopefully, not long at all—assuming they allow me to help in the first place."

The young officer nodded. "All right. I'll check in with Shemar quickly. But afterward, the three of us will look into Anna Schneider and see what we can find on her."

Marco nodded as he slumped in his chair. "That works for me. All I'm good for is busting ghost heads. When that happens, I can be a real participant."

"But you do not have your bat," Aiyana reminded him.

He closed his eyes as if to catch a quick wink of sleep but smirked. "Did you think that was the only one I had? I've played ball for the better part of two decades now." He opened one eye. "Although, before we rush into the next fight, we need to swing past home so I can grab one." His gaze drifted to his sister. "Maybe one for Annie too given what she was able to do with the last one."

Valerie chuckled as she rested her head against her palm. "No kidding. We need to find out what that was, Annie. It could come in handy if another army of those freaks rampages through New Orleans."

Annie looked at her hands. "Yes, but there is a problem

there."

"What's that, sis?"

She clenched her hands into fists before she lowered them and sighed. "I'm not sure what it was either or if I can do it again in the future."

They looked at one another and Marco shrugged. "Eh, We should probably find out as quickly as possible. The sooner we get home and grab one of those bats, the better."

"Are you good with all this?" Big Daddy asked the mafia head, whose head rested against the window of the car. "Working with the cops—I never thought I'd see the day."

"You mean beyond bribes or traitors?" Sergio asked and rolled his lights. "Yeah, me neither. It goes to show how much of a pain in the ass the Axman is."

"I have some idea," Big Daddy admitted and created a spark to light another cigar. "But do you want to clear it up for me?"

Sergio's phone rang and he sighed and reached into his jacket. "You know how far down the line I was to take over this section of the mafia? Thirty-four guys were ahead of me, and they are either all missing or obliterated, or abdicated once they heard they were being sent here, the cowards." He answered the call with a curt, "What is it?" The mafia head was silent for a short while, but Big Daddy could see his lights dim slowly. "What do you mean they are all dead? We're already dead!"

When they arrived at the motel, Johnny immediately flung himself on the bed while Vic continued to mutter.

"Seriously, kid, getting the Wild Hunt involved in all this? I know you might not be as familiar with them as I am—or any ghost for that matter. But I would have thought you were bright enough to understand that they are bad news. Hell, even Big Daddy and the mobsters don't want to bring them in despite everything the Axman has done."

"Oh, I've noticed," he mumbled as he turned away. "And I don't plan to use them to go after the Axman. That's our job. But we have other things to worry about. Besides, right now, there is the possibility of a keeper getting a physical body, the Agency maybe having that bomb or whatever at the ready, or perhaps God himself smiting New Orleans into oblivion. I think we're at the point where we should consider more drastic options."

The ghost detective floated forward to sit on the bed, removed his hat, and sighed. "Eh, maybe you're right. I'm still not all that happy about it but we should consider all our options. Promise me you will go over your idea in detail when you wake up, all right?" He waited for a few moments with no response and glanced at his partner. "Johnny? Did you hear me?" he asked, only to hear a loud snore this time. He shook him, again with no response. "Man, I guess he was out of it." He drifted to the other bed, retrieved the remote for the TV, and turned it on. "Hopefully, he'll be able to get some good sleep after all the shit we went through today. He's earned that much."

Unfortunately for the young revenant, it appeared that whether he had earned it or not, he wouldn't get it.

CHAPTER TWENTY-NINE

When Johnny woke, it was to darkness. He looked at his hands and noticed a red tint to them—the reflection from a red sky with no stars or clouds. He rubbed his eyes and looked at the debris that surrounded him. A sign amongst the rubble caught his eye and seemed familiar. He jogged to it, shifted some of the wreckage aside, and stared at the cracked remains of the Carnivale sign. It took a few moments of confusion before he realized that this was the remains of Romeo's bar.

Shocked, he straightened and backed away while his mind tried to understand what had happened. He turned and gaped at the crumbled remains of New Orleans around him, completely devoid of life and ghosts. What was going on? Were they too late?

A loud sound filled the air—like a deep groan or hum that made his body shake with how loud it was. He jerked his head in every direction to try to find the source and finally noticed a massive, dark figure in the distance. The skeleton Samedi had shown him was now complete.

Slowly, two large white orbs appeared as its eyes. The figure seemed to rest on a makeshift throne of buildings that had broken beneath it. It cocked its head to one side before it lurched forward onto its feet and revealed that it was far bigger than he had realized. While he had seen it in the path, it had floated so high above them he couldn't grasp the sheer scale of it. In reality, it was far bigger than any skyscraper he had seen, even in photos.

A cold feeling began to swarm over and through him. It felt similar to the feelings he experienced around ghosts but this was beyond bone-chilling and more extreme than any previous experience. He thought he might turn to ice on the spot and wondered if this was a power of the skeleton. Or was it his fear consuming him?

"It appears," it croaked in a voice that threatened to burst his eardrums, "that I missed a soul. How could that be?" Light appeared all around him and a boom accompanied its approach. "Ah, the revenant." It cackled and when he looked up, he was almost blinded by its eyes that had fixed on him. With another sickening cackle, the shadow of its giant hand descended on him. "I wonder how you will taste?"

Johnny resisted as the hand closed around him and his body cracked as it squeezed him so tightly he was not able to draw enough air to scream. He thrashed against it but was only able to wiggle his shoulders and hand a little when the skeleton opened its jaw and revealed the dark void within. Various lights appeared and ghosts reached out and clawed at him from within the creature's maw. Somehow, he was able to drag in enough air to utter a cry as he was shoved in and his body was slowly torn apart and thrust into the chasm of the skeleton's collection of souls.

He woke with a start and flung the covers off as he looked around in panic before he heaved a sigh of relief. Thankfully, he was in his room.

Wait—his room?

Confused, the revenant noted the posters on the wall, the black desk in the corner, and the computer on it—all from his childhood. A familiar red-and-blue comforter covered the rather small bed. He stood warily and moved to the center of the room, then paused for a moment as he made a more detailed scrutiny. His gaze settled on a black splotch beside the fan, one he had made when he was a kid and had fooled around with small fireworks. Without a doubt, he was in his room.

Johnny first went to the light switch and flipped it. When nothing happened, he tried to turn the fan on with the switch and then by the cords but with no success. He opened the door and peered into the hallway but saw nothing but darkness. He didn't see his old cat Ebony anywhere, although since she was a Bombay, that would have been difficult with the lack of light.

His next step was to walk down the hall to his parents' room and knock on the door. "Mom? Dad?" When he had no response, he turned the knob gingerly and walked inside. Their bed was made up but they were not there. He turned and left the room, but when he passed the stairs, he noticed a flickering light below.

Reflexively, he moved his hand to his chest and sighed inwardly with relief to discover that his pistol was with him. He drew it and descended cautiously. At the bottom, he crept around the corner before he turned quickly and prepared to fire, only to realize that the light came from the flickering static on the television screen.

He frowned when he noticed another bright light behind the curtains of the large window in the living room. Without thought, he walked closer and pushed the curtains aside, and his eyes widened. He ran to the front door of the house, yanked it open, and stepped out to gape at a wall of light that surrounded his childhood home. What the hell was going on, and why was this light so familiar?

A hiss inside the house might have been from the TV. The young detective retraced his steps, his pistol at the ready as he attempted to find the cause of the noise. He walked through the halls and checked each room and closet, but nothing was out of place—at least as far as he remembered. He wondered if whatever had created the barrier was somewhere within, or if they hid behind it and tried to keep him trapped inside. If that were the case, what were they keeping him there for?

Another hiss distracted him from his thoughts, this time clearer. He recognized it but couldn't remember from where. When he returned to the living room, he stared at the flickering TV screen. It took a few moments for him to see that the static wasn't as random as he had thought it was or seemed to be. A figure of some kind seemed to form amongst the random jerk and flurry of the display. For some reason, he remembered this...was this that night? Was this what had taken him?

He fired his gun but the ether passed through the device. Quickly, he kicked it and his boot destroyed the screen. He would not let whatever it was out or allow it to get him again. A crash from his parents' room made him realize that he might be too late, but there was a difference this time. He could fight back.

To hell with stealth. The revenant raced up the stairs. If this was the monster that had taken him to Limbo, he wanted it obliterated. He had his weapon ready as he ran into his parents' room but didn't see any creature or person inside.

Johnny walked to the far side of the bed and noticed that a porcelain figurine of a dancer had fallen from the nightstand, a cherished present from his grandmother to his mother. His wariness increased. Unless the light or creature had somehow granted inanimate objects the ability to move—which wasn't too farfetched at the moment—something had knocked it down.

He left the room and continued to check each room upstairs but found nothing. Despite this, he began to feel a chill as well as nausea, which told him something was certainly there. The upstairs seemed clear and left him with one last place to check—the downstairs studio.

As he descended the stairs and moved toward the hall that led to it, he could swear the shadows around him were shifting, but even with his eyepatch off, he couldn't identify anything. When he approached the studio, he was sure he saw the outline of something skittering within for a moment. He'd caught a glimpse of a thin frame and long, wiry arms and hands.

The young detective drew a deep breath, opened the double doors, and looked around the barren room. Three walls were made of glass and a lone easel stood in the middle. Everything else had been moved to storage—they were moving soon, he recalled. Again, he found nothing and tried to think of what he might have missed.

He was about to leave the room when he glimpsed a sign that he wasn't alone in there. Some of the dust on the floor had flurried slightly as if someone or something moved along the floor. An unnerving chill shivered along his spine, the same unease he'd experienced when he first faced a supernatural terror.

His instincts clicked in and he threw himself across the floor and rolled as he heard the loud crack of wood around him. He stopped himself, stood, and he saw that the wall that was previously behind him had been ravaged. Two long cuts had sliced into it and along the floor. Something was there and he could not see it.

Again, the feeling of dread overwhelmed him and he leapt to the side, but something collided with him and he tumbled awkwardly. He scrambled to his feet and moved back with an intense pain below his ribs. A worried glance confirmed that he had been wounded and blood flowed over his stomach and thigh as he steadied himself.

Johnny focused on his gun and charged it. When the ether within began to emit a low glow, he held it up and noticed that the light seemed to contort around the being's body but no features were present. Still, it appeared humanoid and the light outside that passed through the glass walls seemed to shine through it.

For a moment, he and the being simply stared at one another. He tried to determine what it was as it raised its elongated arms toward its face, moaned solemnly, and lunged in an attempt to snatch him. The young detective fell back and fired, and his adversary fell on all fours. He noticed its long legs and pointed knees as it uttered a hollow hiss and skittered away

Cautiously, he stood and waited for the creature to attack again. He would let it come to him but could feel the apprehension creeping over him. Whatever this was, it was unlike any supernatural terror he had faced before. He couldn't even see it with his ghost eye.

Johnny checked his stomach and felt some relief that the wound had shut and only dry blood remained. Another jolt of the sickening feeling warned him that the creature was about to strike. He spun to face the glass walls, held the trigger of his gun down, and aimed as he slid the power up. With no experience he could draw on, he would have to rely on his instincts.

The glass shattered as the creature barreled through it from outside. Its body was refracted in the light and he discharged the large ball of ether from the barrel with a steady hand. He was hurled away by the force of the shot and glass shards rained around him.

Ether streaked toward the apparition but before it connected with its head, it vanished and the blast disappeared into the light. He continued to feel chills and knew the creature would not give him another chance to collect himself. At least the cold discomfort would enable him to track it. He lowered the power on his weapon slightly when he sensed that it was somewhere behind him. As he turned, the dust on the floor shifted again and small marks appeared as the creature dragged its long arms behind it.

Prompted by pure reflex, the young detective fell back as the dust spun and the creature surged toward him. He landed heavily but thrust his pistol up and fired, still with enough power to crack the boards beneath him. In the next instant, he rolled to his feet as the creature finally made a sound—a screeching, ghostly howl of rage and pain.

Finally, he saw it fully. Its transparent cloak had fallen to reveal gray, cracking skin. It was ghastly—like an emaciated corpse with thin, dark hair—and its long arms twisted around each other while its thin black lips pursed. The being's head moved erratically and tilted toward him with its eyes closed. It lurched onto all fours before its arms snapped forward to snatch his gun and tear into his flesh. He cried out in pain as his hand was sliced viciously. The creature yanked the gun away and flung it behind it before it pounced and drove him to the floor, where it snarled over him and opened its eyes.

Johnny gaped in shock. Its eyes glowed with the same unnatural light that surrounded his home, but as it stared at him, he realized it was the same light he had seen in the path.

Not only that, it was the same light of his ghost eye.

The being fixed him with an emotionless gaze as its jaw unhinged to reveal black teeth before it lowered its head and bit into his neck.

Johnny awoke with a shout and Vic lurched to his feet and looked at him. "Good Lord, kid. Are you all right?" He approached quickly and rested a hand on his shoulder. "You began to toss and turn something fierce. Was it a bad dream?"

He dragged a couple of large breaths in and pinched

one of his hands surreptitiously. The small sting confirmed that he was awake now. "Yeah…a couple." He placed a hand over his eye. "We have to destroy that skeleton, Vic."

The ghost regarded him thoughtfully. "Well, yeah, that's been my plan—beat the Axman and cut the connection. Did you have something different in mind?"

"No." He shook his head. "What I mean is we have to destroy it first. Or, rather, get the Wild Hunt to do it."

CHAPTER THIRTY

Sergio strode into the lobby and greeting area and barely gave his secretary a glance as he hurried to his office. "Lola, cancel everything I have for the rest of the evening. I have something I need to deal with." He yanked his office door open before he slammed it behind him.

The ghost mob boss crossed the room, retrieved a glass and some stygian wine, and placed them on his desk before he activated his monitor to access a list of every remaining soldier under his command. Unfortunately, it grew ever shorter

He was supposed to still be in discussion with Big Daddy about their plans moving forward but had received a report on the way back that changed his priorities. The Axman had reappeared at one of their operations on the pier. It could only be him. The workers who found their colleagues said that the ghost bodies looked like they'd had their life sucked out of them, exactly like all the others, and the few living mobsters who stood guard were nothing but decayed, hollow bodies. They also reported slash marks throughout the warehouse and a trail of what appeared to be dark phantasma. Not a single person on duty was spared.

Over fifty soldiers—his soldiers—gone in a night.

Sergio felt the loss keenly, and not only the goods that were destroyed during the fight. He had worked through the ranks, even if he'd acquired his current position a little more quickly than he'd expected.

As such, he knew what it was like to be one of the guys working those types of gigs when needed. He didn't see them as mere grunts but brothers in arms and even if he didn't personally know all their names, they still shared that bond. Now, they were all gone and he didn't know if they were obliterated or not and couldn't decide what was better—to be destroyed for all eternity or to be in the Axman's grasp? Which was the lesser of two horrifying endings?

What affected him more was the sense of failure, the feeling that he had been made to look like a fool. The Axman was a psychopath but he had dealt with freaks like that before. They always wanted the same thing—their vices catered to and their sick fantasies realized. If you could find out what those were, you could take care of them and maybe even get them under your thumb if you were desperate for some muscle or leverage.

But the Axman? He had begun to think that he was very different from anything he had faced before. First was the fact that he was something beyond simply a terror—anyone who had laid eyes upon him, even in photos, could see that. But he hadn't run rampant and attacked people in the streets until now. He had been methodical, used goons to do his dirty work, then used the shades and chose his battles carefully. Hell, he almost seemed to do things like some mob leaders did.

He wondered if this would compromise his position with the mafia commanders. But no, they wouldn't risk letting him go. Who would take the position? They at least knew his ability and where he stood. He wasn't sure who was next in line and if they would even take the job at this point.

Besides, under normal circumstances, they would worry that he would talk. They would probably have him obliterated if they wanted him gone. He looked at the bottle of wine in his hand and flung it against the wall with a pained shout before he collapsed onto his chair again.

Where did he go from there? He had already sent teams to the warehouses with the weapons to clean up there and given orders for over a dozen search parties to comb the area around the pier and city. But the Axman could have been long gone by this point. Still, he would be found as he wouldn't risk leaving New Orleans right now—that's what they had said in the meeting.

The general consensus had been that he had to be there for something and so wouldn't flee. The mob boss had no issue with that as he already wanted to see that bastard dead, but he now wanted to do it with his skeletal hands. He had already sent a tip to the police about his thefts. They would be on high alert and knowledge of their adversary's last location would also make them look around the area. Fortunately, the workers they had paid had already moved what remained of the goods out of there.

Sergio knew he needed to calm himself. This wasn't

something to be concerned about. His priority was to decide what to do about the organization. They would want answers and what could he say? He should have acted faster? What could he do that the previous bosses hadn't already tried? Now, he had to work with the cops, not to mention the Agency, and it seemed pretty damn out of left field to him. Shit. He hadn't consulted anyone on that. This was his city now and he needed to make sure it was taken care of and damn the risks. Still, he wondered if it would come back to bite him once it was all over—if it ever was.

He was thinking about the Axman again, dammit.

To help him to focus, he checked his messages but nothing had come back from the people he had sent instructions to. His teeth clenched so tightly that they could have cracked. Everyone was under orders to reply as quickly as possible when contacted. Were they defying him now? He began to feel like they considered him a joke and his anger surged again as he drove his fist into the monitor. It would have cut him if he still had flesh. He thumped it onto the table before he rested his head on it and scratched the back of his skull in frustration.

After a long moment, he straightened and pressed a finger on the button of his call pad. "Lola, call Tony and have him ready a team and prepare a car," he demanded and waited for a response. "Lola? Did you hear me?"

The lights in his office began to flicker like they did during a surge. Suddenly, they cut off and plunged the room into darkness. He heard the shutters fall in place around the large windows and jerked to face them.

"What's going on?" he screamed in the darkness.

"Why soundproof the room if you intend to yell like that, Sergio?" a gravelly voice asked.

If he still had a heart, it would have stopped. He opened a drawer in his desk quickly, snatched the pistol within, and spun to fire into the darkness. Brief flashes of light illuminated the surroundings but he saw nothing and hit nothing except what he owned.

"Where are you?" he demanded, withdrew a black box, and opened it to reveal ether bullets. Even inside their casings, it burned him to touch them. In his panic, however, he barely felt the pain as he shoved them into the gun's chamber and shut it.

"With you." the Axman replied. His voice sounded like he was both in front and behind him, but when the mob boss turned, he saw nothing. "Your little gang has been both a nuisance and a boon to me. As much as you've caused me to slow my plans, you've also almost delivered a platter of souls so I let you continue your pointless attempts to stop me. At least until I saw your men working with the agents to try to end me. That was a surprise."

"D-do you r-realize what y-you done? How many people you've killed? My brothers?" Sergio stammered as he circled in one place and aimed the pistol, although he could see no target.

"Of course. I have to keep track. I need to know how close I am to completing my plan," his unwelcome visitor responded. His voice made it seem as if he had answered a mundane question. "I will admit that most of my actions in the last few hours have been more malicious than usual but I was dealing with some issues stemming partially from you and your mafia."

The mob boss crept toward the door to his office and tried to phase through it, but the burn that seared him during his attempt made him back away. He frowned when he realized it was coated in dark phantasma. Panicked, he began to fling himself against it, hoping it would either break or someone would hear him.

"I would imagine you paid top dollar for those doors so they wouldn't budge an inch whenever you had to take your frustrations out on them with all that petulant door slamming," the killer mocked. "Are you hoping your secretary will hear you?"

"What did you do to her?" he demanded.

"The same thing I did to everyone on this floor."

"Everyone? When? How long were you here?"

"Not long at all, at least to me. I've learned patience over the last century," the intruder responded flatly. "You are alone, Don Sergio—is that the title? When I was in the mob, it was a different organization than it is now. I wonder if respect is still as valued as it was in my time."

Sergio fired a shot, more to appease his anger than to try to hit the killer. "What the fuck do you know about respect, you freak?" Silence followed and stretched for what felt like hours. It was more distressing than hearing the cold words.

When the Axman finally spoke again, the flat, casual tone was gone, replaced by a grim, hissing voice. "Tell me, Sergio, what do you know of respect? You certainly haven't shown any to me. When I was alive, I knew what it was and what it meant to respect my betters but in exchange, I got none. I was only good for taking care of the dirty jobs. Now, I return and hold this entire city in the palm of my hand, and I see that nothing has changed. You don't respect me, my power, or my title. You see me only as a pest to exterminate, and that will be your downfall."

It went quiet again before a shocking noise erupted and Sergio felt a searing pain in his leg. He cried out and fell and when he tried to stand, he couldn't find his balance. Confused, he groped to try to find out what was wrong and his hand landed on something. He brought it to his face and recoiled that he held a shoe—one filled with his foot.

As the realization dawned, a boot drove into his chest. He winced and recoiled as the Axman loomed over him with a glowing ax in his hand. The mob boss frowned as he noticed a new hole in his side that let out a white light. "It seems I need to send a stronger message. Killing scores of your goons wasn't sufficient but let's see what happens when it's one of the heads."

He tried to respond, but only grunts and mumbled words formed around the pain of the Axman's boots crushing his chest. His attacker knelt and held the blade of his ax to his face so it was visible in the darkness. He was emotionless and stared sharply but blankly at him as if he was looking through him.

"I considered bringing you into my fold. I invited several mafia members but it was a waste as none responded. It seems I unwittingly killed a few—or at least my minions did—over the last few months. You inherited their mistakes but you should have learned from them. What point is there in not learning from the past, especially for a ghost?"

"J-just do i-it, already!" Sergio couldn't form the words

and his adversary maintained his cold stare as he twirled the plasma blade in his hands.

"Speak up. What am I going to do?"

"Y-you already s-said it!" he replied and struggled to push his attacker off him. "K-kill m-me and s-spare me y-your bullshit!"

"Eventually." the Axman agreed and his mouth formed into a small smirk as his monotone returned. "I suppose how this all ends is up to you, but you shouldn't be all that surprised if I do." He leaned down so his victim's vision was filled by his white lights. "You've tried to kill me for months." He lifted his boot and kicked him across the room. The mafia head pounded into a wall and wailed when his back burned. Was the whole room covered with this shit?

He leaned back to pick the pistol up, turned, and fired at the Axman, who stood motionless as the ether bullets pierced him. Without thought, he continued to pull the trigger and fired spectral bullets, but his opponent merely raised a hand and a ball of ether formed in his palm.

"If that was effective, you would have succeeded by now." He lobbed the ball at the ghost, who cried in pain as the ether burned his form. His clothes disintegrated around his chest and the color faded from his bones.

Sergio lowered his head in defeat and the Axman snorted. "Disgusting," he muttered and moved forward to finish the job. He knelt and positioned the side of the blade against his victim's cheek, who winced when it marked it with the black phantasma. "It is a pity you did not play along. You could have lived to see a world without the fear of death—or, at least, one where the difference between living and dead is almost nonexistent. But what awaits you is only oblivion."

The mafiosa did something that caught his attacker genuinely off-guard. He began to laugh. "Have you gone insane now, Sergio? Don't be so boring."

He looked at the Axman and despite the pain, his face wore a smile. "No, I'm laughing at myself." His lights began to dim. "Before you arrived, I thought you were something to be afraid of—something I couldn't understand." He chuckled. "But nah, you're merely a psycho. You might be in a new freak package but you have the same broken head."

Sergio's laughter pushed the killer over the edge. He raised his ax and swung the blade into his chest several times before he buried it in his throat and yanked it across. The mob boss' phantasma spewed from him and his body slumped before it began to disintegrate. His adversary stood over him and his fist trembled around his ax, both in anger and because he'd allowed himself to lose control. His weakness had cost him a soul.

"You couldn't even die right. How pathetic," he murmured. With a flick of his hand, the lights in the office came on and he sighed and looked at Sergio. "Unlike my life, yours will be forgotten quickly."

The steward knocked on Sergio's door. "Sir? It's getting late. Would you like me to drive you home?" He knocked again when he received no reply. "Sir? Are you in there?" He turned the knob of the door and walked in. The mannequin body he had possessed fell when shock overwhelmed him and he couldn't retain control of it. The room he'd stepped into was covered by phantasma, and the only piece still left of his employer was his skull. He gaped when it began to dissolve into nothing.

CHAPTER THIRTY-ONE

"So will we look for this broad in old yearbooks or what?" Marco asked as Valerie walked him and his sister to her station.

"You could do that—not that it would matter as Anne was older than a teenager when she was attacked," she replied dryly as she sat and activated her computer. "I will personally check the databases as I have a hunch that after the attack, Anne Schneider is no longer Anne Schneider."

"You think she went into hiding?" Annie asked.

The officer sipped her coffee and grimaced at the taste. "Possibly, but her name could also have changed if she remarried. Either way, we need to find the connection between her and the—" She was interrupted when her phone rang and she answered quickly. "Hello, Officer Simone here."

"Hey, Valerie, it's Donovan," the agent replied. "I'm with a team and we've checked a couple of places—a church and an abandoned auditorium— but found nothing so far. We'll separate to check other sites on this side of the city and wondered if you could tag along? I have kind of an ill feeling about this."

She thought back to their ride-along. "I'm surprised you haven't been able to use your empath to find him. He left some of his phantasma in the store parking lot."

"I tried but when I held my orb up, it shuddered and disappeared. I've never seen anything like it," he admitted, his tone weary. "So are you coming?"

Valerie considered it for a moment. "I can't. I'm with the Maggios right now but I could probably send you some backup."

"Who are you thinking?"

"Send me the coordinates of your next stop and I'll see if he's back yet." She ended the call and scrolled through her phonebook for Johnny's name and pressed it.

It rang twice before there was a click and a gruff voice answered. "Howdy, how's it going over—Vic, would you quiet down for a second?"

She stifled a chuckle at Johnny's terse tone. "Man, you sound like you need a nap."

He sighed over the line. "I had one but it didn't go great. What do you need?"

"Donovan—the agent I rolled with earlier—needs someone to hold his hand. I'm with Annie and Marco trying to trace this Schneider lady. Do you think you can help him?"

Murmuring on the other end sounded like Johnny and Vic discussing it. "He's with the group looking for the Axman's hideout, right?"

"Groups, yeah."

"I'll help him check a couple of places, but I need to know where Big Daddy is if you know."

The officer looked around the station. "The purple one, right? He left with the mafia boss a little while after you did."

"All right. See if you can get in touch with him and tell him to call me or something."

She leaned back in her chair and tapped her pen on the desk. "From what I saw, I thought you two were chummy."

Johnny snorted. "He seems to think so too but until last week, we only saw him a couple of times. We did gigs for him and didn't work directly with him. Until he calls, I will babysit your agent." He yawned. "Do you have a location for me?"

Valerie checked her phone and copied a text from Donovan. "Yeah, I've sent it to you."

"Man, this is almost out in the sticks," Johnny muttered as she heard the loud jingle of car keys and ruffling of a coat on his end. "All right, we're heading out. Get back to me when you find Big Daddy, all right?"

"You got it. Be safe." She ended the call and leaned forward as her computer beeped. "Okay...it looks like we got a hit. Let's see...wait—what?" She looked at the screen, then at the siblings before she focused on the data again. "It seems we now know why the Axman is so interested in you two."

"What do you mean?" Annie asked as she and her brother leaned in. The screen showed an image of Anne Schneider with other pictures beneath her arranged as a family tree. At the bottom were two very familiar pictures to the siblings—their own.

"Ah, shit," Marco muttered as he gripped his head. "We're ax baby babies."

It was well past dark by the time Johnny and Vic arrived at their destination, an old building called the Crescent City Theater. When they stepped out of the vehicle, they were immediately flooded with lights and could hear the clicking of guns trained on them.

"Hey, you guys called me!" the revenant shouted as he looked at Vic. "Do you wanna say something? You're probably in greater danger if these are agents."

His partner flicked his cigarette into the dirt. "It's standard for agents to wear at least two different weapons, one with ether bullets and one with live rounds. We're both fucked here, bucko."

"Great."

"Stand down! That's our backup," a slightly familiar voice cried. The lights finally dimmed as one of the agents approached. "Sorry about that, you two. We're all a little on edge now."

"Donovan?" Johnny asked. With the glare gone, he was able to see the proffered hand, which he took for the sake of politeness and to steady himself. "You're worried about a sweep?"

The agent nodded and glanced at the barricaded doors to the theater. "We're all feeling a little ill around here, and one of our guys has an empath that makes him more sensitive to abnormal supernatural presences."

The young detective looked at his partner. "Does that mean Vic will make him hurl?"

Donovan chuckled. "Nah. Normal ghosts are fine, although I guess as a revenant, you would be abnormal in a way, no offense."

"None taken. It's a great icebreaker amongst certain people." Footsteps drew his attention to the three other agents, who walked toward them. All wore masks and helmets and the Agency white jumpsuits. Besides their body types, the only way Johnny could tell them apart was by what appeared to be their rankings.

One had a white triangle on his suit, one had two, and the third had a red triangle. He looked at Donovan, who had three red triangles, which probably made him the head honcho of this little party.

"So, you're the rev, eh?" the man with two white triangles asked in a thick New York accent as he looked from Johnny to Vic. "The bounty hunters? Reports said you took out the Axman double. Good work but a shame it didn't pan out."

"Yeah, that's been the feeling these last few days." He pointed a finger at all three of them. "This is possibly a stupid question, but you're all specters, right?"

A chorus of, "Yeah," came from them.

"It's a standard requirement in the Agency," the woman with the single red triangle explained in a high but somewhat monotone voice. "Even the lab kiddies who don't go into the field need to be. You can't exactly work on ether tech when you can't even see it."

Donovan pointed down the line as he introduced them, starting with the one with a white triangle. "This is my team—well, part of it. Agent Coleman, Agent DeSando, and Agent Anderson."

Johnny nodded and tipped his hat. "Pleasure. You can call me Johnny."

"Vic Kane, detective." He looked at Johnny. "We both are."

"Detective?" DeSando questioned. "We were told you were hunters."

He shrugged. "We're working on that."

Anderson held her hand up. "Do you feel that?" she asked. The two partners looked at the theater. "I'm not sure if the Axman is in there but this place is haunted."

"Technically, you could say that about a large chunk of New Orleans," Vic pointed out.

The revenant removed his eye patch, approached the door, and noticed traces of a dark substance. "Well, there is certainly something here—or was here, maybe."

Donovan and his team joined him and Coleman examined the area he was looking at. "I can't see anything."

"That's not surprising. Does your eye look like that?" Donovan asked as he took a box out, ran it over the door, and raised his eyebrows when the device pinged. "Damn, we got a big hit."

"How big?" DeSando asked.

"Big enough that a Hollywood type would probably want to shoot a horror movie here for realism." He craned his head back. "I can't specify what it is, though. Estimates say maybe wraith or maybe demon."

Vic floated closer and poked the dark spots before he rubbed his fingers. "As best we've been able to tell, the

Axman is a chimera of terrors. If that is his spook juice, the reading would certainly fit."

"If it is not, we should still take this opportunity to rid the haunt of its terror," Anderson suggested and made her point by turning her rifle on.

Donovan looked at Johnny, who drew his gun along with Vic. "After you—pearls before swine and all that."

The agent chuckled. "First into the fire?"

"I'm wearing a shirt and jacket and you're wearing Agency tech." He shrugged. "You can probably take a beating."

He looked at Vic, who nodded, became intangible, and eased half his body through. "It looks clear to me," he said as he pulled out. "At least of traps or hostiles. The building hasn't had a good scrub down in a couple of decades, at least."

A loud thunk behind them made them turn as Coleman walked from behind their vehicle. "Well, we don't have a power washer." He held the tool up in his hands. "But we do have a crowbar."

The young detective nodded. "That'll work. Let's get in there."

CHAPTER THIRTY-TWO

With some grunts, cracks, and more effort than one would think was required to open a derelict building barricaded by old wood, the group was finally able to open the doors and entered with their weapons at the ready. When Johnny took his first cautious steps inside, he was relieved that it was less the death house he had worried it would be. It appeared to be nothing more than an old, rundown theater.

"Hmm." DeSando looked at the cracked and rotted roof. "Do you think this is another miss?"

"There's no way to tell at the moment," Donovan replied and crept up to one of the hallways. "Johnny, you were there with the shaman, weren't you? She said it looked like there were rows of chairs behind the Axman, right?"

"Right." The revenant moved to the opposite hallway and Vic was careful to shine his lights around the dark areas. "He seemed to be on a stage or platform of some kind."

"We need to check the individual theaters then," Anderson suggested as she and Coleman walked behind Donovan. "Be wary for traps."

"Traps?" the ghost detective muttered and adjusted his coat. "I suppose it couldn't hurt, but I doubt the Axman is too worried about not being able to deal with any idiots who creep around his secret base."

"I guess that makes us the idiots, then?" DeSando asked as he came up behind them. "I'll go with you two if that's all right. Keep the teams three and three."

Johnny nodded, peered down the hall, and counted. "I see about five doors along our side. Donovan?"

"It seems the same, but the end is kind of dark," the agent replied, looked at DeSando, and pointed to a walkie-talkie on his belt. "Stay in contact. After we clear this floor, we'll go upstairs."

DeSando and Johnny nodded as the two teams separated and proceeded through their halls. The first door opened into a small space with rickety shelves. The young detective looked back and pointed his thumb farther down the hall. "It looks like a maintenance room or supply closet."

The other man grunted agreement and looked around again before he moved forward. "Honestly, it feels more likely that we'll get tetanus than be possessed around here."

Vic scowled when he noticed a damaged archway with black markings on the wood. "I feel like I'm coming down with something and that isn't even possible for me." He nodded to another doorway, this one with an elaborate surround. "This looks like the first theater."

Johnny nodded but scrunched his nose up as he approached. "Do you smell that?"

DeSando pointed to his face. "Not much. The mask blocks most of it." He pressed a button and immediately recoiled. "Good God! What is that? Is it the building or something in there?"

He waved a hand in front of his face. "This place isn't pleasant in general, but the smell is coming from behind the door." Cautiously, his weapon ready, he turned the knob and the door opened into a large, dark room. He pulled a flashlight out while the agent activated a lamp on his shoulder, then handed him a few glowsticks.

They broke a couple each and tossed them around the space. One of Johnny's caught the edge of a stair, tumbled as far as the middle of a row of seats, and illuminated something draped over the side of one of the chairs. "Vic... DeSando," he whispered and pointed to it.

In silence, they crept down the stairs and Vic's lights grew when he seemed to realize what it was before his companions. They reached the step and stared at the chair with wide eyes. Long-decomposed bodies were strewn across the seats and the floors beneath.

"Shit," DeSando muttered, checked the other areas of the room quickly, and took a step down to look at the next row and its grisly contents. "If this isn't the Axman's hideout, we've stumbled upon a serial killer's dumping grounds."

Johnny studied one of the corpses and while it was certainly decomposed, it resembled something along the lines of mummification rather than natural decomposition. "Is it weird that I want to say we aren't that lucky?"

he muttered and gestured to DeSando to tell the agent to join him. "When the Axman first came to town, he and his cronies stole the souls of their victims. At the end of the process, they initially looked like this. Then, as the perpetrators became stronger, they simply turn to goop."

DeSando shook his head and reached for his radio. "Hey, Donovan. We're in the first theater room— number six on our side—and we've got bodies."

After a click, his colleague responded. "Same here. Coleman and Anderson are examining them. Do yours look shriveled?"

The agent nodded. "Yeah. Johnny says that's what happened when the Axman sucked the soul out of his victim."

A brief beat of silence followed. "Well, shit. The readers don't pick up anything abnormal so it looks like we arrived while he's out running errands. Proceed with caution and continue scouting. I'll call Lovett."

"Understood." When he ended the communication, the two partners nodded to him and he mirrored the gesture to agree that there was nothing else and to move on to the next room. Johnny coughed and sputtered as they left the theater and the smell overpowered him for a moment. His two companions gave him time to lean against the wall as they looked at the next room.

"Do you want me to go in alone in case there's another batch?" the agent offered sympathetically. "I've got a filter in this so it doesn't bother me."

The young detective shook his head, straightened, and held his gun up. "I ain't going to wuss out like that. Besides,

I think another body dump like that would be the lucky thing to find in here."

DeSando cocked his head. "Do you think the Axman might be around? Like the boss said, there's no spike or anything in the readings. It's very unlikely that we'll run into him."

"For now," Vic muttered and peered at the dark sky between the cracks in the ceiling. "It doesn't mean he won't appear when we least expect him. Plus, we also have his buddy to worry about, although I'm not sure how much he can harm us at the moment."

"The keeper?" The agent frowned and he fell silent for a moment. "Donovan gave us the rundown. It's still kind of hard to believe that we might be facing a keeper and even harder to believe that one might be responsible for all this."

The ghost nodded. "We have it on good authority, trust us. Although I do agree that they aren't usually this malevolent, merely kind of smartass when they get bored." A click behind them made them turn to where Johnny stood at the next door. "Hey, we get it, kid. You're hardcore. But if you need a break we can—"

"It wasn't only the smell," he replied and pointed to his ghost eye. "Can't you feel it, Vic?"

The ghost detective looked at him in bewilderment. "Feel what exactly?"

His partner didn't reply but pursed his lips and beckoned for them to come to the door. They joined him as he turned the knob and opened it into another theater, this one faintly illuminated. Inside were more rows of seats but fortunately, no bodies were strewn about this time.

The stage, however, was filled with items ranging from

stacks of books to jars and boxes, and various sigils marked the curtains. As they approached the stage cautiously and stepped on it, he noticed more, including a very large one burned into the floor that seemed to take up half the area.

"Does this seem familiar to you?" DeSando asked and glanced at them.

Johnny nodded and pointed to one of the wings. "It does, but if you want another clue, take a look over there." Vic and the agent looked to where several axes leaned against the wall in the shadows of the curtains.

"I'm very sure that is enough to provide probable cause," the ghost detective commented and narrowed his focus on some type of decoration or device shrouded in a large sheet in the center of the stage. "What do you suppose this is?"

Johnny discerned an odd glow around it with his eye. "Something weird, for sure." They gathered around it and each looked at the others for confirmation on whether or not they should pull the sheet off.

Before any of them could attempt to do so, however, the few lights around them began to flicker and a moment later, they shut off completely. They all jerked back and raised their weapons and the revenant felt a terrible chill slide over him. The sheet draped over the object began to spin before it elevated sharply and disappeared into the catwalks above. It had covered a shrine filled with liquor, cigars, colorful decorations that looked like dolls, skulls, and animal remains, and a picture of a man in a black suit with red trimming on it.

"Oh, shit." Vic growled in disbelief. "Johnny, does that look familiar to you?"

The young detective studied the picture for a moment. The garb was certainly familiar and looked much like Samedi's, but the red color and longer, dreadlocked hair of the man was different. Not to mention the visage, which wore a smile similar to the baron's but seemed more devious. Samedi might have some fun alongside you, but this guy looked like he would have fun *with* you.

"Kriminel" he whispered before a loud, boisterous laugh filled the air.

CHAPTER THIRTY-THREE

The last of the lights went out before the candles on the shrine flared and the flames billowed much higher than they should. The shadows appeared to stretch around them before they twisted from the floor and amassed above the shrine in a ball before they grew larger and assumed a humanoid shape.

It expanded to at least ten feet tall and continued as the shape began to reveal more detail and took the form of a man in a suit and top hat who twirled a cane. His dreadlocks hung over his back and shoulders and small red lights appeared where his eyes would be to look mockingly at them.

He snickered again as the candles' flames settled. When he smiled, he showed no teeth and only a hollow void. He chuckled. "Well, well. Someone called my name, did they?"

No looks were exchanged between the companions. They knew what they needed to do—or what they all wanted to do, at least. They fired at the being while they retreated and vacated the stage.

"Donovan! We got a hostile in theater seven. Get over here!" DeSando shouted into his radio but got no response. Unfortunately, their attacks had little effect and the best they seemed to do was make him wince.

The being's eyes narrowed and he pointed his cane at the agent. "Your little toys will do nothing in my presence. I have no liking for them."

Johnny had hoped that he was somehow tied to the shrine and some border existed that he could not cross. Those hopes were dashed immediately when he swooped toward the agent and ran a fist through him. The man's body was unharmed but his shriek was followed by a long, shrill gasp as he was lifted high.

"DeSando!" the revenant shouted, powered his gun to maximum, and fired. The blast fared little better than his earlier shots, but it seemed to at least draw the keeper's attention enough for the agent's body to slide off his arm. As the loa turned toward him and raised one of his arms with anger boiling in his crimson eyes, more ether shots drove into his back and surprised him.

The young detective used the distraction to roll out of the way as both he and Kriminel looked to where Donovan and his teammates rushed into the room. Even if the keeper was able to tamper with the tech, in a derelict structure such as this, all the chaos of the skirmish would inevitably raise a ruckus.

Vic floated to DeSando, became tangible, and lifted him. "He's not moving!" he shouted and carried him to the side of the theater. Johnny continued to fire powerful rounds while Anderson switched her gun for something that looked like a box. When she pressed a button, however, it unfolded into a rifle and she fed glowing rounds into it.

"Where is that fool? He should be the one dealing with uninvited guests," Kriminel muttered and lifted his cane. "I guess I'll have to bring in the help to tend to ya." An orb of shadow appeared above the top of the cane and shades poured from the sphere as it shrank.

Coleman helped Vic to move DeSando closer to the team as Donovan and Johnny began to target the shades. Anderson readied her rifle, aimed at the keeper, and fired one of the glowing rounds. Kriminel held a hand out as if to attempt to catch the bullet but it barreled through and into his neck before it erupted into a ring of light and his head disappeared.

"What the hell is that?" Vic shouted as she yanked something on the rifle and a casing fell out.

"Ether halo rounds—something the lab techs developed about a year ago," she explained as she pushed another bullet into the slot. "It's meant to deal with demons but I thought I'd give it a try."

"The real question is whether it worked or merely made him mad," Donovan muttered and eliminated another shade with a shot through the chest that made it explode into a shadowy mist. "If these shades aren't disappearing and he made them, we probably shouldn't get too hopeful!"

He was correct. The remnants of the beings they were destroying seemed to pull toward Kriminel's body and swirl around his head as the essence coalesced to remake him. Once his red eyes returned, they glared at the intruders. "You dare to defile a loa?" he roared and his body shifted from an opaque, almost transparent look to an inky black. "The Axman would give you too quick a death. I will do my duty one last time and send your ghosts to the depths of the furnace!"

Vic looked at the stage. "Kid, the shrine!"

Johnny glanced at it. If it acted as a tether or anchor for the keeper and he destroyed it, perhaps he could banish him from this plane or at least buy them some time. Either way, it seemed better than standing where he was while Kriminel's form continued to grow and he raised his massive cane and swung it as a weapon.

Donovan and Coleman picked DeSando up and leapt away while Johnny, Vic, and Anderson moved closer to the stage. They all continued to fire on their adversary, and while their attacks seemed to have more effect now that he was tangible, it didn't mean they did any real harm to him. Even Anderson's more powerful halo rounds that had seemed like their best bet until that point were seemingly nullified as anything she blasted off reformed quickly.

He bounded onto the stage, ran to the altar, and began to knock the tributes off before he kicked the bottom of the elaborate table to upend it. Although it didn't budge, he was able to make a hole in the bottom and saw a glowing sigil of some kind.

This confirmed his suspicion that this was more than merely a traditional ceremonial altar. From what he could tell, it was coated in phantasma, which wasn't something he could simply wipe away. Fortunately, he did have something a little stronger than spit and elbow grease. He took the ether cartridge from his gun, retrieved the ectofire cartridge, and shoved it in.

By this point, Kriminel had looked at him and his eyes

widened.

"Get away from there!" he demanded and pointed to him, and several shades converged. His gun was still charging and he was about to draw his blade when Vic appeared in front of him and fired six rapid shots. All the shades were hit in either the head or chest and they burst apart and covered the two of them with an odd black substance.

Johnny grimaced and wondered how long he'd have to wait before he could take another shower. He turned and squeezed the trigger, and the ectofire blazed into the sigil. His partner fired more rounds as Kriminel lurched toward them with his cane held ready over his head to crush them.

Before he could complete his attack, he began to shrink and he growled as his body began to turn transparent again and shifted between its darker physical form and the spiritual one.

"Get going!" Vic shouted to the agents. "We've got our way out of here!"

"We do?" the revenant asked and his partner pointed farther upstage. He turned toward an old door and caught on quickly. Although he stopped firing his weapon, the sigil continued to burn and he took Vic's lighter and set fire to the cloth on the altar as Kriminel howled angrily.

"Donovan, you might want to call the fire department," he warned as he kicked the altar hard to dislodge the remaining offering that had caught fire. It shattered on the stage and began a blaze that would soon overrun the building. "Let's go, Vic!"

"You will not escape, you damned pests!" the keeper roared in anger as he lunged at him. He wasn't as big as before but whether he wanted to catch them or crush them, he was still big enough to do either. Johnny raced to the door as Vic flew into him and they fused. He yanked the door open and stepped through as their adversary drove a large fist through it, but they were no longer there.

Johnny tumbled into a mass of ghosts and held his head in pain. He looked up and into the barrel of a gun.

"Who the hell are you?" a gruff voice demanded as more weapons appeared around him.

His gaze swept over several well-dressed ghosts who wielded various not-so-nice weapons. "Vic, do you have any idea where we ended up?"

"It beats me, kid," his partner murmured. "But if I had to take a guess based on the garb of these pissed-off gents, they look very much like mafia members."

"Mafia?" He studied the clothes and guns of the ghosts around him more closely. "They do look like the guys we've seen around New Orleans. That's good for us, right? Since we're working with them."

"Good luck convincing them of that. The ghost mob might be more organized in death than in life but it doesn't mean that if you're good with one section you're good with all of them." Guns were readied noisily around them. "You might want to get to talking. They seem a little testy."

The revenant lowered himself to his knees, placed his gun on the floor, and raised his hands slowly. "Shouldn't you come out and join in? You know, as one of their own?"

"I'm not sure that's a great idea," Vic admitted. "Remember, in my day, I went up against mafiosos. I might have put some of these guys away or killed others. There might be a grudge or two among this horde."

"Good point. Stay inside and shut up."

"What's the racket about?" a shrill but loud voice demanded. "Why have all you guys gathered over there? Is there something I should know about?"

"Yeah, boss!" the goon at the front shouted in reply. "We've got a breather here!"

"Breather?" Both the boss' voice and one strikingly familiar answered. "Get out of the way—let me see!" The group of mafia members moved to the side as a smaller, well-dressed ghost floated up to them. He couldn't have been more than three feet tall but he was immaculately dressed and while he glowed a striking blue, he was not skeletal and had smooth features and long hair tied in a bun. He drifted down until he was able to look Johnny in the eyes where he was still on his knees. "A human? No, you're that revenant, right?"

He nodded. If this guy was the boss, he should be nice and upfront with him to not piss the others off. More importantly, if he was one of the heads of the organization, maybe he knew what was going down in New Orleans and would have heard about the deal by now. "Yes, sir, I'm—"

"Johnny Desperaux and his ghost gumshoe tutor Vic Kane," the other voice answered. The young detective looked at the speaker and didn't know whether to feel elated or aghast. Vic seemed to share the sentiments as he fell out in shock, which resulted in more guns trained on them. They were more focused on the much larger presence who approached, smoking a familiar cigar.

Big Daddy offered the two an equally large grin. "You guys missed me so much you simply had to pop in, huh?"

CHAPTER THIRTY-FOUR

"Marsan?" Vic pushed to his feet. The mafia members moved to apprehend him, but the boss raised a hand to stop them. "What are you doing back in Limbo already?"

The dealer took a puff of his cigar and nodded at them. "What are you guys doing here at all? I thought you would be running around the city looking for the Axman."

"We were," Johnny admitted as he stood and dusted himself off. "We found his hideaway and were attacked by his megalomaniacal boss."

Big Daddy twitched so violently he almost crushed his cigar. "Kriminel? You saw him?"

Vic shrugged. "Some form of him, at least. He was tethered to an altar and looked like a shadow puppet. Still, he was able to take a tangible form and summon shades. We wrecked the altar and he didn't seem to like that. My guess is that he needs it to stick around for any amount of time."

"Whoa, whoa. Hold up a second here," the mafia head demanded. "The two of you fought a keeper and lived?"

The revenant shrugged and shook his head. "We fought

a keeper and survived but had to jump through a crossing point to get away. That's how we ended up here." He looked at the guns still surrounding him. Normally, it wouldn't concern him as spectral bullets couldn't kill him, but there were a hell of a lot of them around. Besides, physical items found their way there on occasion and this was the mob. If anyone had real bullets, it would be them. "Sir."

The mafia leader folded his arms and nodded slowly. "I heard that revenants can cross between Limbo and the living side whenever they want." He studied him speculatively. "It sounds useful. Are you guys in need of work?"

He ran a hand through his hair and chose his next words carefully. "We're already at work, sir. We're investigating the Axman situation with the New Orleans leader, Sergio."

With a grimace, the mob boss said, "Not anymore, you aren't."

Vic turned quickly. "What happened? Did he bail?"

Big Daddy sighed and shook his head. "He probably should have. He's gone."

"Gone?" they asked at the same time and focused on the dealer.

He nodded. "He was obliterated. What was left of his remains was found in his office along with the Axman's phantasma."

It took Johnny a moment to absorb this. His shock didn't come from hearing about Sergio's demise. He hadn't known him for longer than thirty minutes if that. But the fact that he was killed so soon after all the separate organizations had begun to work together was a concern. And on top of that, the Axman hadn't previously attacked the mafia unless they attacked him first, at least as far as he knew. "I can't believe it."

"And shortly before he was whacked, one of the New Orleans mob's stash areas was attacked," the dealer added and folded his massive arms. "Down at the port. The Axman is getting feisty now."

"Is that why you're here?" Vic asked and glanced at some of the soldiers around them. "Getting help?"

Big Daddy looked at the mafia head. "That was the hope. Plus, the New Orleans mob will be in disarray without a boss. I was hoping to kill two birds as it were. Don Pesci and I were in the middle of discussing our options when you appeared."

"Speaking of which," Pesci muttered, "how did you know to come here?"

"We didn't," the ghost detective assured him. "Unless we use specific crossing points, wherever we end up is random."

"And you merely happened to end up here?" he questioned. "It seems convenient."

The dealer chuckled. "Maybe they had a little help with directions," he quipped. Vic glanced wryly at him while some of the mob members looked at each other, utterly baffled.

"So Valerie never had a chance to talk to you?" Johnny asked.

"About what?"

"I needed to make contact and talk about a plan I had."

His partner moved quickly to his side and whispered, "Maybe now isn't a good time for that, kid."

Big Daddy looked intrigued, however. "What are you thinking, Johnny boy?"

"You remember the skeleton Kriminel is building?"

"Skeleton?" Pesci asked. "What skeleton?"

The dealer scratched the top of his head and sighed. "I was hoping to not bother you with that. It seems Kriminel is building some kind of body that would allow him to access both realms."

"What?" the mafiosa shrieked, balled his hands into fists, and shook them. "You didn't think that was important enough to share with the class, you moron?"

"Hey now." He held his hands up. "If we deal with the Axman, it's a non-issue. I didn't want us to focus on two big problems at once. Besides, from what I can tell, we can't do anything about it. He's keeping it trapped in the path."

"That's not entirely true," Johnny began and drew a sharp intake of breath. "I thought we could get a hand from the Wild Hunt." A dramatic pause followed and he looked around at faces that displayed confusion, shock, and even contemplation—maybe some of the others had already begun to consider it? If so, at least he wouldn't be alone in trying to pitch the idea.

He noticed a light at his side and expected to see Vic but was instead greeted by the fury of Don Pesci who grasped his neck. "Are you a fucking idiot, kid?" he demanded as he began to shake him. "Why do you think we've bent over backward to try to get this guy without setting any alarms off? Now you want to send them an open invitation?"

The revenant grasped the boss' hands and managed to

loosen his hold slightly. He was deceptively strong for his height. "Listen for a second! I'm not saying bring them to New Orleans but use them to deal with the body and force the Axman's hand," he explained. "If we make the Hunt think the body is the problem, they can deal with it. If it's destroyed, we don't have to worry about them peeking into New Orleans!

"Besides, it's been months since the killings started. How much longer can you hide it? The Axman and Kriminel may stop most souls from getting through, but people are still dying of natural causes, accidents, and all that. If they get here and start blabbing, how much longer do you have until a big enough ruckus is raised and the Wild Hunt goes out to check?"

Pesci thought about it for a moment and made a noise between a sigh and a growl as he floated down and shook his head. "The thing that pisses me off is that you're already right. We can't stop all info from getting out and it's been spreading for at least a couple of weeks now. But bringing the Hunt in? Your plan still sounds desperate."

Big Daddy chuckled, but this one sounded more mocking. "Shit, we're already desperate. This one at least has a chance at a happy ending."

"Or maybe merely a decent one," Vic added with a sigh and dug his pack of cigarettes out. "The part he's missing for us to have a chance to even try is getting to the hunt in the first place." He patted his pockets for his lighter, remembered that his partner had it, and glanced at him. The young man checked his pockets and shrugged, unable to find it.

His lights dimmed slightly before a large hand stretched

over his shoulder and opened to reveal a lighter. "I can help you with that," Big Daddy offered and handed it to the ghost detective. "And I think we can get you to the Hunt."

"We?" Johnny asked as Vic found an unbroken cigarette and lit it.

Pesci and Big Daddy stared at one another and looked for all the world like they were communicating telepathically before the mafia head sighed. "Like you said, we're desperate. But are we honestly that desperate?"

The dealer rolled his shoulders. "I do know we're running out of time so don't try to avoid this by summoning the council or whatever. The worst that can happen is that the Hunt gets pissed off at a breather on their turf and takes him out. There's no way to pin it on you or the mafia at large."

With a snort, the don shook his head. "No, the worst thing that can happen is that he lets enough slip that the Hunt gets suspicious and takes a look anyway. And might take out a few annoyances along the way simply for kicks."

Big Daddy's lights narrowed and he inhaled the last of his cigar. "Is that any worse than the Axman winning? Make the call. You're the one with the ticket."

"Ticket?" Johnny looked at Vic to check if he knew anything but received an equally curious look from him. "Ticket for what or where?"

Pesci sighed and mumbled something to himself about this coming back to bite him before he raised a hand and waved it. A couple of soldiers in the back of the room turned and entered another area before they approached the boss and gave him a white-and-gold box. He rolled his sleeves and produced a golden key from inside his jacket.

His expression dour, he slid the key into the lock of the box and turned it three times to the left before he turned it to the right. After a sharp click, he opened the box, which produced a glow in various colors and startled the two partners. Quickly, he snatched something from within, shut it, and locked it again.

While the young detective didn't know what he had taken out, the trepidation in the mafia members made him wonder if setting out on this quest was a smart move. He had begun to appreciate everyone else's worries.

In all honesty, he didn't want his epitaph to be *Whoops*.

CHAPTER THIRTY-FIVE

Pesci handed the box back to his subordinates and walked casually to the detectives. "This is a ticket to get you to the Wild Hunt's part of Limbo." He pressed his thumb through his closed hand and a white coin slid up his fingers. "It's more of a token rather than a ticket, but I guess that was merely a metaphor. This isn't an easy item to get hold of, even for us. The Hunt likes to go looking for people—more of a 'we'll call you' type of situation. I respect that and work by similar rules in both life and death. But a predecessor of mine—someone who gave up the life and eventually got out of this dump of a realm—well, he got this."

"A Ferryman's token?" Vic asked as he peered at it and saw the image of a bow on one side and a horse on the other.

"Does this look like simply any Ferryman's token to you?" the mob boss asked and flicked the coin to him. "I never had a use for it until now but it looks like trying to tackle this situation in only one way ain't cutting it. I hate to admit it but we are losing control." He sighed and slipped his hands into his pockets. "You do your thing. Usually, I would send someone I've known for more than five minutes but BD has a point."

He floated up again and made sure they both looked him dead in the eye. "You say nothing about us, you got it? If we somehow survive all this and the Wild Hunt comes looking for us, I'll know why. Then you'll know that what they do is merciful compared to what we will do, capeesh?"

Vic slotted the coin into his pocket as Johnny nodded. "Yeah, we follow. Trust me," the ghost detective answered, took his hat off, and rubbed his skull. "We'll go after the body, which means we'll probably deal with Kriminel again. That leaves the Axman." He looked at Big Daddy. "We need him distracted, especially if he's at breaking point."

The dealer stamped his cigar out. "I haven't heard word that he's been seen but we'll need the manpower—or ghost power—to deal with him once he appears again. We've probably got enough guys still in the city but they need a leader."

Pesci folded his arms. "All right. I'll take over for now."

This drew an alarmed look from Big Daddy. "That seems unnecessary. Think of all the bosses who have already been killed. Before they showed up, I was going to offer my services as a—"

The mob boss made a motion for him to zip it. "Yeah, I've done this for a long time and could see the signs there, buddy. It would take too long to find the next guy in the city to take over, even if they would and especially since they are being targeted now. Getting someone around here to take the reins would also be a pain in the ass."

He spun and pointed to the dealer. "And while you've been an asset to us, you ain't part of the mob and this is a mob matter. I'm up to speed and I want to wring that bastard's neck while I rip the lights out of his eyes with a melon baller. So I'll go up there and handle this myself."

Pesci raised his hand and snapped his fingers. "Get my things. We leave in five!" he ordered. Every mobster in the room hurried in different directions as the don turned to Vic and Johnny. "There's a Ferryman's post northwest and about twenty minutes from here. Get to the edge of the water and wave the coin. They should pick you up shortly after."

"Appreciated," the ghost detective replied as two soldiers walked past him and handed the don a black coat and bowler hat.

The mafiosa adjusted the coat and tipped the hat to the perfect angle before he nodded. "I'll say the same as long as you two don't botch this and remember what I said about blabbing," he warned, turned, and snapped his fingers again. "Let's head up, BD!"

The dealer looked a touch annoyed but an amused smile crossed his face. "I didn't plan on this but it could be interesting," he muttered thoughtfully as he nodded at the partners on his way out. "I guess we'll race you boys to see who gets their big fish first. Best of luck to you and all that and if you die, I'll make the funeral arrangements for the kid."

He cackled as more mobsters ran past them and into the main hall. Johnny and Vic picked their guns up, followed them out the door, and waited while they all piled into long, old-looking black cars and began to move down the long, cobblestone street. The revenant looked over his shoulder at a mansion from which more mobsters emerged, crowded into other vehicles, and followed the mob boss. Before too long, they were alone.

The revenant looked around. "So...uh, which way is northwest?"

His partner flicked his cigarette on the ground. "The moon is always due north in Limbo." He pointed at the sky before he moved his hand slightly. "That way. I gotta say, Marsan seems to like you, paying for your funeral and all."

He frowned. "How likely do you think it is that I'll collect on it?"

The ghost chortled as he produced the coin from his pocket. "What? Are you getting cold feet now that we can put your plan into action?"

He shook his head as he shoved his hands into his coat pocket and began to walk. "Oh, I'm sure we'll get the Wild Hunt to help," he admitted as Vic followed and they headed into a thicket. "But after dealing with Kriminel when he wasn't on his own turf and now heading into his domain, I'm worried that it might not be enough."

Valerie, Annie, and Marco were seated in a diner to consider what they had learned about the Maggio family history while they nursed their drinks and hunched over plates of barely touched food. They needed the calories and energy to keep going but it seemed they didn't necessarily have the stomach for it right now. "So, Anna Schneider..." Marco began and rubbed his eyes. "She's our great-grandmother?"

"Great-great-grandmother." Valerie corrected, finally plucked a few fries from next to her burger, and chewed them slowly. "Her child Margret is your great-grand-mother and her kid Elise is your grandmother."

"I think we could have worked that last one out," he muttered and sipped his coffee. "Granny Elise never spoke about anything like this when we were growing up."

The officer snickered as she lifted her coffee cup. "I imagine it's not the easiest thing to bring up, especially during family visits and the holidays."

"If she knew about it at all," Annie pointed out and pushed the fruit around in her yogurt. "Anna changed her name so we don't know if she talked about it at all after it happened."

"Not to mention that she got married soon after and changed her name again," Marco added. "But I think people would talk about it. Having a baby after someone tried to murder you is fairly unique. I'm sure Margret must have known. At least a couple of clueless guys probably mentioned it while she grew up and maybe she was even in the papers on an anniversary or something."

Valerie shrugged and cut a piece off her burger. "Maybe, but after it happened, it wouldn't surprise me if everyone wanted to forget. The Axman might like to think he's Jack the Ripper, but he didn't capture the fascination the Brit did. I'll look into it more later but I doubt there's much to dig up after the killings stopped."

Annie took a mouthful of her yogurt and let the spoon

rest in her mouth for a moment before she removed it. "So where does that leave us?"

The officer checked her phone on the table. "The next best guess is to talk to that priestess. I wanted to wait for Aiyana to do that but I don't know when she'll be able to get here."

"Right now," the shaman answered and startled them as she sat at the table. She looked at them in confusion. "What?"

"Where did you come from?" Marco asked and relaxed again.

She pointed slowly behind her. "The...front door?"

"I didn't hear you coming at all."

She shrugged and smiled. "I've had to get used to being quiet when on a hunt. I guess it's bleeding into my normal activities too." She looked at Valerie. "I sent you a text. Did you get it?"

The officer looked through her phone and frowned. She sighed and nodded. "I did but I didn't see it. It got buried by all these texts I'm getting from all the teams. We created groups to keep better track of everything."

"Speaking of which, Donovan's team found something," Aiyana told her. "He also tried to get hold of you and said they ran into the keeper at the theater."

"What?" She gasped and startled some of the other patrons. "When?"

"He and his team returned as I was leaving." The shaman removed her satchel and retrieved her phone. "It was at the Crescent Theater in the outskirts of the city. He said he was summoned to an altar in the building and that Johnny burned it before he disappeared through a door."

"Is he okay?" Annie asked, worry visible in her eyes.

She nodded but hesitated a moment after. "Well, I suppose none of us can say for certain. But given his ability to jump between realms, I would guess that he was able to get away."

Valerie checked her phone in case she'd missed a call but found nothing. "I haven't had any contact with him since I asked him to back Donovan up." She felt a pang of worry. If something had happened to him, she was the one who sent him to it.

Suddenly, cries from outside drew everyone's attention. The group stood and turned to gape at a stream of cars that appeared in the streets. Some of the pedestrians were shocked and scattered, while others looked around in confusion.

"Are those cars?" Marco asked and pointed at the glowing vehicles. "From Limbo?"

CHAPTER THIRTY-SIX

"More mafia." Valerie sighed, took some money from her purse, and placed it on the table as they hurried outside. Some of the civilian specters now crowded around the vehicles. She flashed her badge and ordered them to move out of the way as mafia members began to exit the cars.

Others stood around, not panicked or even surprised, which told her they must have been some of the human mob members. One of the ghosts opened the door to a more stylized car. A short ghost stepped out followed by a much larger and purple-clad one.

"Big Daddy!" she shouted.

The ghost looked at her when he heard his name and smiled as he tipped his hat. "Officer, are you here to escort us already? We didn't even drop a line. That's what I call service!"

She gestured around the street. "Yeah, well, this is what I call a scene. What are you doing appearing in the middle of the street like this?"

He shrugged. "It was the most convenient crossing

point without having to pay a Ferryman. And look at all the guys we brought." He flicked a thumb behind him as dozens of mafia members began to slide out of the cars. "That's a shitload of doubloons we'd have to pay to cross over."

"I guess I ain't mad to have some more muscle," Marco commented as a couple of skeletons passed. "Figuratively speaking."

"Mr. Big Daddy, have you seen Johnny?" Annie stepped closer and tugged on his suit. "He was looking for you."

The dealer nodded and snickered as he began to light a cigar. "As it happens, I have. He appeared in our meeting as we were putting this all together. He's still in Limbo right now, bringing in the Hunt."

"The Hunt?" the group said almost unanimously.

"You mean the Wild Hunt?" Aiyana asked.

"Yeah, but don't worry about it," a shrill, more animated voice declared. The group focused on the smaller mafia member. "He's got a plan. It seems a long shot, but we need to get more pots cooking anyway."

"Who are you?" Valerie asked. She noticed that this ghost was far more humanoid and thus had far more access to stygia.

His eyes narrowed as he floated to her height. "Don Pesci. Don't forget it. I'll take over this section of the mafia until we rip that Axman bastard into pieces, got it?" She nodded as he floated down again. "All right, you bums. Get into squads like we talked about and search the area. The rest of you make contact with the topside members and bring them up to speed and this show into full gear!"

"He's got...um, spirit," the officer ventured and Big

Daddy nodded and took a drag. "I'll inform the chief but we can't escort you. We're on our way to see a spirit caller."

His gaze darted to hers and his eyes brightened. "Let me guess—a priestess?"

"Catherine Leveau," she replied with a nod and folded her arms. "You know her?"

He chuckled as he brought his cigar to his teeth with a wry nod. "Funny how things work out," he mused. "Yes, I do. I think we'll join you if you don't mind."

"We?" Marco asked and they all looked at the group of mafia members around them.

"We," he replied firmly. "You know, for protection."

The water—if it could be compared to that—was both enchanting and terrifying. It looked similar to liquid but glowed and dimmed, and its color was easy to see against the dark backdrops that comprised the matter of Limbo. Not only that, it appeared to be bottomless. The partners approached a large river cautiously and Johnny stared across it and into the distance at what appeared to be only a dark, ever-expanding chasm.

"Are we at the edge of Limbo?" he asked

Vic took a cigarette out and lit it with his new lighter. "I doubt it. I don't hear any of the droning you typically do at the edge." He took a quick drag and folded his arms. "It's probably merely another section all the way across—I have no clue which but maybe forty-seven? There's a large river between it and forty-eight, big enough that most would call it an ocean." He picked a rock up and tossed it into the river. The ripples told them that it flowed to the right. "But Limbo works differently, now doesn't it?"

The revenant chuckled as he sat on the pier and gazed at the vast expanse ahead. "How many great artists and creatives wander around Limbo and the best they could come up with to call different landmasses is numbers?"

"There are a hell of a lot of them, kid." Vic took another drag. "Besides, they do have actual names but they've changed so much over eternity that the numbers help to keep everything straight."

"Is there a bridge?" he asked and saw nothing but more tree line as he checked the coast.

"Maybe somewhere. But some sections are cut off from others."

"Why is that?"

"They prefer it that way." The ghost stared into the dark. "You have to remember that some of these guys have been around way longer than you would probably believe. They are stuck in their ways, especially since contact with the living was sporadic until the tear." He let the smoke plume out of his skull. "Despite everything, I consider myself lucky that I never lost that connection even after kicking the bucket."

His partner laughed loudly and smirked at him when he was done. "You don't think you're stuck in your ways?"

Vic pointed at him with his cigarette between his fingers. "Hey, I have preferences. That's not being stubborn. There's a difference."

Johnny stretched his arms. "And I'm sure you can give me a long and unnecessary explanation once we're on the boat." He looked into the water and frowned. "If he ever gets here. What's the deal?"

The ghost detective shrugged, placed the cigarette between his lips, and retrieved the coin. "I don't know. Ferrymen are strange guys. But they usually know when a paying customer is waiting on them to—"

"Uh, Vic?" the revenant interrupted, his eyes wide.

They both stared at a tall being who held a dark oar. He wore a long black robe and only a pair of white eyes broke the monotone appearance. When he extended a long limb, the young detective scrambled to his feet and backed away slightly from the disconcerting figure. Vic looked at the coin and then at the hand before he extended the token and placed it in the figure's palm. The Ferryman closed his wrinkled hands around it and stepped back to reveal that he stood on a longboat and didn't float on the water.

The partners exchanged a long look to confirm with each other that they should do this. Johnny felt he should be the first in as this was his idea so he drew a deep breath, walked down the peer, and stepped into the boat. It was surprisingly slippery and he almost fell, but Vic caught him by the arm—or he thought he did, at least. When he looked up, however, the Ferryman supported him with a firm grasp and pointed to one of the seats at his feet. "Uh... appreciated," he muttered as he sat and waved Vic forward.

His partner got in and sat across from him. The Ferryman raised his oar between them and planted it on the edge of the dock to push off and begin their journey. Johnny let his hand drift in the Limbo water. It felt incredibly chilly and would certainly cause a shock if he fell in, but that concerned him less than the massive shadow he could barely make out deep in the water. He pulled his hand out immediately and looked at the ghost detective. "So…uh, do you have any idea what we can look forward to at the Hunt's HQ?"

Vic shook his head. "I haven't seen it—most haven't, honestly. The Hunt usually stay in their little domain and you don't want to be around when they come out, especially to ask stupid questions like what they decorate with." He finished his cigarette and was about to put it out on his seat when they heard a gruff growl.

The Ferryman stared at him, his oar out of the water. His gaze burrowed into the smoker, who nodded and used his skeletal hand to pinch the top off and shove the remains inside his jacket. The Ferryman nodded approvingly and continued.

Shortly thereafter, they stared at what seemed to be a doorway or something in front of them. A trail of water flowed through it and a familiar light surrounded it.

"Is that the path?" Johnny asked as they approached it.

"It seems so." He was about to lift his pack again, but stopped, folded his arms, and leaned his head back. "Let's hope it's the right one."

CHAPTER THIRTY-SEVEN

Harrison Hargrove had a rough day at the mill. When he arrived home, he collapsed on his couch and fell asleep in front of the television. Much later, he heard a loud bang—loud enough to wake him—and he cursed as he fumbled for the remote to turn the TV off. He didn't find it on the chest or above him on the arm of the couch.

Wearily, he opened his eyes. The light of the TV was obscured by bars of darkness that looked like...a rib cage? He looked up slowly and gaped at a skeleton that stared at him with wispy eyes of light. It raised its arm with an ax grasped firmly by bony fingers.

He muttered the only thing that came to his mind. "What the fu—"

His shocked protest remained unfinished as the killer buried the ax deeply into his head and blood spurted onto the top of the couch, walls, and ceiling. The Axman extended his other hand and a white orb formed in the palm as he leeched the soul from the mill worker's now lifeless body. He looked from the orb in his hands to the wound in his side. It had grown smaller with each kill but those had been ghosts and he wanted to try something fresher.

As he prepared to absorb the soul, a loud, angry, terrible voice hollered in his mind. *"Axman!"*

Unable to withstand the pressure, he collapsed to his knees and held his head. He knew this voice and he certainly knew this anger.

"What is it, Kriminel?" He hissed his irritation. Between the pain in his side and the unwanted intrusion in his mind, he had little patience to spare.

"They found your hole, Axman," the loa growled and the killer was almost certain he could see his visage in the dark corners of the room, although that was impossible. "They burned it to the ground, along with my altar. My connection to this plane is growing weaker, but they sent agents and officers to check the remains. Go and slay them!"

The Axman got to his feet and placed the orb into the wound. It was sucked in and the hole closed, but he could still feel the pain of something piercing his side. Still, it would do for now.

"Before I waste my time with your petty retribution, tell me how they got that far," he demanded and looked at nowhere in particular. "Hmm? I'm sure you would have dealt with any intruders who put your precious altar at risk."

"It was the revenant!" the keeper snapped, his irritation evident and at this point, the killer didn't know if it was at him or the one who had destroyed Kriminel's alter. "Him and those damned agents! I had them in my clutches but he disappeared behind one of the stage doors. Some type of power allowed him to flee."

He knew what that power was and an idea formed in his head. "He has the ability to jump between realms—something you should know as I've told you before." He turned as if to stare through the walls of the house. "But he does not have perfect control over it from what I've been able to gather. This means he is currently indisposed, and if agents and officers are preoccupied with cleaning up the remains of my abode, there is opportunity."

"To slaughter them?" Kriminel asked and a trace of mirth returned to his voice. "To make them pay for their desecration?"

"To finish our work," the Axman clarified. "Without the revenant, the agents, officers, and mafia are all little more than annoyances to me. I should be able to spirit the girl away again, this time for keeps."

His patron clicked his tongue disapprovingly. "Trying the same thing again and expecting a different outcome, are you? I suppose this does prove you to be insane." Again, the shining red eyes at the edge of his vision glared at him. "Dozens of souls await execution and you want to try to abduct the girl again? Your obsession with her grows increasingly tiresome, Axman. I believe I've given you more than enough opportunities to attempt your little side project but I am done with that."

He was growing irate—something that had become fairly common for Kriminel in the brief time he had known him—but he had to placate him lest it create further issues for him. "You are…correct," he stated and looked toward the eyes, although they seemed to have disappeared. "Acquiring the girl has been a more difficult challenge than I anticipated and you have been patient. But this is a golden opportunity for both of us."

"Hmm? And how is that?" Kriminel asked and sounded somewhat intrigued and less angered.

"The revenant is in Limbo now, yes? Your domain, so you could eliminate him there. It wouldn't surprise me if he went there not only to escape you but to meet your brother."

The Axman steeled himself against a shuddering in his head when the connection between himself and his patron made him feel his rage and fear. "He is the one your brother chose, after all. And they have been the biggest thorns in our sides. Your vessel is almost complete, correct? If you can trap them while you have the advantage using the power we've collected thus far, eliminate them. There is no one to stop us since the other keepers have been minding their own business."

He waited once he'd finished his thought and his patron considered what he'd said. "I have avoided Samedi thus far, but since he's been so preoccupied with looking for me, he has not done his job with the proper attention, which has cost him souls. The number of his followers has diminished as well, and both mean that he is not nearly as powerful as he has been.

"The revenant is a gnat but annoying enough and has slowed our work, nonetheless. This could be a golden opportunity indeed." This time, Kriminel's form appeared fully beside him, his arms folded while he tapped his foot. "I would need to find them first and they could be anywhere. And even if I did, what will you do while I am doing the heavy work?" He spun his cane and pointed at the corpse with it. "Simply making small pickings?"

The Axman shook his head and almost crushed the handle of the ax under his tightening grip. "No, I will make good on my promises, Kriminel. We will truly begin our finale." He turned toward the keeper and his eyes shimmered. "I will make sure they know that all they have done was delay the inevitable."

———

"Are we there yet?" Johnny moaned as he leaned over the side of the boat. As impressive as the contrast was between the dark visage of wherever the hell they were and the white flowing river, the journey seemed to take forever.

"Quiet, kid," Vic muttered. His hat was tilted over his eyes and he seemed to try to take a nap despite the fact that ghosts didn't sleep. "There isn't exactly a power engine on this, you know?" He lifted his hat slightly. "Not that you aren't doing a great job," he added but the Ferryman merely grunted in response. "But since we have the time, I should probably ask what your plan is once we get there."

The revenant focused on him and cocked his head. "I thought I'd made that abundantly clear."

His partner tapped his fingers on his chest. "Yeah, I know why we're going and what you hope will happen. I'm asking how we'll get from A to C."

"I don't follow."

Vic sighed exasperatedly. "How will you convince the Wild Hunt to go and take care of Kriminel's...god body or whatever the hell it is?"

Johnny raised an eyebrow as he folded his arms. "What do you mean? That's their job, isn't it? Telling them something screwy is going on will make them want to investigate, won't it?"

The ghost detective straightened and adjusted his hat so it tilted back on his head. "We can hope that's how it works. But let's use our imagination and say they won't simply take the word of a breather that something of unimaginable danger—something they should probably have picked up on by now—involving a keeper was happening under their noses. What then?"

"I would like to think a human—and a revenant— showing up in their domain would warrant at least a little curiosity," Johnny reasoned. "All this time, all you ghosts have told me is how bloodthirsty—or phantasma thirsty, whatever—these guys are. Are you saying this might hurt their pride and they won't investigate simply because they are suspicious of me?"

Vic shrugged. "I'm only saying it's a thought. I can't offer more or any guidelines because I've never been idiotic enough to approach the Wild Hunt until this moment."

He took a moment to think about this. Perhaps it was too hopeful that they would simply follow him into the path because he asked nicely. For a realm of the dead that upended most current beliefs and sciences, there seemed to be as much bureaucratic nonsense as there was in life.

"We have arrived," the Ferryman informed them with a slow drawl. The partners straightened and looked ahead at another large doorway. This one led to what looked like a forest of trees with long, twisting limbs. Black, red, purple, and blues leave glowed with an unnatural shimmer. Johnny swore he could see what appeared to be birds or flying animals in the distance, but they seemed far too large to be anything normal. Given the giant beast he had seen in the water not too long ago, many things about Limbo were still unknown to him.

They passed through the entry and emerged onto another large lake, this one deep red. The Ferryman guided the boat to a simple wooden pier, turned, and helped them off the boat before he raised the oar. "I wish you well," he intoned, turned, and prepared to leave.

"Wait—this was one way?" Johnny asked and glanced at Vic to see if they should try to stop him.

The Ferryman stopped for a moment and looked back with its spectral eyes hidden in the darkness of its cloak. "I will return if you have need of me. But that all depends on your success."

"And you don't believe we'll have much of that, do you?" Vic challenged.

In response, the ghost boatman raised a hand and pointed behind them. "That is why I wished you luck."

CHAPTER THIRTY-EIGHT

The partners turned slowly and stared at several enormous figures who all held very large weapons. They were clad in different varieties of armor. Johnny wasn't exactly a historian but he could see designs that looked Celtic, Norse, African, Roman, and Asian, at least when compared to what he had seen in movies and books.

But they all shared something in common with the Ferryman. Large hoods with emblems he couldn't identify obscured their visages, but their piercing, glowing eyes in various colors were fixed on the newcomers.

He looked at the water but the boatman had already gone so he coughed a couple of times to clear his throat before he extended a trembling hand. "Hello there. My name is Johnny and this is my partner Vic."

"You didn't need to mention me," the ghost detective said through clenched teeth.

The one who wore the Norse armor walked forward holding a large ax, ironically, which he pointed toward the young man. He would have admired the details in the weapon if the blade alone wasn't larger than half his body. "Why are you here, revenant?"

Johnny seemed frozen, his gaze fixed on the giant weapon in front of his face. While he had dealt with axes far too often recently, this was huge and the person who wielded it looked like he could lift his boot and crush him in one gory splat. The Wild Hunt should be ghosts of some kind and therefore couldn't hurt him within Limbo, but he didn't know everything about the inner workings and they were something more than "only" ghosts. He didn't feel like testing that theory.

Vic coughed, nudged him, and leaned closer. "You going to answer the gentleman, kid?"

He opened his mouth but closed it quickly and moved closer to his partner. "Do you wanna give it a shot?"

The ghost detective shook his head. "Nuh-uh. This was your plan so you talk to the crazy…uh, nice hunters."

"And what if I blow it?" he whispered.

Vic's gaze darted to the hunter and the ax and returned to him. "Okay, I might try to step in but I should have said this on the boat. It's been nice knowing you, kid."

"Answer, revenant!" the hunter ordered in a tone that made them both stand at attention. "Why are you here?"

"We need your help to kill a big skeleton," Johnny blurted.

"Smooth, kid," his partner muttered while they awaited their fate. The hunters didn't seem to react much, although a couple tilted their heads to regard them with more curiosity than before.

"Explain," the ax-wielder demanded.

"Right…sure, of course." The young detective drew a

deep breath. "Okay...so one of the keepers, the loa Kriminel, has been stealing souls to create some type of body for him to be able to exist in both realms. He's used a serial killer known as the Axman to do his dirty work in New Orleans. They've played both sides and have gotten away with it for a few months now." He needed to be cautious and steer this in the direction he wanted. "We've dealt with the Axman but we can't take Kriminel on by ourselves. Souls will still go to his domain and if he completes his creation, we're all screwed."

Again, the hunters barely moved although the ax lowered slightly, much to his relief. "If what you say is true, this skeleton that is being created is certainly cause for concern. But how do we know you are telling the truth?"

"If our words aren't enough for you, simply ask Kriminel's brother," Vic interjected. "He guided us to this path and has tried to deal with this for a while."

"Vic!" Johnny hissed. "Do you think it's smart to mention that?"

The ghost shrugged. "The last time we saw him, he admitted he's been too coy about all this. We're here to get these guys' help and the sooner we can get them to agree, the better."

"Samedi?" the hunter questioned. "He and his brother have been warring for ages. I did not think it would escalate to something of this nature."

"I admit, I can't see how this is a trick or joke," another hunter in samurai-looking armor remarked. "But we would have to see this skeleton to assess what needs to be done."

"We need to destroy it," the revenant insisted. "Kriminel is keeping it in his domain. You can access it, can't you?"

"We can, but only in grave situations, however. The domains of the keepers are not ours to frolic in." The hunter raised his ax and rested it on his shoulder. "Aetios, come forward." A figure draped in dark-blue robes with a curved staff on his back stepped from within the crowd of hunters. "See into their souls and tell us what you find." He pointed to Johnny as he spoke the order.

The robed figure nodded and approached the partners, knelt, and stretched his hand toward them. "Wait—see into our souls?" Johnny protested as the man's hand began to glow. "What are you talking ab— Whoa!" Aetios' eyes brightened and filled his vision. Vic stiffened as he was washed by light, but only for a moment as it seemed to dissipate as quickly as it began.

"He speaks the truth." The man pushed to his feet. "He has seen what he describes. I feel no turmoil or chaos in his soul, despite his peculiar nature."

"What the hell was that?" Johnny asked and clutched his chest. "Whatever it was, I'm not sure I wanna go through that again."

Vic motioned for him to silence. "Whatever it was seems to have convinced them to believe us so roll with it."

The hunters now talked amongst themselves. The revenant heard comments and talk of a purge that worried him, but they at least seemed to take it seriously now. "If we destroy Kriminel's creation, we should be able to set all the souls contained within it free, right?" he asked.

The leader looked at him. "Perhaps. Soul weaving is a forbidden art in Limbo, one not to be trifled with."

He glanced at his partner. "Soul weaving?" An unknowing shrug was the only response.

"However, there is the matter of the keeper to be dealt with as well." The hunter looked at the man in samurai armor. "Enji, how many of our forces are available?"

"Currently, about a third. At last count, we were at seventy," the man replied. Johnny was bewildered. The Wild Hunt that caused almost every ghost to have an absolute fit whenever their name was raised had only a little over two hundred members? He'd expected an army and honestly, he kind of wanted one if they intended to deal with the situation in Limbo. If Kriminel appeared, he would be at his true power, not the shadowy being they had fought at the theater.

"We will make do. Aetios, see if you can summon the baron." He looked at the partners. "You will guide us, revenant. We will need someone who has seen the domain of Kriminel to open the gate. We cannot afford to wait for Samedi to join us."

He nodded and finally felt a fire burning in his body again. "Yeah, we need to end this."

CHAPTER THIRTY-NINE

"It's up there on the left," Big Daddy stated as the driver turned the corner. "Little Cathie. It's been a while since I've seen her face to face."

Aiyana looked questioningly at the ghost. "How did you get acquainted with a priestess? Was this before or after your passing?"

Marco frowned. "That seems a little forward, Aiyana."

"Does it?" she asked with a small frown. "I didn't mean to offend but in my experience, ghosts are usually more at ease with death than we are."

The dealer chuckled. "Oh yes, very much so. In a few more years I'll have been dead longer than I was alive, so it ain't no biggie to me." He raised his cigar to his lips. It wasn't lit out of respect for his passengers, but the habit was deeply ingrained by this point. "I got to know the family shortly before I bit the big one. Since her mother was a priestess as well—most of the women in the family are—we kept in touch afterward. If anyone could have a unique perception of what's happening, it would be her."

This caught Valerie's attention. "Then why have you not talked to her before now?"

They approached the entrance of the house and the car began to slow. "As foolish as it may sound, I didn't want to get her involved in all this. Her mother was more active with things on both sides of the underworld, figurative and literal, but she didn't want that for her daughter. Catherine mostly works for those looking for a séance or for those in the religion who need guidance or assistance in a ritual, but she's not exactly one to shy away from looking into supernatural matters.

"I'm sure she's been looking into this ever since the Axman appeared, although who knows how far she's come." The car door opened and he stepped out with his entire group behind him. At least a dozen mafia members surrounded them. "It looks like a slow day here, or maybe she's off. Either way, she would probably enjoy the company."

"Even if we're here to tell her that the Axman is working with a loa and then drag her into it?" Annie asked.

Big Daddy looked thoughtfully at her. "I should probably do the talking. At least in the beginning." He looked at the mafia members. "Hopefully, nothing should happen. But be alert, all right?"

"Got it," one said with a nod and held his gun up.

The dealer raised a hand in protest. "You might want to keep the guns on the down-low. This is a nice neighborhood. Don't go scaring the people now."

With that, he opened the gate in front of the house and ushered everyone in. He walked up to the door and made his hand tangible to press the doorbell before he took a small bottle from his coat, held it to his mouth, and drained the contents.

"I should probably have made sure to stock up on stygia before we headed out," he muttered as the group saw purple skin appear around his form with long dreadlocks that hung down his back.

By the time the door opened, he looked more human while still clearly a ghost. None of the group was able to see the woman as she was blocked by Big Daddy.

"Hello, how can I be of—Marsan?" She gasped when she recognized the ghost beaming at her with a wide smile. "Marsan! I haven't seen you in so long!" She hugged him warmly. "It's good to see you." She strained to look around him. "And you've brought friends?"

"Associates," he clarified and broke the hug to rest a large hand on her shoulder. "I'm sorry it's been so long, Cathie, and I wish I had only stopped by for some friendly conversation and to catch up. But we have something going down—something you might be able to help with."

"I see." She sounded understanding. "Come on in. I have some tea and beignets ready."

Big Daddy laughed as they entered the house. "What? Did you have a vision that you would have company?"

"That's not how it works, Marsan, and you know it," she chided. Her home was decorated in an older style and filled with pictures, both photos and artwork. "For a believer, you certainly like to make fun of Voodoo."

"It's all good-natured," he responded as they entered a dining room with a long maple table and over a dozen chairs. Everyone sat while Catherine went through a door into the kitchen and returned with a tray of tea, several glasses, and a plate of beignets.

Now that she wasn't blocked by the giant ghost, they could see she was a pretty young woman in either her late twenties or early thirties. She wore a green-and-purple dress and a brighter purple headwrap.

"Help yourselves," she told them as she placed the tray in the middle of the table. She moved toward the seat at the head of the table but stopped and looked at Aiyana. "Pardon me for asking, but are you a spirit caller?"

She nodded. "I am—a shaman. It is a pleasure to meet you." She proffered her hand.

Catherine smiled and gave her hand a playful shake. "Same here. I don't get to meet many other callers and I don't think I've ever met a shaman, at least not knowingly."

"We can be very secretive and we move around much of the time," the shaman conceded with a chuckle, although her mirth soon faded. "It's a big reason why we are here. We were hoping you could help us."

"Help you?" she asked as she sat. "What with? I imagine it's something quite important if you are rolling with Marsan."

"Oh, it's very big," Marco told her after he'd eaten half a beignet. "We're after the Axman."

"The Axman?" She looked speculatively at Annie. "Wait...I've seen you on the news. You were there when he attacked the main street." She looked around the table as realization dawned in her eyes. "All of you were!"

"Yes, we were." Marco confirmed with an exaggerated smile. "I guess many people have been in the news because of that bastard. The difference, you'll notice, is we're alive."

"For now." Big Daddy chuckled. "But we would like it to stay that way. We were hoping you would be able to give us some advice on the matter, Cathie, because of the Axman's partner in crime—Kriminel."

If she had been holding anything, Catherine would have dropped it. Her body tensed and her hands seemed to clench and unclench reflexively. "Kriminel?" she asked, almost in a daze. "Surely it can't be. He might be one of the more…ornery of the loa, but he would never stoop to this. Even if he did, Samedi and his family would put him in line."

"He's been trying to," Annie interjected. "But it hasn't been easy as he's tried to not alert all of Limbo about his brother's crimes."

The priestess turned to her. "Then you've seen him?" she asked and received a nod. "Not to presume, but…well, I suppose that is exactly what I'm doing, but you do not follow the faith, do you? Voodoo?" The young woman shook her head. "And yet a loa appeared to you?"

"The Axman wants her badly," Valerie explained. "At this point, she's joined Daphne from Scooby-Doo in terms of attempted kidnappings."

Annie rolled her eyes but nodded dejectedly. "We learned that my brother and I are descended from one of his victims. But Baron Samedi appeared to Johnny well before he did to me."

"Johnny?" Catherine chewed on her lip. "Johnny Despereaux? The revenant?"

"You know him?" Big Daddy asked.

She nodded and hurried across the dining room into the living room. "I've heard of him from other spirits. But

I've seen a man in my dreams, surrounded by fire with blood dripping off him and a horde of ghosts at his back." She returned with a notepad, placed it in front of Valerie and the others, and gestured at the sketch in it. "Is that him?"

Marco nodded approvingly. "Man, you've got talent." The image showed exactly what she had described. A lone figure with many spirits behind him stood before a larger one in the foreground. "Who's that?"

"My guess would be the Axman," she responded. "I am not completely sure, however. I can never get a clear picture and I do not hear names."

The young officer pulled the pad closer and tried to identify the figure. "You said you saw this in a dream?"

Catherine nodded. "In Voodoo, we believe that dreams can show us visions or instructions from the loa. However, they can occasionally be opaque or unclear."

"Have you ever seen the Axman in person?" Marsan asked.

She shook her head and rubbed a hand up one of her arms as if she was cold. "No, only in the news footage. Fortunately, it doesn't seem that I have— What is that noise? Music?"

The group all froze. It was indeed music. The familiar drone and scattered jazz began to play a little louder.

"No," Valerie whispered and looked wildly around. "No, no, no!"

Big Daddy was the first out of his chair and he rushed into the hall. "Frank, what's going on out there?" Rain began to patter on the windows and walls of the house. "Frank! What's happening?" He attempted to exit the front door but when he grasped the knob, he immediately jerked his hand back like it had burned him. "Gah! What the hell?" He scowled at his hand and a dark substance that coated his palm.

"What's going on?" the priestess asked as Valerie drew her gun. "Is this some kind of sign?"

"A very bad one," Marco told her brusquely and looked around. "Do you have a bat?"

"A what?"

"Bat—you know, a baseball bat? Wooden, preferably."

She looked toward the hall. "There's a small storage area under the stairs. I think one of my nephews might have left a couple in there."

He ran to it, opened the tiny door, and rummaged around inside before he emerged with a dark oak bat that was immediately coated by blue phantasma. "It'll do." He found the other and tossed it to Annie. "Do you think you can whip up whatever you did last time?"

His sister caught the bat and held the grip tightly as she lifted it in front of her. "I'm not sure what I did last time to make it happen. I...I don't know."

"How the hell did he find us?" Valerie demanded, her voice terse as she fought to stay calm. "Is he clairvoyant now?" A thought occurred to her and she turned to Catherine. "Do you speak to the loa or communicate in any way?"

The woman nodded. "Of course. That's my primary function as a priestess."

"Which loa?" she asked and shook her head quickly. "Have you ever talked to Kriminel? Does he have a connection to you?"

She looked at her fingers and counted them off as she tried to recall all those she'd communicated with. "Kriminel? Not directly, but I suppose the path is open to any loa who would hear me—oh no."

"The path is open to any loa and their friends, priestess," a grim, echoing voice responded. Everyone tensed for a moment before they turned toward the living room, now darkened due to the lack of lights and the storm but from which a pair of glowing white eyes peered at them. "I thank you for your service. The other plans I had to find them were far less convenient."

CHAPTER FORTY

"Felix!" the lead huntsman shouted as they approached the end of the track. "Ready the bridge! We are headed into the path." When they reached the clearing, Johnny and Vic marveled at the sight before them. A large obelisk made of dark stone—or Limbo's approximation of it—stood behind a circular altar and a long path that seemed to lead off a cliff. The hunter turned to Johnny and pointed at him. "Revenant!" he shouted and drew their attention. "Get on the platform."

"The platform?" Johnny asked and looked at the circular area as another huntsman in robes placed crystals around it. "What for?"

The man looked somewhat irate, probably at being questioned. "You wish us to rid both realms of this keeper's terror? You need to be the conduit."

"Conduit?" He looked at all the huntsmen, who seemed to grow more impatient by the minute. "But I thought you guys could travel to the path any time you needed to."

"We can travel through it," the leader corrected, turned,

and looked at the platform. "Only on rare occasions can we access the path itself, and even then, where we end up is not known."

Vic bumped Johnny's shoulder. "It sounds like how we cross over."

"So you will be our guide," the man stated. "You still have the essence of the path or what remains of it on your soul. We can pinpoint the location of Kriminel's domain and follow you into the breach to destroy his abomination."

"Oh...uh, okay?" he muttered and walked slowly to the platform as he questioned his life choices. "This won't hurt all that much, will it?"

The huntsman's eyes narrowed. "We do not feel pain."

He sighed as he stepped onto the platform. "That's not helpful," he commented under his breath and turned as the robed man, who he thought was called Felix, positioned the last of his crystals and nodded to the group of huntsmen. They moved to the carved road in front, all brandishing their different weapons.

"Open the bridge!" the leader shouted. Warcries resounded from the group as the robed huntsman stepped to the side and clasped his hands together before he pointed at the crystals. They hummed, elevated slightly, and began to glow with a green light.

"Whoa—what the hell?" Vic protested as he was forced into his partner's body.

"It looks like there's room for one body on this trip," Johnny remarked before he began to float. He had no control and could only stop himself from flailing about as he hovered over the huntsmen. The crystal's color changed from green to white and streams of it connected to his body. It flowed from him to the earth and illuminated the bridge before a portal began to form at the edge. He was pushed forward at increasing speed and pressed his lips together to stop his instinctive scream.

"Forward, my comrades!" A large cheer echoed behind the revenant as he was catapulted through the portal into the white void of the path. He began to fall and fear caught hold of him as he looked at the bottomlessness of the realm. In a moment, however, his descent slowed before he came to a stop.

"Are you okay, Vic?" he asked as he got his bearings.

The ghost detective emerged and brushed himself off theatrically. "I would have liked some warning." He groaned and looked into the sky. "God, that is ugly."

Johnny scowled at the skeletal body still hanging life-lessly above them with dark pits for eyes and the storm of souls that swirled around it. He studied it carefully and noticed that its legs were only half-formed. "Well, at least it doesn't look like he has made much progress."

"It's only been a day," his partner reminded him, checked his jacket for his pack of cigarettes, and found nothing. "We'd be in a real mess if it was being built that quickly. Not that it matters." They both turned to the portal, where the Wild Hunt now strode through. "The wrecking crew is here."

"By God!" the leader shouted as the hunters formed rows behind one another and stared at the body. "It is a creation of soul weaving!"

Enji placed a hand on his shoulder. "I still sense souls who can be saved within that beast, brother." As if to prove his point, faces pressed against the insides of the ebon body. "We must destroy it quickly and free them so the cycle continues."

The huntsmen cheered in agreement as the leader nodded. "If I had to guess, the loa plans to end it for good." He pointed his ax at the body. "And our duty is to uphold the cycle. Wild Hunt! Destroy that abomination!" The partners moved aside as the dozens of huntsmen attacked the skeleton, their weapons ready to destroy it.

Vic placed a hand on Johnny's shoulder. "I have to give you props, kid," he remarked. "It looks like I might have been too paranoid. Your idea worked."

The young man grinned and folded his arms. "I'll try to stay modest, but don't expect me to—wait. The body!" Their jaws dropped when they saw the head twitch and as the huntsmen were almost in range to strike, one of its massive arms sprang to life and swiped violently to hurl them all away.

"What the hell?" The ghost detective gasped.

"I thought it wasn't ready?" his partner yelled as the huntsmen recovered and the body lifted its other arm. "What's going on?"

His answer came in a loud, vicious cackle that filled the void. "You thought you could come into my domain and break my valuables?" A "tsk tsk" sound almost sounded amused but for the rage laced through it. "You should have known better, Wild Hunt. You are not keepers and cannot hide your presence from me in my abode."

A figure emerged from within the chest of the skeleton. It was a man with dark skin who wore dark clothes accented with red trimming and a red dress shirt. His face was adorned with a skull-like visage similar to Baron Samedi, but his was more angular and demented.

He raised his head and opened his blood-red eyes. This was Kriminel, not the shadowy apparition they had fought shortly before they'd arrived. He appeared before them now in his full splendor. "I hope you understand that while I am here, no one can come in or out without my blessing. So why don't we have a nice chat?"

"Keeper Kriminel!" the lead huntsman cried and brandished his ax at him. "You owe us an explanation! What is this travesty?"

"Travesty?" the baron asked and placed a hand on his chest as if he were hurt by the accusation. "I've worked hard on this body. It could use a little color, perhaps, but it is a work in progress."

"Then you do not deny that this is your work? That you exercise the craft of soul weaving?" the huntsman demanded. "You dare to turn your back on your duties and bring madness to the realms of life and death? The only answer for that is to be obliterated!"

Kriminel straightened and his wry grin changed to a furious glare. "Madness? This whole thing is madness already!" He stretched his arms and the skeleton mimicked him. "I am to be a slave for eternity? To be nothing but a glorified valet for souls? I have watched my worshippers and power diminish over the centuries because of this pointless cycle, and the breaking of the veil has only worsened it all."

His cane appeared in his hand and he spun it and planted it in front of him. "No more! I will break this cycle —this pointless relic we only keep because the supposed almighty cannot be bothered to change it. I will rule in his stead, separate the veil once and for all, and bring a new era to both realms by making them one."

"So that truly is his grand plan?" Vic questioned. "Bringing a sledgehammer to the wall between life and death?" The partners' gazes faltered when the loa looked at them.

"Ah, if it isn't the boy and his pet ghost. Or is it the other way around?" he asked with a dark chuckle. "It seems the Axman had a good idea what you would be doing. This works out perfectly. I'll take care of you and your new friends here while he deals with your friends up top."

"What?" Johnny and Vic looked at one another in dread. They both reached for their guns, knowing that it might be fruitless but determined to not stand around.

"Wild Hunt! Destroy both this false keeper and his creation!" the huntsman ordered. He and the others surged toward the loa, who regarded them with contempt.

Kriminel looked at the portal, stretched his hand toward it, and closed his fist and the gateway collapsed on itself. He then pointed his cane at them and the skeleton extended its pointed claws. "At least make this fun for me. I haven't had much in so long."

CHAPTER FORTY-ONE

Valerie was the first to act and yanked an ether barrier from her coat, which she tossed onto the wall. It created a shield that extended in front of the Axman. "Get outside!"

"He's blocked us," Big Daddy exclaimed.

Marco ran to the front door. "Maybe for you, spooky!" He delivered a powerful kick to the door and the black phantasma that covered the exit. His bat lit up and he swung, but any of the substance that he managed to knock out of the way merely seemed to reform.

"Do you think this will do anything to stop me, Officer?" their adversary asked as he pounded his large black hand against the barrier with a loud thud. "You haven't paid attention." He formed a fist, drove it into it, and caused a massive crack to form.

The young man continued to batter the phantasma fruitlessly until Aiyana stepped in. "Allow me." She raised her hands as white flames formed around them and blasted the phantasma to force it to part, but the darkness licked at the fringes of her flames. "Everyone out!" Marco and Annie complied and Big Daddy ushered Catherine through.

Valerie and Aiyana looked back as the Axman struck the barrier and shattered it. Both women bounded through the doorway seconds before the black phantasma engulfed it again.

"Big Daddy!" one of the mobsters shouted as he and the rest ran up. "Thank God. We wondered what was going on. We called the boss when the black stuff appeared but I don't—"

"Get the guns!" the dealer ordered as the rest of the group began to scatter. "The Axman is here. Get the guns and blow him to hell!" The gravity of the situation finally dawned on them and the cars' trunks were opened and guns were passed around quickly. Big Daddy yanked his shotgun from the car and racked it. "Come out and play, Axman!" he roared and aimed at the house.

Silence descended when he didn't appear and the dark phantasma that coated the building began to disappear. They all stared in bewilderment. "He ain't calling it quits, is he?" Marco asked.

"Don't be stupid." Valerie growled and scanned their surroundings continuously. "He won't waste this moment. There are only a few of us here so he has the opportunity to—" She was interrupted by a gurgling sound. Everyone turned to where the Axman stood on top of one of the cars and held two mobsters by their necks. He crushed their spines and the color drained from their bones as he tossed them aside. "The opportunity to take my prize?" he asked and held his hand out as his ax appeared. "That I do. But I also have the opportunity to rid myself of you pests."

Several hunters dug their blades into the hand of the skeleton and cuts appeared and a white, airy light began to slip through. Cries could be heard until the hunters were forced back and souls from the storm above sank into the enormous body and the wounds began to repair themselves.

Johnny, for his part, wanted to fight but could not decide on a plan of attack. He watched as the majority of the huntsman attacked from various angles and tried to inflict real damage. It seemed that no matter how much they sliced the body or tried to break it, the excess souls would pour in to fuel it and repair it.

Kriminel battled a group of huntsmen but fortunately didn't dominate them like the revenant had feared when he arrived. Still, between his rapid movements and ability to attack from a distance by firing some type of red energy or phantasma, he was able to outmaneuver the hunters before they could inflict any real injury.

He had also begun to summon shades, which were what the two partners were dealing with, but it almost seemed like an illusion. While the young detective had not kept count, no matter whether he eliminated one, two, or ten, they always seemed to stay at the same number and even began to feel like their ranks were increasing.

A dark figure at the edge of his vision caught his attention and he spun and fired. The blast destroyed half the skull of a shade in the form of the Axman. The body disappeared and he looked at Kriminel in anger. They needed to finish this. If the Axman had targeted his friends, they would need to go in as backup, although he hoped someone had already been called in the living world. Otherwise, all those mafia members would have made a pointless trip.

Vic fired a couple more shots before he grunted in annoyance. "This is beginning to feel fruitless." He growled and looked at his partner in concern. "Simmer down, kid. I know things are bleak but don't do anything half-cocked."

The revenant turned the power to his gun up and moved toward Kriminel. The ghost detective tried to stop him but a group of shades descended and forced him back. Johnny was able to outmaneuver the shades in his path and even use them for cover as he snuck up on the loa.

A hunter with a claymore clashed with the keeper, who blocked the strike with his cane. His red eyes glowed almost fire-like as he kicked his attacker away and blasted him through the chest. The impact catapulted him back and another hunter caught him, only for his wounded comrade's body to fade and turn into a traditional blue skeletal body before it lost its color and disintegrated into dust in his arms.

Johnny tensed and floated behind the loa as three other hunters attempted to strike. The leader noticed him and hunched over, awaiting his moment. When the keeper was able to slip away from his attackers and readied himself to retaliate, the young detective fired a charged blast into the back of his head. Slivers of darkness and red phantasma were knocked loose.

The keeper stilled but his head suddenly jerked toward him, his eyes full of wrath. The lead huntsman saw his moment and lunged at the loa while he swung his ax overhead. Kriminel turned but had no time to block it with his cane. He grasped the head of the ax as it plunged to sink into the "flesh" of the keeper's hand, and red phantasma poured out, looking very much like blood.

"You should have struck me together!" he chastised, tightened his hold on the blade, and with shocking strength, ripped it from his attacker's hands. He flipped it so he held the haft before he slung it at the huntsman. The ax buried into his shoulder before the loa spread his arms wide and another torrent of shades appeared in front of him out of nowhere and swarmed the members of the Wild Hunt.

Kriminel turned toward Johnny, snapped his fingers, and appeared directly in front of him. He towered at least five feet taller than him and while his rage was still evident, he also seemed to regard him with a hint of curiosity or possibly amusement.

"So, my brother's chosen flesh puppet," he muttered, leaned forward on the balls of his feet, and twirled his cane absentmindedly in his hands. "I'm not sure whether I should find humor in the fact that he had to settle for you." He thrust his cane forward suddenly and the golden tip stopped barely an inch from the young man's face. "Or be angered that he sent you instead of facing me himself!"

He found it in himself to push the cane aside. "Give it time. He'll be here."

The loa threw his head back and laughed. "Samedi can't come in while I am here. Didn't you hear me earlier, boy? He has no back doors or tricks to stop me now." He straightened quickly and raised his cane. "This is my domain and I have no use for you."

Johnny fired as Kriminel swung. While the blast seemed to do little to hurt his adversary, the force of it pushed him back and he avoided having his head caved in. The words replayed in his head, however. A back door?

Samedi seemed crafty so it wasn't a stretch to think he would have had something like that in place. Without one, even if the runner sent to get him arrived, he wouldn't be able to help if he couldn't get in. As he considered this, an oddity he hadn't given much thought to until now took on new relevance. Samedi was somehow able to direct his ability to cross over and put him where he needed to.

He wondered if it could work in reverse.

"Johnny, get out of the way!" Vic shouted and flew closer. He snapped out of his distraction and scowled as a ball of red light streaked toward him. Even if he wasn't a ghost, he was still very sure it would inflict real injury if it didn't kill him outright. He turned, fired another shot, and went lower so the projectile sailed over him.

Quickly, he holstered his gun, removed his jacket, and once it was off, he extended a hand. "Vic, get over here!" The ghost gave a him quizzical look before he fused with him.

"Are we bailing?" he asked as the young detective stopped and held his jacket up. "I'm not sure if we can."

"I'm trying to see if we can make a door," he responded and held his jacket out. "But we won't use it. I'm hoping someone else will come through." He flipped the jacket quickly but nothing happened. Shit. Kriminel prepared to fire another blast, but his focus was broken by something. From the look on his face, it was something that terrified him.

CHAPTER FORTY-TWO

A sly, whimsical laugh came from behind Johnny, who dropped his coat in shock as Vic reappeared and drew his gun. Both paused and grinned as a familiar figure in black-and-purple and skeletal face paint smiled at the other loa.

"Have you finally stopped hiding, brother?" Samedi asked as he twirled his cane theatrically. "Do you know how annoying it was putting all the pieces in place when I couldn't show my full hand? You've made our reunion quite bothersome." He floated toward his kin and seemed to grow larger. "Kriminel."

The other keeper clenched his teeth. "Samedi!" he cried in rage as he fired another blast. The baron simply turned to the side and it rocketed past him. He pointed his cane at his brother and tendrils of purple smoke emerged, swirled around him, and bound him.

"Don't be in such a rush," he chided as he dragged Kriminel closer to him. "I'm making your grave today, Kriminel. I want it to look nice." He looked at the group of huntsmen who had fought the loa and flicked a thumb toward the skeleton. "Go, free the ghosts!" he instructed and turned to his brother. "I have something else to finish." He thrust his hand into Kriminel's chest and the keeper uttered a pained cry that filled the entire void.

The streets were scarred by fissures and littered with the remains of ghosts. Big Daddy slumped against the bars of the gate to Catherine's home, his shotgun still in hand as wounds on his body leaked phantasma and made him shrink slightly.

"Is that all you got?" he asked and raised the shotgun shakily as the Axman approached. "So you think you are hot shit? You killed people in their sleep in life and rely on powers that aren't yours in death. I, on the other hand, am a self-made badass!" He fired once and struck his adversary in the chest, then fired twice, one into his shoulder and the other into the side of his head. He prepared to fire again but the killer struck quickly. His shotgun and most of his left leg were sliced off, but the dealer only reacted with a pained grunt.

"Strong last words," he remarked and raised his ax. "But last words nonetheless."

A shot rang out and hit the side of his namesake weapon. He looked at Valerie, bleeding and still on the ground next to the unconscious bodies of Marco, Catherine, and Aiyana. "You need to learn when to play dead," he remarked, shouldered his ax, and approached her.

"Stop!" Annie shouted, stepped out from behind one of the cars, and held a bat up. "Don't get any closer."

He did stop, but only to look at her. "Ah, little Annie. There you are." He smiled coldly, his eyes alight. "I assumed you couldn't have gone very far. But this is still convenient." He looked at her bat, hesitated for a moment, and seemed uncertain. "I don't see any of that odd phantasma glowing, so I suppose you don't have a strong grasp of your empath. Is this another attempt to parlay like you did with my henchman? I spare your friends or you'll kill yourself? It's more difficult to do that with a bat, I'm afraid."

Something on the horizon behind her caught his attention and resolved into a fleet of cars similar to those around him, along with police sirens that gradually grew louder. "Hmm, more? I couldn't. Honestly, I'm bored now."

"Annie, run," Valerie implored and struggled to keep her head raised. "Let the others...deal with him."

"Deal with me?" He growled in annoyance and glared at her over his shoulder. "You don't seem to understand. I am beyond anything you can hope to defeat. All you have done is delay my plans and I am done with you—all of you." He raised his ax in a challenge. "You will not stop the return of the terror of the Ax—"

His jaw dropped and his weapon slipped from his hand and clattered on the streets. He fell to his knees and clutched his head. "Aaaaggghhh!" The dark phantasma on his body began to fall off and turned to sludge as it landed on the asphalt. "What's happening? *Kriminel!*" he cried as his dark bones turned into a decayed-looking gray.

The cars pulled up and dozens of mafia, cops, and agents exited the vehicles. The Axman crawled to one of the crevasses. For the first time in his long existence, desperation drove him and he couldn't think clearly. He knew without a doubt that he faced ultimate defeat—but there was someone who could save him. It was a wild beacon in the waves of despair. If he could only accomplish this one small thing, he would have what he needed to reverse his failure.

"Stop him!" someone shouted and blasts rang out in unison. Some made impact and they seemed to do real damage as he reacted with unnatural sounds. Despite this, he reached one of the fissures and fell inside.

Dozens of humans and ghosts rushed past Annie to inspect the chasm and some fired into it. "Is he there?" Don Pesci demanded as he pushed through the group. "Dammit!"

Annie sighed as she fell to her knees and a couple of agents approached her and asked if she was all right. "I'm fine. Please—go look after my friends," she pleaded. They nodded and jogged to the group with some cops to assist them while Pesci had some of his soldiers tend to Big Daddy. She leaned against one of the cars and dragged shaking hands through her hair. While she wasn't sure what had happened, the Axman had certainly looked afraid for once and they finally had a victory.

She drew a deep breath, stood, and took a step toward her friends but couldn't lift the other leg. Was it wounded? She recoiled when she realized that a gray skeletal arm had emerged from the fissure beside her and grasped her ankle. Shocked, she had no time to utter a warning or scream before she was yanked into the pit.

Samedi had pulled a black-and-white orb from his brother's chest and now stared grimly at it.

"The skeleton—it's stopped moving!" one of the hunters shouted. It was stuck in a position where it reached forward with an open jaw and looked like it was about to snatch a group of the hunters. Frozen in time, it looked like a macabre art installation.

The baron looked at his brother, who was still bound, his head slack and lolled to the side and his eyes now white instead of red. "It seems my brother is a little tired." He held the orb between both hands and crushed it, and an explosion of dark phantasma erupted around him. "The skeleton should be nothing more than a disturbing decoration now. It still traps the souls, however, so destroy it!"

The leader held his recovered ax up. "With pleasure." He struck one of the fingers while the other hunters also began to dismantle the skeleton and release souls from their confinement as long cracks of white began to form along the body.

Samedi dusted his hands off. "I destroyed my brother's crux—the 'heart' of us keepers. It takes most of his power with it and his connection to the Axman. That spry little fiend should be nothing more than a normal bag of spectral bones now."

Johnny and Vic hovered beside the loa and both nodded. "Thanks for the save," the ghost remarked.

The keeper turned and grinned. "I wouldn't have been able to do much of anything without you enabling me to cross into this domain."

"Then it's a good thing I can pick up on context clues," Johnny muttered and folded his arms. "Did you have to be so cryptic? Couldn't you give us more of a clue about this potential plan? It could have gone south real quick if your brother was the strong, silent type."

"I couldn't take the risk that he would catch on." The baron shrugged. "Or cross certain boundaries that could have caused more problems."

Vic shook his head and rolled his lights. "More of that keeper law bullshit."

Samedi looked at the skeleton. "You've had a taste of what the repercussions could be if we try to take the cycle of life and death into our own hands." He shrugged and adjusted his hat. "I agree, it is quite annoying, but look at it this way. You only have to deal with it. I have to live with it."

"Live in a manner of speaking." The ghost detective chuckled but his eyes dimmed as he tilted his head and pointed to the skeleton. "Hey, I know this is kind of a unique case, but is that a good or bad thing?"

The cracks forming along the skeleton crept rapidly down the body and began to consume it, and bright light flowed from within. Even the Wild Hunt backed away from the body, as bewildered as the two partners. A low, rumbling chuckle made Samedi look sharply at his brother. Kriminel raised his head weakly and grinned at them. "Mind your heads," he warned as his smile turned manic.

The baron lunged at him. "Kriminel!" he roared as the cracks began to brighten before they consumed the body and erupted in a flash of light. Johnny and Vic were dragged deeper into the void of the path.

The revenant's vision went black for what felt like only a moment before it cleared and he squinted at the red in the sky and felt powerful wind all around him. He thought he heard Vic say something, his voice frantic and shrill, but he couldn't make it out and his vision went black again.

The ghost detective tried to wake his partner as they plummeted earthward. He looked around frantically and saw members of the Wild Hunt falling alongside them. That seemed odd but he would worry about the implications of it later.

He located Johnny's jacket, darted forward, and snatched it. An idea came to him—a long shot and probably insane, but so was their current predicament. He dragged it onto the young detective, then possessed it, yanked it up, and slowed his fall. It certainly wasn't as much as he would have liked but he was already screwing physics over as it was and even as a ghost, there was only so much that supernatural ability could muster.

They landed on the top of a hotel with a large sign. When they came to a stop, he quickly slid out of the jacket and attempted to flip Johnny, only for him to cough loudly and turn while he held his head.

"Vic?" he asked and shook his head groggily.

"Yeah, I'm here, kid," he said and laughed with relief. "Are you all right?"

Johnny nodded and scrambled to his feet. "What the hell happened?" He walked to the side of the building. "Are we back in New Orleans?"

"We seem to be," the ghost detective said with a nod. "I'm not entirely sure how that works, but we can think about it in a minute. See if you can get hold of Val or someone and find out what's going on with the Axman."

He nodded groggily. "Right. Right, one sec." He

retrieved his phone, slightly annoyed to find there was now a crack in the corner but then reminded himself that it was probably one of the better outcomes given how his night had gone. He opened his contacts and called Valerie. She answered after only two rings. "Hey, Valerie, what's going—"

"He took her!" she interrupted. "The Axman has Annie!"

"What?" He almost toppled over the side of the building as his balance suddenly failed him. "How? What happened? He should be weak now."

"Something did happen before he disappeared. He lost all that dark phantasma on his body and he crawled around in pain but he disappeared into one of the craters he made. We thought he had run away but now, Annie is missing. He must have come back and taken her, Johnny!"

The revenant grasped his partner's shoulder. "Vic, we need to go. Annie is missing and it's possible the Axman finally got her." The ghost did not move. "Vic! Did you hear me?" When he looked up, the ghost stared wordlessly into the sky. He followed his gaze and his eyes widened as well. He lifted the phone to his ear. "Valerie, we're on it, we promise. But you need to prepare yourself for something too."

"What do you mean? What happened to you?"

He swallowed. "We're all right. But New Orleans—" In the red sky, a large portal surrounded by dark clouds shimmered with the glaring white of the path. It looked like a scar or gash in the sky and hundreds of souls streamed out of it and fell to earth. "New Orleans will have a whole lot of somethings going on."

The story continues with *Jazz Funeral,* available at Amazon and through Kindle Unlimited.

Claim your copy today!

First, thank you for not only reading this story, but these author notes in the back as well.

I am presently on a 'direct' train from Nice to Paris in France.

By the way, you pronounce Nice as 'neese.'

Now, what I was unaware of was that a direct train does not mean no stops. It merely means you don't change trains.

I have changed trains before, and I wouldn't recommend it if you don't have to.

I wasn't the guilty party for believing that the direct train meant no stops. That will be the person who purchased the tickets, and that person's name will remain 'anonymous.'

I didn't believe a six-hour train trip would be non-stop, but two things allowed me to be swept up into the confusion of the illusion. First, the tickets (sent to me as images) only showed Nice and Paris. It did not mention any stops on the ticket.

Second, and possibly more important, was I seem to remember a bullet train in China being non-stop. Unfortunately, with my mind always seeming to create stories out of thin air, this memory is *highly suspect.*

So, with these two hard and soft facts, I believed I might be on a train that would be non-stop.

WANTING TO BEAT MY HEAD UNTIL MY EARS COULDN'T HEAR

Having many stops wasn't so bad except for the *damned* chimes that come on every few minutes while we are in transit and an explosion of times as we enter a village... during the stop itself... as we get ready to get underway again... and for whatever reason, they decide to chat with us from the front of the train.

Which would be great if I understood French - but I do not. My languages are English, bad English, cursing (very fluently in English), and a smattering of Spanish...Like, very smatter...ing. Plus, I can only figure out words in Spanish when written – not when spoken. The speakers are too fast.

So, in short, I am no polyglot.

** UPDATE **

As I am typing this, the train has stopped at a station, picked up and dropped off passengers, and is now on the way again. I have successfully not beaten my head in frustration.

** END UPDATE **

It would be really fantastic to understand French (never mind the annoying chimes) to find out what the hell they are saying and why all of a sudden we are taking off going backward. I should probably find one of those iPhone apps that will translate languages on the fly. Downloading and using one of those would not only be smart...

It would be sci-fi-*SEXY!*

At this point, the author looks over at *anonymous* and realizes she won't find me using an app sci-fi-sexy as she knows the language already. Since she doesn't know why we are now going backward, I can presume they didn't explain jack-shit over the loudspeaker.

That's ok because I have GPS BITCHES!

...

...

Well, *shit*. We just went into a tunnel. The GPS doesn't work. Not any small tunnel either. This tunnel is apparently kilometers long. My grand plan to know where the hell we are going is dashed due to rock.

When the hell is sci-fi going to make me cool, I wonder?

Post Update

I found out about 10 minutes after finishing these author notes that I had my maps zoomed in and couldn't 'see' the whole country. Therefore, the GPS didn't look like it was working at all to me.

My GPS app was probably looking at me, thinking I needed to buy a clue more than worry about looking sci-fi-sexy to my wife.

** End Post Update **

I look forward to talking with you in the next book!

Ad Aeternitatem,

Michael Anderle

*** P.S. We made it out of the tunnel... My GPS still doesn't work because the local phone system won't connect with my AT&T phone.*

The Astral Wanderer

(with Michael Anderle)

A New Light (Book One)

Bloodflowers Bloom (Book Two)

The Oblivion Trials (Book Three)

Revenant Files

(with Michael Anderle)

Back from Hell (Book One)

Axeman: Cycle of Death (Book Two)

Jazz Funeral (Book Three)

CONNECT WITH MICHAEL

Connect with Michael Anderle

Website: http://lmbpn.com

Email List: http://lmbpn.com/email/

https://www.facebook.com/LMBPNPublishing

https://twitter.com/MichaelAnderle

https://www.instagram.com/lmbpn_publishing/

https://www.bookbub.com/authors/michael-anderle

Lightning Source UK Ltd.
Milton Keynes UK
UKHW011302280322
400721UK00005B/1391

9 781685 005016